CINN-FULL SECRETS

CINN-FULL SECRETS

AUNTIE CLEM'S BAKERY
BOOK TWENTY-TWO

P.D. WORKMAN

ISBN: 9781774686751 (KDP Paperback)
ISBN: 9781774686768 (KDP Hardcover)
ISBN: 9781774686775 (Large Print)
ISBN: 9781774686799 (Lulu Paperback)
ISBN: 9781774686782 (ePub)
ISBN: 9781774686805 (Accessible Audio)

ALSO BY P.D. WORKMAN

FIND MORE BOOKS AT PDWORKMAN.COM

Auntie Clem's Bakery
Culinary & Pet Cozy Mysteries
Gluten-Free Murder
Dairy-Free Death
Allergen-Free Assignation
Witch-Free Halloween (Halloween Short)
Dog-Free Dinner (Christmas Short)
Stirring Up Murder
Brewing Death
Coup de Glace
Sour Cherry Turnover
Apple-achian Treasure
Vegan Baked Alaska
Muffins Masks Murder
Tai Chi and Chai Tea
Santa Shortbread
Cold as Ice Cream
Changing Fortune Cookies
Hot on the Trail Mix
Fateful Plateful
Cut Out Cookie
On the Slab Pie
Wedding Cake Crush

A Waffle Death

Murder Meringue Pie

A Fowl Play on Christmas Day (Christmas crossover story)

Cinn-Full Secrets (Coming Soon)

Muffin to Lose (Coming Soon)

Custard Cream Conspiracy (Coming Soon)

Recipes from Auntie Clem's Bakery

Parks Pat Mysteries

Police Procedural Set in Canada

Out with the Sunset

Long Climb to the Top

Dark Water Under the Bridge

Immersed in the View

Skimming Over the Lake

Hazard of the Hills

Knows the Hills

Spanning the Creek

Sanctuary in the Stream

Echoes of the Engine

Bench with a View

Beneath the Icy Depths

AND MORE AT PDWORKMAN.COM

To all of those in toxic relationships.

CHAPTER 1

*A*ll you need to do is tell me where she is," Simon growled. "Come on, you can help a guy out."

Erin shook her head. She continued to line up portions of cream cheese icing in tiny paper cups along the tray, deliberately avoiding eye contact with him. The rich, spicy smell of the freshly baked cinnamon rolls filled the bakery.

"Sorry, can't help you," she told Simon. As if she hadn't already told him a dozen times. She would just keep repeating it calmly as if he were a child and, sooner or later, he would leave. At least, that was the theory she was operating under. She hoped that it would unfold the way she planned. She didn't want there to be any trouble.

"You know where she lives," Simon insisted. "Where she works. You know where in town she might be."

Erin shook her head. "I don't keep track of Adrienne, sorry."

"Where's the other one? Bella? She would tell me where Adrienne is. She knows that we're back together again. You think you're protecting Adrienne from something, but you're not. We're together; I'm just wondering where she is right now. I need to talk to her."

Bella came out of the kitchen and stood back behind the

1

counter with Erin. She was an older teen, still in high school. She had a brilliant business mind and wanted to own her own business after college. She was one of Erin's most dependable workers and always came up with good ideas. She was slightly heavy, with wavy blond hair and a ready smile.

At least, she usually had a smile on her face. Today, she was obviously not entertaining friendly thoughts about Simon.

"You and Adrienne are *not* together again," she told him icily, "and Erin and I are not helping you find her or talk to her, or passing a message to her, or anything else. Why don't you go back to Las Vegas or wherever you were? Adrienne doesn't want anything to do with you."

"My wife is in Bald Eagle Falls, Tennessee, so I am in Bald Eagle Falls, Tennessee," Simon said in a sharp, flinty tone. "And I'm not leaving here unless she and the kids are with me."

"That's not going to happen," Bella told him flatly.

Erin would never have had that kind of confidence as a teenager. She hated confrontation and would do just about anything to avoid it. But Bella was a dragon, standing up to a man twice her age, protecting Adrienne and her children.

Erin had been worried that Adrienne would get back together with Simon. Despite their efforts to keep Simon from tracking her down over the past few weeks, he had met up with Adrienne in town a couple of times. Bald Eagle Falls was not a big place; it wasn't that hard to find her if she were in town instead of at Bella's family farm, or wherever else she and her children might be squatting now. Erin wouldn't be surprised if Adrienne had moved her family deeper into the bush. Simon could find out from anyone in town where the Prost farm was if he knew that was where his wife and children were. People were always trying to be helpful and put families back together, even when you told them there was good reason to keep them apart. Friends and family members were notorious for feeling sorry for a wrongly done husband and father who just wanted to make things right.

They had looked pretty cozy when Erin had seen them together. Erin worried that Adrienne would take him back and put the children at risk. Adrienne had told Erin that she didn't want anything to do with Simon, but her actions didn't bear that out. It was obvious that she was attracted to him. They had been together long enough to produce several children—Erin didn't know if all of the children were his or not, but at least a few of them were—so the relationship was a comfortable place for Adrienne to return to. Being with Simon would feel natural. It would be easy to be seduced by his lies and believe that he was now going to support her. He was a changed man.

Only he wasn't. A leopard didn't change its spots.

Adrienne wanted to believe Simon would support her and her children now. That he wouldn't abandon them again, or do whatever other stupid stuff he'd done in the past. Adrienne admitted they had already broken up and gotten back together more than once. Erin was reminded of Adele, the gamekeeper who lived in the woods behind Erin's house and helped to keep them free of trespassers. Despite Adele's saying that she never wanted to see her husband again—and hadn't even told anyone she was married when she had first moved into town—Erin had seen how Rudolph Windsor had still persuaded her to take him in. He was bad for her and had a criminal past, but that had not stopped her from allowing him into her life again. Though, of course, it hadn't lasted.

Erin had her own history too. Would she have fallen back in with Brandon if he had shown up unexpectedly in Bald Eagle Falls and tried to woo her instead of stalking her? She would like to think that she would not have been tempted. She had lived with him out of desperation when she hadn't had anywhere else to go. It hadn't been a matter of loving him. She supposed that was the difference between her and Adrienne or Adele. It was a lot harder to resist a man you loved.

As far as Erin knew, Simon wasn't a criminal, just a lowlife. Someone who had abandoned his wife and kids one too many times. Gathering what she could from Simon's and Bella's words, Adrienne had finally decided to be tough and kick Simon to the curb.

And he was desperate to get back together with her now that she had money.

CHAPTER 2

$\mathcal{I}$f you're not going to buy something," Erin told Simon, "please move on. Other people are waiting to be served."

Simon's small, black eyes flashed. He wasn't going to be put off that easily.

"Buy something? All of these empty carbs?" He looked over the items on display in the bakery case.

It wasn't like he was an athlete, keeping his body in pristine condition. He was on the short side for a man, with skinny arms and a gut. Not someone who worked out or watched what he ate.

Erin didn't bother to explain or excuse the preponderance of carbs in the display case. It *was* a bakery. Simon had known that when he had shoved his way through the front door.

"What are these?" Simon pointed to the sample cups Erin was preparing.

"Cream cheese icing for the cinnamon rolls. These ones are dairy," Erin pointed, "and these are vegan. Non-dairy."

"Non-dairy cream cheese?" he scoffed.

"Not everyone has the benefit of being able to eat dairy," Erin said evenly. "There are a lot of people who are allergic or intolerant. And they would still like to be able to enjoy their cinnamon rolls."

"They are cinn-fully delicious," Vic intoned from where she stood at the register.

Simon barely spared the pretty blond a glance. Most men would have at least given tall, slim, Vic a look of admiration. But maybe Simon had learned from Adrienne that Vic was trans, so he ignored her.

"All this stuff about everybody being intolerant or allergic to everything these days is just a crock," Simon asserted. "Sure, there are a few people who have celiac disease or will actually die if they eat something, but that's just a few people out of thousands. Everybody else," he shook his head in disapproval, "they're just being trendy. Pretending they are doing it to be healthy when they're just being difficult."

Wasn't he the one who had just complained about all the carbs?

"This is a gluten-free and specialty bakery," Erin pointed out. "If you don't want gluten-free, dairy-free, or another special diet, then there isn't anything here for you." Erin looked at the clock on the wall. "And I think it is time for you to go." Erin leaned to the side to see who was behind Simon, even though she knew very well who was behind Simon and didn't need to be so dramatic about it. "Mary Lou, what can I get you today?"

Mary Lou stepped forward, so she was beside Simon rather than behind him. She looked into the display case, smoothing her pantsuit over her hips.

"I'm sure Joshua would like to try some cinnamon rolls," she said. "The regular icing will be fine."

"Great," Erin agreed. "Do you want just a couple?" She knew that Mary Lou was on a budget. She wished she could do more to assist the family, but they wouldn't accept any "charity." Mary Lou also didn't usually eat any desserts and was very careful of the number of calories she ate to avoid putting extra pounds on her slim figure. Joshua, Mary Lou's son, and Roger, her husband, would each eat one. But six or a dozen was not in their budget.

"Yes, two should do it," Mary Lou agreed. "And a loaf of bread," she pointed to the multi-grain-crusted loaf she wanted. "And... maybe a pizza shell. The herb one."

Erin proceeded to serve Mary Lou, ignoring Simon, who didn't move out of the way.

"Do *you* know Adrienne?" Simon asked Mary Lou.

Mary Lou looked at Erin, raising her brows as if she didn't know how to respond to his question. Erin gave an infinitesimal shake of her head. Of course Mary Lou already knew not to tell him anything. Erin was confident that she wouldn't.

"I'm sorry, no," Mary Lou told him coolly.

"You don't know who Adrienne is?"

"I'm afraid not."

Simon didn't believe it for a minute. "In this small town? Everybody in Bald Eagle Falls knows everyone else," he insisted. "If they're not actually related to each other. I know who you are. You're the wife of the man who tried to—"

"Simon," Erin interrupted, trying to avoid a painful topic of conversation. "Did you want a cinnamon roll? You really need to buy whatever you're going to and get out."

Erin hated to be rude. She didn't routinely tell people to leave Auntie Clem's Bakery, but she was tired of Simon and his antics and didn't want him harassing all of her customers.

"You're the only one new here," Simon told Erin. "I know everyone else."

"I'm not exactly new," Erin pointed out. She had been there for a couple of years now, longer than she had lived in most places.

"You're new," Simon told her flatly, shaking his head. "Families like mine and Adrienne's have lived on the mountain for generations. We are real Tennesseans. Living here for a year or two doesn't qualify you to make any judgments about me or my family."

"I'm not making any judgments about you or your family," Erin told him, bemused. "And my family has lived here for generations; I'm the only one who has not. I don't see what that has to do with anything. You're in a bakery. Buy something and move on."

"You can't talk to me like that."

There were increasingly restless movements from the other customers. No one had come to get in the middle of some domestic situation. Mary Lou gave Simon a disapproving look and walked past him to the register to pay for her purchases.

Erin took her phone from her apron pocket, tired of dealing with Simon. She tapped the screen a couple of times to call Terry.

That is, Officer Terry Piper.

He and K9 would be happy to get Simon on his way. They were probably bored with a quiet patrol day and could use some excitement.

"Erin," Terry's voice was warm, but also concerned. She didn't normally call him when she was on shift at Auntie Clem's. "What's up?"

"I have a trespasser at Auntie Clem's who is causing some problems, Officer Piper," Erin told him, her eyes on Simon. "I could use some help."

"I'll be right there," Terry growled. He terminated the call.

Erin slid her phone back into her pocket. She looked past Simon again.

"Betty, what can I get you?"

Betty Thompson was a senior who usually came in with her husband and was notoriously slow in choosing what she wanted to buy. Best to get her up to the counter so she could start pondering her choices. At least now that she had been coming to Auntie Clem's for a couple of years, she didn't have to ask for the ingredients in each item or to ask Erin where each had come from or to debate the benefits and drawbacks of each.

Betty shuffled up to the display case to have a look, giving Simon a wide berth.

"Okay, give me a cinnamon roll," Simon snapped. "You see? I'm a legitimate customer. I'm not trespassing."

He'd been back in town for long enough to know that Terry Piper was, in fact, law enforcement and that he would be on Erin's favorite contacts list. It wasn't just a bluff.

Erin got a single cinnamon roll for him and put it in a sleeve. She did not ask him, as she would have asked any other customer, if he wanted her to warm it in the microwave for a few seconds so that the icing would soften and run into the spiral layers.

"Did you want the cream cheese or non-dairy icing?" she asked him politely, as if she hadn't heard his earlier diatribe.

Simon choked, swore under his breath, and then apparently decided that if he were trying to be a legitimate customer, he'd better watch himself. "Cream cheese," he snarled.

Erin nodded and added a plastic knife and a little container of cream cheese icing to his bag. She briefly entertained the idea of giving him the non-dairy icing to see if he noticed the difference. But she had seen enough people caused harm by restaurant employees "testing" to see if someone really would react to a small bit of a food they claimed to be allergic or intolerant to. She would never give someone anything other than what they had ordered. It just wasn't in her makeup.

She put the bag on the counter next to the cash register for Vic to ring up.

The bells on the door jingled as it was pushed open, and Terry came in, devastatingly handsome in his police uniform, a bit of a five o'clock shadow on his jaw after a long patrol. K9 walked briskly at his side, ears pointed alertly forward as he looked for any sign of trouble.

"You're having a problem?" Terry asked Erin, not seeing any immediate issues.

Erin indicated Simon. "Mr. Simpson is ready to leave."

Simon glared at Erin. "I'm a customer," he said, holding up the bag containing the cinnamon roll. "I have a legitimate reason to be here."

Erin folded her arms. "And now that you've completed your transaction, you're ready to leave."

He opened his mouth to argue. But where was that going to get him? If he had already purchased what he needed, then there was no need for him to stay around. If he was there for another reason, like to threaten Erin into revealing where he could find Adrienne or to cause problems with the other customers, he obviously couldn't do that in front of local law enforcement.

And even if he didn't happen to think that Terry Piper was a formidable force, he had to consider whether he would win or lose in an argument with K9. And most people Erin knew would choose not to be on the receiving end of a German shepherd bite.

"You're ready to go?" Terry asked.

Simon looked at Erin and Bella, then back at Terry and K9. There wasn't any way for him to save face or to stay there any longer, so he gave up.

"Yeah, I'm leaving," he agreed. He shook his head and departed the bakery.

A collective sigh went up from the remaining customers. And staff.

"That guy is trouble," Terry observed.

Erin nodded. "That won't be the last we see of him."

"Just keep calling me. Or the dispatcher if I'm not available. Don't try to argue with him or convince him to go. Just call me the second he walks in the door. It shouldn't take too long to discourage him from showing up here."

"Okay. I'll let everyone else know," Erin agreed.

But Erin was wrong, because it *was* the last time that Simon would set foot inside Auntie Clem's Bakery.

CHAPTER 3

"Wow, what a day," Vic sighed, stretching her arms and shoulders and letting her hair down from its bun now that she had her baker's hat and apron off. Few things were more satisfying than shaking off the day and heading home to relax.

Erin rubbed her shoulders and the back of her neck. She could tell that she had been holding herself tense for much of the day.

"I kept thinking Simon was going to come back."

Vic nodded. "Simon Simpson is more irritating than a mosquito bite on your backside. At least your man is willing to step in and take care of him."

"Yeah." Erin had to admit that she felt a lot better knowing that if Simon stepped through her door again, all she had to do was call Terry. She didn't have to try to talk him into leaving, misdirect him, or come up with something that would satisfy his demands temporarily without actually giving him any new information or leads. "Do you think he'll give up? I mean, sooner or later, he has to accept that he and Adrienne aren't getting back together, doesn't he?"

"Sure… sooner or later. We all know the only reason he's

here at all is because Adrienne came into money. When he finally accepts that he isn't going to get his hands on it... he'll be gone again. Back to LA or wherever he's been since Sarah was conceived."

"Is Sarah his?" Erin asked tentatively. From what she'd heard, Simon had been gone for at least a few years, and Sarah was still an infant. Had Simon been back during the interim, or had Adrienne been with someone else?

"Uh..." Vic reddened. "I wouldn't want to say one way or the other. That's Adrienne's business."

Erin agreed.

"Do you know where the cake knife is?" she asked, hands on hips, looking around at the counters and anywhere else someone might have put it down. "I'm missing one."

"Are you sure?" Vic opened the utensil drawer and moved things around. "Yeah, you're right." She opened the fridge and looked inside. Sometimes things ended up in the oddest places. "I don't know. I'm sure it will turn up."

"I'm sure it will. Are you and Willie taking off anywhere this weekend?" Erin asked.

"I doubt it. He hasn't felt like going anywhere lately."

"Still not feeling very well?" Erin asked sympathetically.

Willie was undergoing chelation therapy for heavy metal poisoning and, from what Erin had gathered, the "flu-like symptoms" and "irritability" they had been warned to expect had been a lot more severe than the words suggested.

"No. And you know how men are when they are sick." Vic rolled her eyes. She looked at the clock on the wall. "I should be getting him something to eat before long... are you going to be much longer?"

"I want to do a few more things. Accounting, planning, all that kind of fun stuff. Charley and I are supposed to meet on Monday, and I should have everything caught up and ready to present."

Vic's eyes went to the clock again, and then the door. "So...
do you want me to wait around?"

Erin shook her head. "Just lock the door on your way out.
I'll be fine here."

Vic hesitated.

"Go take care of Willie," Erin urged. "You don't need to
hang around here."

"Yeah, okay. Don't work too late, okay? Even if you don't
have to get up for tomorrow's morning shift, you know you'll
wake up anyway."

It was true. Try as she might to sleep in, Erin was never very
successful in sleeping past her usual alarm time or going back to
sleep once she had awakened.

"I won't be too long," she promised. "Maybe just an hour.
Then Terry will be off his double shift and we can chill tonight
and tomorrow."

"Sounds heavenly," Vic said a trifle jealously. Willie's
demands must be wearing on her if "chilling" sounded that
desirable. Vic usually liked being off adventuring, not just sitting
at home.

"See you later," Erin promised. Since Vic lived in the loft
over Erin's garage, they frequently had tea together in the
evening, and it sounded like Vic might need the break even
more than usual.

CHAPTER 4

On Sunday mornings, Erin held the ladies' tea for the church women who wanted to socialize after Sunday morning services. It was something that Erin's Aunt Clementine had done for them back when the bakery had been a tea shop, but she'd had to stop when she got too sick and frail to continue. Erin had been asked to reinstitute the practice when she inherited the storefront after Clementine's death.

It might seem like a strange service for an atheist to offer, but most of the ladies had accepted by now that Erin did not have any interest in their religion and they were not going to convince her to join them for church services. They were happy to have somewhere to go afterward to drink tea, nibble snacks, and gossip.

Teacups clinked softly as the women gossiped and discussed their week.

"How is Adrienne?" Erin asked Cindy Prost as she refreshed the platter of sweets at her table.

Cindy was not one of Erin's favorite people. Unlike her daughter Bella, who was endlessly positive and upbeat, Cindy usually had something to complain about. She was critical of pretty much everyone and everything. But Erin had seen her soften around Adrienne's children, transforming into an aunt or grandma figure who enjoyed doing things for them, feeding them, or playing with them.

Cindy turned her eyes on Erin, pushing a hank of blond and gray hair that had come loose from her bun back over one ear. She glanced at Erin as if about to assert that it wasn't her business. Then she gave her head a little shake.

"She'd be better off if that idiot was gone for good," she said, her mouth twisting into a snarl. "I don't know how he heard she'd come into money. Whoever told him has got somethin' to answer for. His kin were never anything but trash. She should have known better than to get together with him in the first place."

Erin nodded. She supposed she wasn't going to get a real answer from Cindy. The woman was just going to vent her spleen about Simon and his forebears, and Erin didn't really want to hear that.

She took a step away from Cindy to attend to another of the tables. Cindy put a hand on Erin's arm. She had a strong grip.

"She's going to be fine," Cindy told Erin. "As long as she stays away from Simon and he stays away from her, she'll be just fine."

The woman had been through a lot lately, and Erin hoped she was right. Adrienne deserved a break.

"I haven't seen Simon for a couple of days. Is he still around? Or did he decide to take off again?"

"I hope to heaven that he is gone. And that he never comes back again. She doesn't need his influence on the children. Adrienne always goes back to him. She needs to cut him off once and for all."

"Well... I hope she does. I hope that he's already gone and none of us have to deal with him again."

"Your lips to God's ears," Cindy agreed.

≈

After the church ladies were gone, Erin and Charley did the cleanup. There wasn't much to do. Erin had learned to minimize the amount of preparation and cleanup needed for the ladies' tea so that she could have as much of Sunday to herself as possible, since they did not open for business on the Sabbath, as dictated by those same church ladies.

Erin checked to see if anything else needed to go out in the garbage. It looked like she had gotten all the used napkins and other detritus.

"I'm just going to toss this," she informed Charley and headed out the bakery's back door toward the dumpster.

Her nose wrinkled as she got closer to it. She knew her nose was more sensitive than that of anyone else she knew, but the bin smelled much worse than usual. Either the garbage hadn't been collected during the week, or someone had decided to dump their own garbage into the dumpster because there wasn't room in theirs.

The bakery did use eggs and dairy, so sometimes their garbage got pretty rancid by the time it was picked up, but what Erin was smelling wasn't the normal Auntie Clem's trash. It smelled like meat. Meat well past its prime. She gagged.

They rarely had any meat in Auntie Clem's. Erin didn't make meat pies or other prepared meals. Sometimes bacon for break-fast muffins or maple bacon muffins, but that was about it.

Someone had definitely put something in the Auntie Clem's bin that wasn't supposed to be there.

She held her breath as she approached the bin and threw her bag into it. She took a quick look for anything that shouldn't be there but could only see the trash she had previously disposed of. All of the trash bags were the same color and size.

Erin stepped back, shaking her head, and took several steps away before taking a gulp of air. She breathed in a few times through her mouth.

If the smell wasn't coming from something that someone had put into her bin—unless they had used exactly the same bags as Erin herself, then where was it coming from? She held her hand over her nose, looking around.

It was summer in Tennessee, which meant it was hot enough that her shirt was already sticking to her even though she had barely stepped out of the air-conditioned bakery. It might be an animal. A bird or mouse killed by a cat or something larger killed by a car going too quickly down the back alley at night.

She checked around the bins and back fences of each of her neighbors, but that seemed to be taking her farther away from the stench. Erin returned to her bin, looked in again, and still couldn't see anything to explain the stench. She leaned on the fence and looked into the space between the bin and the fence.

Charley looked over as Erin staggered back into Auntie Clem's Bakery, opening her mouth to ask a question. But when she saw Erin, whatever she had been about to ask was quickly forgotten.

"Erin? What's wrong? Are you okay?" Charley hurried over to her.

Erin tried to protest that she was fine but couldn't find the words. Her stomach roiled and she couldn't say anything or explain. She dashed for the powder room and slammed the door behind her. She luckily reached the toilet before she lost the contents of her stomach.

"Erin? Are you okay?" Charley shouted through the door.

Erin didn't hear what else she had to say. She wasn't okay, but she wasn't in any condition to talk. Charley was still speaking, but Erin couldn't make out any of it. Her ears were ringing and she was afraid she was going to pass out.

It was a while before she was able to calm her heaving stomach and consider standing up again. She eventually struggled to her feet and splashed cold water on her face. She was sweating like she had a fever. The cold water felt good and soaked down into the collar of her shirt.

When she opened the door, Charley was not in the kitchen,

which she thought was odd. She knew Charley wouldn't have just gone home, leaving her throwing up in the bathroom. They were more than just partners in the business. Charley was Erin's half-sister and, even though they hadn't grown up together or even known of each other's existence until a couple of years ago, they cared for each other. As rough around the edges as Charley was, she wasn't the type to walk away from someone who was sick or in trouble.

There were low voices in the front of the store. Charley had let someone in through the front door.

Charley walked Terry and K9 into the kitchen.

"Erin? Are you okay?" Terry asked, going to her and putting his hands on her shoulders as he looked into her eyes. "Charley said you were sick. You don't look so good. Did it just hit you suddenly?"

Erin shook her head. "Out back," she croaked.

"Out back? What?" Terry looked toward the back door. "What are you talking about?"

"He's out there." Erin swallowed, trying to keep from reacting to the sight and smell again.

"Who is out there? Did something happen?" Charley demanded. "I didn't hear anything," she told Terry earnestly. "Erin, did someone hurt you?"

Erin gulped air and turned back toward the bathroom again, unsure she could keep her equilibrium.

"Simon." She gagged. "Simon Simpson."

"He was back there?" Terry hurried to the back door and looked out. "I don't see him now. What did he do?"

"Behind the bin. Behind the garbage bin."

Terry gave her a look that told her he thought she was off her head. He walked out the door. K9 led him unerringly to the new discovery, his doggie nose even more sensitive than Erin's.

Erin could see Terry through the doorway as he pulled out his phone and started making calls.

CHAPTER 5

"hat's going on?" Charley demanded. "What are you talking about? Simon isn't back there."

They both watched Terry from inside the kitchen, not going out to join him. Did Charley have an inkling of what was going on, and that was why she was staying with Erin rather than going outside to see what Terry had found? Or was she just staying with Erin to keep an eye on her because she was sick?

Erin grabbed one of the stools she sometimes used in the kitchen when her legs grew tired, as it was tall enough to reach the counters comfortably. It took a couple of tries to get settled, and Charley helped her to make sure she was stable. Erin put her elbows on the counter and her face in her hands.

"It's Simon," she repeated. "He's back there between the dumpster and the fence."

"What's he doing back there?"

Erin had a sudden vision of what Charley must be picturing, rough-looking Simon crouched between the garbage bin and the fence, lying in wait for Adrienne. But that wasn't even close to what Erin had discovered.

"He's dead," she told Charley. Tears were leaking from her

eyes but, with Erin's hands over her face, Charley wouldn't be able to see. "I could... I could smell something out there."

"Oh, yuck," Charley said. She patted Erin on the back and rubbed in slow, soothing circles. "How could something like that happen? I'm sorry, Erin."

How could something like that happen? It wasn't like it was the first death that Erin had discovered in Bald Eagle Falls. Or even the second. She didn't know how she always seemed drawn toward them. This time, it had been the smell. She should have known better than to look too closely, leaving it for someone else to investigate. Called Terry to look for her. Even if it had just been a dead animal, then who better than her boyfriend to find it and deal with it, protecting her from seeing what had happened or smelling the stench close up.

She gagged just thinking of it. She held her arm and then her shirt to her nose, checking to see whether she had carried the smell of the decomposition with her. She would have to wash everything. Shower for an hour to ensure it didn't cling to her skin or get into her hair.

"Can I get you something?" Charley offered. "A glass of water? Would that help?"

Erin nodded. "Maybe."

"Or some tea? I can heat a teakettle."

Charley was not the best in the kitchen. She had grown a lot and could now follow most of the recipes in Erin's big reference binder. Most of them. As long as she was careful and followed the step-by-step directions exactly. She was distractible and had been known to mess up an entire batch of dough more than once.

Erin nodded. Charley left her side to put the kettle on to boil. Erin sniffled.

"You might as well use the big boiler. If the police want anything..."

"Oh, yeah, I suppose," Charley agreed. She turned off the

kettle and looked at the big boiler they used for the ladies' tea and other events. "This thing always scares me a little."

"You just need to turn it on and make sure the tank is full."

Charley looked at the boiler dubiously, but followed Erin's instructions. The boiler started to tick, warming up.

"Ginger?" Charley asked, looking at a selection of teas in the ladies' tea basket. "That's supposed to be good for stomachs."

"Yeah." The pungent smell would help clean the smell out of Erin's nose as well as the tea reducing the nausea. There wasn't anything left in her stomach to throw up, but that didn't mean she couldn't try.

The sound of approaching sirens reached into the kitchen, tinny and far away at first, but quickly homing in on the bakery and its latest, deadest customer. The wails rose to an unbearable level before finally stopping outside and cutting off abruptly.

Terry spoke to the sheriff for a couple of minutes. They both walked behind the fence, looking down at the ground, their heads close together as they discussed the discovery.

They were both experienced law enforcement officers and it certainly wasn't the first time they had been faced with a decomposing body. Still, she couldn't understand how they could stand that close to the remains without covering their mouths and noses. Or getting sick.

After a few minutes, Terry left the sheriff there and he and K9 returned to Auntie Clem's, joining Erin and Charley in the kitchen just as Charley was putting a mug of ginger tea in front of Erin.

Terry stood a few feet away from her, unsure of how to approach the subject or treat Erin. She was, she supposed, a person of interest by virtue of being so close to the dead body. And the fact that Simon had been harassing her about Adrienne and then he had disappeared, only to turn up dead.

Surely, he knew by this time that there was no way Erin could have killed Simon or anyone else. And there was no way that she would have put herself in the position of having to see and smell the body in that condition. If Erin were to commit a murder, she would be more likely to kill and dispose of someone in a big walk-in freezer like the one in Buttermilk Biscuits, a restaurant in Whitewater Junction, than she would leave a body out in the Tennessee sun to putrefy outside her back door.

"Erin, are you okay?" Terry asked, still a couple of steps away from her. Did he maintain that distance because he was still acting in his role as a law enforcement officer, separate and emotionally distant from Erin? She had thought the sheriff would have taken him off the case.

"Mm-hmm," Erin murmured. She took a tiny sip of the ginger tea and waited for it to start working before filling her stomach. One small sip at a time, until she could get the whole cup down. Then she should feel much better.

"Can you tell me what happened? How did you discover the body?"

Erin shook her head.

"You can take your time," Terry said. "If you're not ready yet."

"She was just taking the garbage out," Charley informed him. "We were cleaning up after the ladies' tea."

Terry nodded. He looked at Erin for more details, but she just shook her head. There wasn't much else to say about it. She didn't want to relive the experience. If she kept going over it, the discovery would just be indelibly impressed upon her memory, so she could never forget it.

"It isn't exactly in plain sight," Terry pointed out. "How did you end up looking behind the dumpster?"

"The smell."

"It is pungent," Terry admitted. "But you didn't think it was just the garbage?"

Erin shuddered and shook her head. "Does it smell like garbage?" she challenged.

"Well, yes. To me... it doesn't smell any different than any other rotting garbage."

Erin shook her head. "Ugh. Rotten garbage doesn't smell like that."

Terry looked at her, his face a study of concentration. "I'm glad I don't have your sense of smell," he told her, not for the first time.

Erin nodded her agreement. As delightful as it was to have her sense of smell when there were cookies or a nice turkey dinner in the oven, her sense of smell was more often an inconvenience than a helpful tool. It might be fun to identify the ingredients in a tea or recognize what brand and variety it was, but garbage, dead bodies, and other terrible smells were not things she enjoyed.

Erin took another sip of her tea. She could hear the muted voices of the other law enforcement officers talking or yelling back and forth as they secured the scene and looked for any forensic clues that would tell them what had happened there.

Erin, Charley, and Terry said nothing for a while, each pondering their own thoughts.

"When was the last time you saw Simon?" Terry asked. "Before this, I mean. The last time you saw him alive."

Erin swallowed. "The same time as you did. When I called you to get him out of the bakery."

"You had to call him to get Simon out of the bakery?" Charley repeated, not having heard this detail previously.

Erin nodded and looked at Terry. "He was harassing me. Wouldn't get out. Blocking the other customers or asking them uncomfortable questions. I asked him to leave and he wouldn't, so I called Terry." She nodded to him. "He got Simon on his way, and that was the last I heard from him. I was expecting him to come back... he kept coming back to demand to know about Adrienne. Where she was or if I could get her a message."

"But he never came back after that?" Terry asked.

"No."

"That was... Friday afternoon."

Erin nodded. She thought about the state of decomposition

of the body. It wasn't a fresh kill. Someone had made sure that Simon would never come back to the bakery to harass Erin again.

"I guess that's about right," Terry admitted. "He must have died soon after that. It's been more than a few hours. More than a day, I would say, but we'll have to see what the medical examiner has to say about it."

"Who would do that?" Erin demanded. Who would kill Simon? Who would leave him right outside Erin's back door, rotting behind the dumpster like that? There were so many questions whirling through her head as she tried to make sense of it.

"How was he killed?" Charley asked sensibly. She was the only one of the three of them who had not seen the body, so she would need to be filled in on the details of the murder.

Because Simon *had* been murdered.

CHAPTER 6

*T*erry looked at Charley and didn't answer the question, obviously trying to keep the details of the investigation under wraps.

He was the one who was required to keep the details confidential, not Erin.

"Stabbed," Erin told her. "That's what it looked like."

They both looked at Terry for confirmation. He just shrugged. No comment.

"Stabbed," Charley repeated. "Up close and personal, then. A face to face confrontation." She looked at Erin. "Was it face-to-face?"

"Stabbed in the front," Erin agreed. "Chest or stomach… maybe more than once, I didn't get close enough to investigate."

"Anger," Charley deduced. "Rage? How many stab marks?"

"Don't know," Erin reiterated. Charley looked at Terry, but he didn't help out.

"He was so well-liked," Charley said sarcastically. "It's going to be hard to find anyone who wished him dead."

Terry snorted. K9 looked up at him with a doggie expression of concern.

"Who did you see around here Friday?" Terry asked Erin. "After

I left. Who was around the bakery in the next couple of hours? Customers, employees, anyone you saw walking down the alley?"

"I didn't see anyone walking down the alley. I don't stand out there watching for people to go by. The only time I open the back door is for deliveries or to take stuff out to the garbage."

"Did you have any deliveries Friday afternoon?"

"No."

"Anyone come by for the day-old bread?"

That was another thing that people came to the back door for, and Terry knew that. Anyone who needed help with their groceries, who couldn't afford the bread that the family needed, could come by Auntie Clem's to get day-old bread and baking from the freezer. Whatever they needed, no questions asked.

"No. Not Friday."

"Did Adrienne ever come to the back?"

Erin shook her head. "Not on Friday."

"Did she ever?"

Erin balked at revealing anything sensitive to Terry. "I don't see what that has to do with it. That's confidential."

"If Simon knew that sometimes she came by for day-old bread, he might have camped out there to watch for her."

"And then stabbed himself?" Charley asked sarcastically.

"And then... had a confrontation with Adrienne or someone else."

"Adrienne didn't come by," Erin repeated.

"No one else came by?" Terry verified.

"No."

"And you didn't... hear anything strange out there Friday or Saturday?"

"It's a heavy door. And we often have machines or water or fans running back here. So we don't really hear anything from outside."

"Did you hear anything?" Terry repeated. Erin could hear the frustration in his voice. She didn't mean to answer ambiguously; she just felt that his questions needed more context. She meant to answer.

"No. I didn't hear anything."

"Any of your employees? Anyone mention hearing or seeing anything unusual?"

Erin looked at Charley and shook her head.

"I don't know of anything," Charley confirmed. She wasn't in the bakery very often but, hopefully, her confirmation reassured Terry that Erin was telling the truth and not just trying to brush him off.

Sheriff Wilmot entered the kitchen. He stomped off his shoes at the door in case they were dusty and wiped his sweaty forehead. It was evening, but it was still pretty warm out.

"Miss Erin," he greeted. "Mind if we have a chat?"

Erin nodded. "Of course."

She was glad that he had come in himself to interview her rather than assigning the job to Rodney Stayner, whom Erin had never really gotten along with.

He nodded toward Erin's tiny, closet-sized office and asked, "Shall we take your office?"

But there really wasn't room in there for two people. There was no guest chair and Wilmot would have to stand or sit on the edge of the desk. And it would be very close and warm.

"Why don't we grab a table at the front instead?" Erin suggested.

The sheriff nodded his agreement, and he and Erin sat down at one of the small wrought iron tables in the front of the bakery that they used for the ladies' tea and that customers occasionally used if they needed a quiet place to have their tea or cookies before going back to the office. Everything was clean and tidy. Erin and Charley had just wiped everything down, swept, and wet-mopped.

Sheriff Wilmot sighed as he sat down opposite Erin. "So... Another day, another body," he joked gently.

"I think it's time for someone else to take a turn," Erin said ruefully.

"Yes. You seem to have had to deal with more than your own share, haven't you? How are you feeling? You're a mite pale."

"Well… I was sick. But I guess I'm okay now. As long as I don't think about it too much."

"We'll try to avoid that the best we can, under the circumstances. I'm sure you've already walked through it with Officer Piper, but if you could outline things once more for me…"

"I was just taking the garbage out. I could… smell the decomp. I looked around, thought it might be an animal. And then… I saw him."

"Quite a shock. Despite your experience in these matters."

"It's always a shock. And it's not something that I go looking for."

"Certainly not," he agreed. "Was there anyone else around when you found the body?"

"Just Charley. And she was inside the bakery, not out there."

"Anyone walking by? Did you hear anyone out there earlier? Yesterday?"

"No."

"I'll need a list of your employees and when they were on shift."

Erin thought about that. She wasn't sure how knowing the bakery shifts would make any difference. If someone were working a shift, did that make them a suspect? Or did that mean that they had an alibi? It could go either way.

"Okay," she agreed. But she didn't really think it would help him.

"Have you seen Adrienne the last few days?"

Erin shook her head. "No. She hasn't been around town very much." She gave a little grimace. "Almost as if she was avoiding someone."

Wilmot chuckled. "Almost as if she were," he agreed. "Do you have a phone number for her that works?"

"Um… I might."

He frowned, brows drawing closer together. "Miss Erin. Do you have a number for her or not?"

Erin sighed. "Yes. But it is supposed to be private. I'm not supposed to share it with anyone."

"You're going to need to give it to me. We need to get in contact with her to notify her of Simon's death and discuss the circumstances with her. We can't get around that."

Erin nodded. "Okay. But can you not put it on anything that others will see? If it leaks out to other people in the town… then it's not exactly private anymore."

"It is going to need to go into our official records." He held up his finger to stop Erin from objecting. "Again, no way around that one. We have to keep accurate records. It won't be available to anyone outside of the police department."

Unfortunately, Erin knew the police department had at least one very large leak.

She pulled out her phone and found the number for Wilmot. "Just please… keep it as private as you can."

"Isn't the danger already past? Wouldn't you say that the one person she needed to keep that number from is past being able to use it?"

Clearly, Simon was dead. But was he the only person who would show up interested in Adrienne's windfall? She was reclusive and liked to keep herself and her family apart from mainstream society. She wouldn't want just anyone calling her.

"It's not a public number," Erin reiterated. "Keep it as quiet as you can."

Wilmot nodded his agreement. "When was the last time you saw Simon?"

"Friday. When I called Terry to get rid of him."

The sheriff raised his brows. "To get rid of him?"

"From Auntie Clem's. He was making a nuisance of himself and wouldn't leave when I asked him to. So I called Terry, and he saw him on his way. That was the last I saw of him. I expected him to come back, but he didn't."

"Very good. That's helpful. And you didn't see or hear anything else in the back?" He gestured again.

"No." Erin tried to think of whether she had heard the trash pickup or whether she had seen or heard anything else over the past two days. "No, I can't think of anything at all."

"How late were you here Friday night?"

"Uh… maybe seven. I'm not sure."

"And you didn't hear anything out there? Shouting? Anything like that?"

"No. I was in my office, and you really can't hear anything in there."

"Who else was here? Miss Vicky?"

"No. I was… just by myself. The bakery was closed. I had some accounting and planning to do while it was quiet."

"You were here by yourself."

"Yes." Erin swallowed and tried to meet his eyes. "Is that really a problem? You don't think I did it, do you? I wouldn't take on someone like Simon physically. That would be stupid."

"People do stupid things. And desperate things. And they even up the score with weapons or other advantages. No, I don't think you had anything to do with Simon's death. But I still have to follow up and make sure I have everything documented. I still need to follow proper investigative procedures."

"I know."

"What time did Victoria go home?"

"Six o'clock, maybe. Roughly that. And she said she was going to cook dinner for Willie, so she had an alibi. She wasn't hanging around waiting for Simon Simpson to show his face."

Wilmot nodded. "Fair enough. I will talk to her and confirm that. As well as the rest of your employees. What about other people you saw in the bakery that day? Who was around?"

"Friday and Saturday? That's a pretty tall order… I can make copies of the sales for you. But I can't tell you everyone that we sold something those days. Or that might have come in with someone who bought something."

"You have a lot of turnover," Wilmot joked.

"No, we're out of turnovers this week," Erin deadpanned. "We've been focusing on cinnamon rolls."

"Mmm. I might have heard something about that. Cinnamon rolls with cream cheese icing." He licked his lips.

"I'll pack you some to take home."

Wilmot grinned. "I would be much obliged, Miss Erin. Although my wife might have something to say about my expanding waistline."

"She'll have to take you for a walk."

He guffawed at that. "She will indeed."

CHAPTER 7

By the time Erin and Terry got home, word of Simon's death had spread over the Bald Eagle Falls grapevine, and everyone wanted to talk to Erin. Her phone kept ringing until she turned it off. When she arrived home and went to put tea on in the kitchen and scrounged for some leftovers from the fridge, she was counting the seconds until Vic descended the stairs from her loft apartment, crossed the yard, and showed up at the back door. She was not disappointed. The motion detector lights went on, and Erin went to the back door to disarm the burglar alarm and open the door for Vic. Vic had her own code for the alarm, of course, but Erin thought she would eliminate any concerns Vic had about intruding during a difficult time by opening the door for her.

"Oh my word," Vic exclaimed, fanning her face. "I can't believe it! Simon Simpson is dead?"

Erin nodded and let Vic in. Willie was just a few steps behind her.

"Are you okay, Erin?" he asked.

Erin nodded. "I'm tired," she admitted, shaking her head. It wasn't quite bedtime for her yet, but it was close, and being interviewed by the police always tired her out. "But other than that… I'm just fine. Peckish." She turned to look at the fridge again, feeling too exhausted to do much more than defrost a couple of cookies, which wasn't a good idea for her figure.

"Shoo. You sit down," Vic ordered, waving her hands at Erin. "I'll pull something together for you. The least Officer Handsome could do is take you out for something to eat after he interrogates you." She raised her voice to make sure that Terry would hear her.

"I just put in a double shift," Terry shot back. "I'm going to shower off the sweat and dust from the day, and then there'd better be something on the table for me."

Vic laughed. "What does he think, I'm his servant?"

Erin smiled. She melted into the chair—as much as one could melt into a straight-backed kitchen chair—and mentally reviewed the evening. It had dragged by but, at the same time, it was all blurred together. She couldn't have put everything into a perfectly coherent timeline if she'd had to.

"But you're okay?" Vic asked as she worked at the counter to pull the leftovers into something appetizing.

"Yes. I'm just fine. It isn't like they think I had anything to do with it. They have to investigate all avenues of inquiry."

"That sounds like something that came out of the sheriff's mouth," Willie observed.

"Yes… him, Terry, everyone. It's just one of those things. If they didn't get all of my information, the investigation wouldn't be complete, and they could be in trouble. Or might end up missing something important."

"With the number of deaths around here, you would think they'd had plenty of practice," Willie said. "This should be a cinch for them."

Erin shrugged. She looked around. "Where is Orange Blossom? Usually, when I'm late getting home, he has a fit." The noisy orange cat had not put in an appearance when Erin had opened the door. He might be sleeping in one of the bedrooms, pouting because she had neglected him.

"I came over and fed him a couple of hours ago," Vic assured her. "I figured you wouldn't get home until late."

"Oh, you're the best. And now you're over to feed me, too! What did you guys have tonight? Do you want anything? Dessert?"

Vic glanced over at Willie to see what he thought. He sat back in his chair, arms folded across his chest, and shook his head. "I'm supposed to be watching what I eat," he advised. "No junk food or sweets."

Erin admired him for sticking to his diet. "Good for you. I don't know if I could give up sweets," she admitted.

"Well, it's not forever, but while I'm in treatment... to tell the truth, I want it to be over as soon as possible."

"It's been pretty rough, hasn't it?"

Willie looked over at Vic. "It has probably been even harder on Vic than me. I can grouse around or sleep half the day and everyone just accepts that I'm sick and puts up with it. But they don't have to be around me all the time like she does."

"You *have* been a grumpy old man," Vic agreed cheekily.

Erin laughed. Vic put a sandwich and bowl of soup in front of her. Looking over at the stove, Erin could see that there was more waiting for Terry when he finished his shower.

"This is really nice, Vic. Thanks for the help."

The soup was warm and soothing. Erin closed her eyes and savored it.

"So...?" Vic sat down at the table. "Spill. What are all of the details of Simon's death? There are so many rumors going around right now, I have no idea what to believe."

Erin sipped her soup, thinking about it. She had gone over it and over it with the police. That was how they worked, repeating the same material over and over again and seeing how much each repetition varied. Digging up more details. Examining anything she might not have been entirely forthright about. Although there was no reason for her not to be completely forthright about it. It wasn't like she had anything to hide. Everyone already knew about the animosity between Simon and Erin. And that the reason she was at odds with Simon was because she was protecting Adrienne. She didn't have any previous contact with him or any other reason for arguing with him.

"Someone said he'd been dead for a long time," Vic prompted. "It didn't just happen today."

Erin nodded. "I guess that depends on how you define a long time. But yeah… the body was in pretty bad shape."

She had to swallow and take a few deep breaths to fend off the nausea.

"But we saw him on Friday. So it was after that," Vic contributed.

"Probably pretty soon after that, they're thinking. I don't know; we'll see what the medical examiner says and who had seen him since he was at Auntie Clem's. But in this heat…" She swallowed again and shook her head. She sipped more soup. She hoped eating would help settle her queasy stomach rather than making things worse.

"How was he killed?" Willie asked. "Finding him in the back alley like that… was he hit by a car? Thrown to the side? I'm not sure how he wasn't discovered right away. It isn't like it's a big town. People use that back alley."

"Stabbed," Erin told him. "And he was… out of sight. Back behind our dumpster. I guess… maybe someone dragged and dumped him there. To where no one would see him right away. But I could smell something that wasn't just the garbage…"

"Erin and her super smeller," Vic said.

"It isn't the first time I've wished I didn't have a good sense of smell. Believe me… there are many things I would rather not *ever* have to smell."

Willie chuckled. "I can believe that."

Erin went back to her soup, inhaling the savory scent deeply before taking another spoonful.

"So, stabbed," Vic said meditatively. "I'll bet there are a lot of people who would have liked to have stabbed him. I know I would have."

Erin nearly choked on her soup. She swallowed her mouthful and looked at Vic, shaking her head.

"You can't just go around stabbing people."

"Well, I *know* that. That's why I say, I would have liked to have stabbed him. But I didn't do it. I controlled my homicidal instincts." She looked at Willie. "I have a lot of practice with that."

"You see, there is a benefit to me being a cranky old man," Willie teased. "If you didn't have all of that practice restraining your homicidal impulses, you could be in jail right now."

"I could be," Vic agreed.

"It's a good thing you're not," Erin told her. "I'm going to need some extra help the next few days. You know how crazy Auntie Clem's gets when something like this happens. And I don't know how well I will sleep tonight."

"That's right," Vic agreed. "We should call someone right now for the morning shift so you don't have to worry about getting up early. You can sleep however late you need and just come in when you feel up to it."

"People will want to talk to me."

"No problem. We'll just feed them a bunch of wild gossip until you get there to keep interest high. We always get the best business when there's something juicy to talk about."

Erin laughed. "You are *not* going to feed them a bunch of lies until I get there to tell them the truth."

Vic shrugged and fluttered her lashes at Erin, putting on an innocent schoolgirl act. "Well, we'll just have to see what happens until you get there."

CHAPTER 8

*E*rin knew that Vic was only joking about spreading gossip about the murder until she got there to answer people's questions about what she had discovered. But she still couldn't help feeling like she had to be at the bakery to make sure that there weren't any false rumors spreading about Simon's death. She had seen how quickly stories could spread through Bald Eagle Falls. No one seemed to care whether a story were true or not. They just wanted something juicy to chew on.

Erin would prefer that whatever was circulating was the truth. She didn't want to spend the next few days or weeks trying to quash false rumors about what she had seen or done.

So, despite a restless night, she was up early as usual the next morning and was in the kitchen dressed and ready to go, fresh hot coffee in her travel mug, when Vic made her way down the stairs from the loft.

"I thought you were going to sleep in," Vic teased. "You didn't get enough sleep, did you?"

Erin shrugged. "Enough to get by for one day. I'll get Charley to close and come home for a nap."

Vic laughed. "No, you won't."

"I could."

"Yes, you could, Miss Erin. In fact, you could have slept in this morning. But you didn't."

Erin handed her the second mug of coffee. "This sounds like a discussion that could be carried on at Auntie Clem's while we get ready for the day."

Vic took the mug, and she and Erin climbed into the yellow bug for the drive to Auntie Clem's Bakery a few blocks away.

Erin had called in Cheyenne the night before in case she couldn't make it, so there were three of them to get the ovens going and to prepare for the morning rush, which was bound to be even busier than usual with the news of Simon's murder.

They were all familiar with all of the morning routines and recipes, so they worked together efficiently and had the display case filled and labeled well ahead of opening the doors, and were able to sit down for a moment to finish their coffee and fortify themselves for the flurry of activity that was a few minutes away.

Then Erin arose and unlocked the front door, flipping the sign over to Open. A number of customers were already waiting, gossiping over their morning coffees and eager to hear the details of Erin's discovery from the horse's mouth.

Erin didn't want to rehash the details of what she had seen—and smelled—over and over all day long, but she knew she would. And their sales would skyrocket because of it. A murder in Bald Eagle Falls was like free advertising. Especially one that happened right behind the store.

Erin was not surprised that Melissa Lee was the first one in the door. Melissa was one of the worst—or best—for spreading gossip in the town. And since she worked part-time for the police department, she often had little snippets of information that she should not, and was eager to share. She liked to make a splash and would take every opportunity to do so.

"Oh, Erin," she gushed, reaching for Erin's forearm and squeezing it as if comforting her for a terrible tragedy. "I couldn't believe it when I heard what you had found." She had a broad smile, as she always did while spreading gossip. She shook her head, dark spiraling curls bouncing in every direction. "How do you do it?" She laughed.

"Don't ask me," Erin told her dryly. "You're welcome to spread the word that someone else could take over the honor any time now. I'd be quite happy to have someone else stumbling over the bodies."

Melissa giggled. "I'll make sure people know."

She made a show of looking over the display case. "Everything looks so good. And I always love the smell of fresh bread first thing in the morning." She took a deep breath of the sweetly scented air. "If you could make that smell into a drink… you could make a fortune. Because that's all I want to do, just drink it in."

"I made some of the white chocolate chip brownies you like," Erin pointed out the brown bars with white dots of chocolate chips. "Not what you want for breakfast, I don't suppose, but you'll need something for dessert tonight."

"Yes," Melissa agreed, "I'll take a couple of those. And I should probably take something in for the police department. Maybe a muffin assortment."

Erin nodded. "Sheriff Wilmot has money on account for the police department. So you don't have to pay for those."

Melissa's brows rose. "Sheriff Wilmot?"

Melissa had recently complained that she was the only one who ever brought treats in for the department, and paid for them out of pocket. Erin had spread the word and ensured that Sheriff Wilmot had liberated some funds from the department budget and donations from the other members of the police department to ensure that Melissa did not have to continue to pay for them herself.

"Yes. You don't need to pay for them. They're covered."

"Oh!" Melissa's cheeks flushed pink. "Well, thank you, Sheriff! I'll be sure to thank him."

"No reason you should have to pay for them all the time,

especially when you are only—when you only work part-time hours there."

Melissa nodded. "It's so nice to have someone else step forward."

For a moment, she had been distracted by the food but, as soon as she had picked out the muffins for the department, her thoughts returned to the latest gruesome discovery.

"I can't believe that Simon Simpson was killed right behind your bakery," she told Erin, making sure that her voice was loud enough to carry to the other customers. "What are the chances of that?"

Erin had no idea what the chances were. It seemed to be a fairly common occurrence since she had moved to Bald Eagle Falls. Bodies in the bakery itself or on the property were more common than she wished.

"I didn't have anything to do with it," she pointed out.

"Oh no, of course not. I wouldn't suggest that. Even though…"

Erin eyed her. She wasn't sure she wanted to hear Melissa's latest news.

"Even though what?" she asked eventually, since Melissa would not go on until she'd leaked whatever information she had come to share.

"Well… I wouldn't want to say. The body was picked up by the medical examiner's office this morning, so it isn't like we have his report yet. He hasn't even looked at it. But some things were obvious…"

Erin shrugged. If they were obvious, then she probably already knew them. But Melissa hadn't really come to share her observations with Erin, who had seen the body. She had come to share them with the rest of the town.

"Well, I couldn't help noticing the knife Simon was killed with," Melissa said.

CHAPTER 9

*E*rin's stomach tightened. She didn't want that news to get out. But the police department was bound to find out exactly where that knife had come from. And they probably wouldn't hold the news back from the public.

Nor would they be able to if Melissa was going to announce it in Auntie Clem's.

"Do you really think you should be sharing that?" a voice behind Melissa asked.

Melissa turned partway around to look at the speaker. Erin was surprised to see that it was Lottie Sturm. She was more used to Lottie stirring things up than her being the voice of caution.

Melissa's mouth hung open for a minute as if she were astounded that Lottie would suggest such a thing. She closed it and shook her head. "Everybody is going to find out anyway," she pointed out.

"What if the police aren't ready to release it yet? As someone who works in the police department, aren't you required to follow their lead?"

"Nobody has said anything to me about it being kept quiet," Melissa informed her. "I'm not doing anything wrong."

"Aren't you?"

There was silence in the front of the bakery while everyone waited for Melissa's answer. Erin could hear Cheyenne in the kitchen, pulling pans off of oven racks.

Melissa's generous mouth twisted into a grimace. She tried to blank her expression, but still looked like she was pouting. She stepped over to the cash register to pay for her order, which Erin placed on the counter. Vic rang up the brownies, and Melissa paid and left, scowling at Lottie as she walked past her.

Vic rang up the muffins separately and put the receipt to the side for Erin so she could keep track of how much money was left in the police department's charge account.

She raised her brows at Erin. Erin recognized the expression of disbelief that Melissa would listen to what Lottie had said instead of just steamrolling over her, as Erin would have predicted.

Erin shrugged in response. They would have to discuss it later.

Lottie approached the counter and looked over the baking in the display case, her expression serious. Erin didn't know whether to make a joke or thank her for her intervention, or to go on as if nothing had happened.

Since Lottie didn't look at her or say anything, Erin decided that the best thing was just to let it go. Whatever Lottie's reasons were for jumping in and stopping a discussion she would normally have encouraged, Erin wasn't going to argue.

Lottie ordered what she wanted in a clipped, no-nonsense tone. She paid for her treats and shot each of the remaining patrons an angry look as they parted to let her pass back out of the store. Erin shook her head and smiled at the next customer.

It was early afternoon, after the lunch rush had passed, that Terry stopped in with K9. Erin refilled his water bottle and offered him a cookie, which he declined. He was trying to stay in shape despite always having multiple desserts available at home. Erin always had the freezer packed with bread, rolls, cookies, and other treats. He was trying to hold himself to one small dessert after supper, and that was it. Erin knew how hard it was to resist the allure of the baking. She felt it too, but didn't want an ever-increasing waistline to take over her life and threaten her health.

Terry didn't leave again immediately after Erin handed him his water. He lingered. There was only one other customer in the bakery. Erin served Mrs. Peach, her next-door neighbor, and Terry was still there after she left.

"Was there something else?" Erin asked. "Are you sure you didn't want a cookie?" She couldn't think of what else he might want.

"No, not a cookie. I just wanted to talk to you alone for a minute. I was hoping that you could help me to find Adrienne."

He stood there looking at her expectantly. Erin opened her mouth and didn't know what to say. Nothing came to mind. She just shook her head. "No... I don't really know where she is right now."

"No?" He studied her. "Are you sure?"

"I know some places she could be, but no, I don't know for sure where she is staying or where she is right now. You know that she's hoping to build a place of her own. I don't know if she has picked out a property yet. She might have."

"Nothing has been registered at Tennessee Land Title. There's nothing in her name. And I somehow doubt that she has set up a shell company while she has been squatting."

Erin shrugged. "Well then, I really don't know."

"What about Bella? Is she here?"

"She won't be here until after school. A few more hours. She'll help with closing."

"Can you call her? Ask her where Adrienne is?"

Erin shook her head. "She's at school. I can't call her while she's in class. They're not allowed to have their phones out during class and I don't want to get her in trouble. You'll have to wait until school lets out. And then… I don't know if she'll talk to you about it."

"We need to talk to Adrienne."

Erin nodded. "Uh-huh."

"Do you have a phone number for her?"

Erin looked for a way around the question. Terry was a law enforcement officer and she was always careful not to lie to him. She sometimes left him with the wrong impression, but she tried not to actually lie. Unless there was no way around it. And then not if it was part of a police inquiry. If it were something about her private life… she felt she still deserved some privacy. But this was a police investigation. A murder investigation.

"A phone number?" Terry repeated. "One that works?"

"I have one, but I don't know whether she will answer it. Or if it is still good."

"Give it to me and I'll see."

Erin reluctantly pulled out her phone and gave him the number she had for Adrienne. Which she very well knew *was* the right number and that if Adrienne didn't answer it, it was because she had it turned off or didn't want to talk to whoever was calling.

"Why don't you call her and see if it works?" Terry suggested. "If she answers, you can give it to me."

"No!" Erin was appalled at the idea. "I'm not setting her up."

"No one said anything about setting her up," Terry said reasonably. "We just need to get in touch with her. We haven't even been able to do the death notification yet. She is the next of kin."

"I'm not calling her for you. If she wants to talk to the police, she can answer when you call."

"What are you protecting her from?"

Erin rolled her eyes. She didn't know why he even bothered to ask. It was perfectly clear what she was trying to protect Adrienne from. She didn't want the police to pursue her as a suspect.

It was ridiculous to think that Adrienne had left her children to come into town and stab her estranged husband to death behind the bakery.

There was a pain in her chest when she thought about it. She knew that Adrienne couldn't possibly be involved. Adrienne was very thin. She couldn't have a lot of strength. Her husband would have been able to fend her off easily. Statistics might say that the likeliest suspect was the spouse or ex-partner, but that wasn't always the case. There were plenty of people who were killed by strangers, enemies, or in the course of committing a crime. It wasn't hard to imagine Simon as a criminal. He was a tough character.

"Will you let her know that the police would like to talk to her?" Terry asked.

Erin thought about how that conversation would go. They hadn't yet done the death notification. Did Adrienne know that Simon was dead or not? Erin certainly didn't want to be the one to tell her. If she had already heard it from someone else, maybe from Bella, then she would know why the police wanted to talk to her. She was already dodging them.

"You'll just have to try to reach her," Erin said. "I don't want to get involved."

Terry shook his head. "*You* don't want to get involved. You, who I have to keep out of every other murder investigation in Bald Eagle Falls, you don't want to be involved in this one."

"No. I don't want anything to do with it."

"What about Cindy?" Terry asked.

Erin was thrown. "What about her? I don't remember if... I don't think she was in the bakery that day. But you were there. What do you remember?"

"Cindy is not being helpful either. I'm sure she knows exactly where Adrienne is, but she won't say a word about it."

Since Adrienne had been living on the Prost farm the last time Erin had seen her, Erin was sure Terry was right. Cindy probably had a very good idea of where the family was. She was probably one of the few people who knew exactly where Adrienne and the children were staying.

"I'm sure that when Adrienne is ready to talk to you... she will."

He grunted, not liking her answer. They were impatient to find out where everyone had been at the time of the murder and to be able to pin it on someone.

"You were quite likely the last one to see Simon alive," he told Erin.

"If I was the last one to see him alive, then you were too. Everyone in the bakery Friday afternoon was. Because I didn't see him again after that."

He stood there, looking like he would say more. Maybe he, like Melissa, wanted to talk to her about the murder weapon. Get her take on it. Lay the evidence before her and see what she had to say about it then.

Eventually, K9 whined and nudged against Terry's leg. Terry petted him and scratched his ears. "I'd better be getting on my way."

"See you tonight."

"See you then."

Erin did not wish him luck as he left.

CHAPTER 10

*E*rin had expected to be the one to run out of energy before the end of the day, but she caught Vic yawning several times in the afternoon and eventually sent her home. She could nap before having to make supper and look after cranky-pants Willie. Or maybe Willie could step up and take care of Vic. Make her a nice dinner and show her how much he appreciated her.

Erin understood that there was a reason for his irritability and mood swings. A real, physical explanation. She had fully expected that Willie would not feel well and would have problems with brain fog, focus, and being able to follow all of the routines that had previously been easy for him. But that would all go away quickly enough, and then he would have more energy than ever and be able to go on with his life.

She had not anticipated the extent of the problems that Willie would have. She had expected that he would go on just as before, only with a little more difficulty. But he seemed more like a cancer patient—little energy to do anything, weight loss, no concentration, always upset about something. Vic found him difficult to cook for. He said that everything tasted like metal.

It was a wonder that Vic was still putting up with him and

hadn't just kicked him out until he could be civil again. He had his own house. He didn't need to hang around the loft. Vic was a better partner than Erin would have been if Terry had behaved the same way.

So Erin and Bella were alone at the bakery at the end of the day, counting up the day's deposit, sweeping the floors, wiping down the counters, and prepping the batters that they would put into the ovens first thing the next morning.

There was a knock on the back door. Erin checked the peephole, worried that it would be a reporter or a cop or someone else with questions about the murder. She didn't want to talk to anyone about it.

But it was not someone in uniform. Or a reporter. Erin slid back the bolt and opened the door.

"Adrienne!"

Adrienne looked around quickly, head tilted, like a little bird. She made a motion with one skinny arm that Erin took as a request to enter, so Erin stepped back and let her in. She closed the door and threw the bolt again. If anyone had followed Adrienne, they were not getting in.

"Adrienne, how are you? Are you okay?"

Adrienne's eyes were rimmed with red and her face was blotchy. She had obviously been crying.

"I can't be long," she said. "The kids are watching Sarah."

Sarah was her baby, far too young to fend for herself or be watched by preteen siblings.

"I guess…" Erin trailed off awkwardly, unsure what to say to the young woman. "The police must have managed to get ahold of you."

"The police?" Adrienne's eyes widened. "No, I've been able to avoid them so far."

"Terry Piper… he asked me for your phone number. I hope you don't mind that I gave it to him. I didn't know what else to do. I didn't want to be guilty of impeding an investigation."

"It's not even on most of the time. Just when the kids might need to get me." Adrienne sniffled and wiped her red eyes.

"But someone told you… about Simon."

"Yes." Adrienne nodded. She sniffled again and shook her head. "I don't know why I'm crying about it. Do you know how many times I wished that man dead? He was so aggravating. I just couldn't deal with him and his nonsense anymore. I wanted to be done with him." She quelled a sob. "And now I am. No more problems from Simon."

"I'm so sorry." Erin wanted to hug her but wasn't sure how it would be received. She touched Adrienne's arm lightly, then withdrew.

CHAPTER 11

I should get some bread," Adrienne said abruptly. "Could I get some bread?"

"Of course. Let's get what you need from the freezer."

She escorted Adrienne to the freezer full of day-old bread and baking that Erin did her best to give away to those who needed it. She had been able to give some of it to Adrienne before. And she had also donated some through Adele when Adrienne was still too shy to have anything to do with Erin directly.

Erin pulled out several loaves of bread. Straight white bread. She knew what kids liked. They wouldn't want the multigrain or herb stuff. They would want snowy white, evenly sliced bread that they could use for peanut butter and jelly sandwiches. "And some muffins," she murmured. "And cookies. What else do you want? Some pizza shells? Tortillas?"

Adrienne nodded. "Not too much," she cautioned, "I don't want to take more than my share. Just a few things to keep us going."

"There's plenty more; you're not taking too much. Anything I can't find a place for in Bald Eagle Falls, I have to take to the city. I would rather get rid of it here."

Adrienne helped herself to some more muffins and a couple of bags of waffles. "Everything is always so good. You're an angel."

"I'm a baker. That's all."

"You're a good baker. The kids always love your stuff."

"How are they all?"

Adrienne shrugged. "They're okay," she said tentatively. "They don't know yet about Simon. I don't know how I'm going to tell them."

"Are they all his?"

Adrienne hesitated, then nodded. "Yes… we had such an up-and-down relationship. He would be out of my life and I would think I was never going to see him again, and then one day he would show up and… I just couldn't tell him no. I especially couldn't keep him from the kids. It wouldn't be fair to them. But now… I guess I didn't do them any favors letting them develop a relationship with him. Now they will all be upset that he is never coming back again."

She swallowed, and she and Erin filled up a couple of grocery bags with the baked goods.

"Maybe I just won't tell them," Adrienne said. "They're used to him taking off. They'll think that he's just skipped out again. And that one day, maybe he'll come back again."

"I don't know if that would be the best thing," Erin ventured. But what did she know? She wasn't a mom. She hadn't raised any kids. Not with a partner and not by herself. She didn't have any right to think she knew better than Adrienne about how to raise her children.

"I know," Adrienne admitted. "But it's just not fair. It is… so unfair. They're just little children, and now they'll grow up without any dad in their lives. Ever. Do you know what that's going to be like for them?"

"I grew up in foster care," Erin told her. "At least they still have you. They don't have to be passed from one family to another, thinking no one wants them."

"How am I going to raise them by myself? How can I be everything to them? What if something happens to me? Then what?"

"Don't think about the worst. It won't help them. You were raising them by yourself anyway. Before Simon came back. And you were going to kick him out, not let him stay around to raise them."

"I was trying. I don't know if I would have been able to keep saying no. He always… wore me down sooner or later. That was why I was trying not to even see him. If I didn't respond to him, he couldn't find me in town or anywhere else, then he would give up eventually and go somewhere else."

And what would have happened if Simon had refused to give up? If he had waited back behind the bakery watching to see if Adrienne came by to collect some day-old bread for the family? What if there were a confrontation and Simon wouldn't just give up and go somewhere else?

But it still didn't fit. Nothing that she had thought of so far had worked.

"It's better with him out of your life," Bella told Adrienne, her voice sharper than Erin would have expected. "Now you can move on and you can be in control of your life and your family. You don't have to worry about him tracking you down and showing up. You don't have to worry about his influence on the kids or him taking all your money." Her voice was angry. "Can you imagine if he had cleaned out your bank account with all the settlement money sitting there?"

Adrienne's face was already pale. But at Bella's words, she looked even whiter. The money was her one chance to build a home for her children instead of living in a tent in the woods or with other people. It was her one chance to have a permanent home and the stability the children needed. If Simon had taken that away or threatened to…

"When did you see him last?" Erin asked. "He was in here on Friday looking for you, but I just kept shooing him out. Even called Terry to get him out of here the last time. Then he stopped coming."

"He was persistent," Adrienne said. "He didn't like to give up. He always had dreams, ways he was going to make it big. He would go from one thing to another, but he always had something... some kind of plan to finally get all the money he wanted, or the fancy car, or watch, or whatever the new thing was. He had it all figured out, and this time, it was all going to work out. But if it worked out... it was never enough. He'd go on to the next scheme and he'd lose it all. He always bragged that he'd made millions." Her mouth twisted into a tight grimace. "And I don't think he'd made that much. But he always said that he had made millions but lost millions, too. He said it wasn't so hard, making a million dollars. The hard thing was hanging on to it."

"I think if I ever made a million dollars, I would be able to hang on to it," Erin said. "I think I'd hold on to it pretty tight."

"The man never made a thing," Bella said. "Forget making millions. He hardly ever even walked away from the table with a profit. If he made ten bucks on one hand, he'd lose fifteen on the next."

"You don't know all of that," Adrienne said, looking away from Erin, clearly embarrassed.

And she was probably right. When had Bella ever had the opportunity to watch Simon playing cards?

"I have ears," Bella countered. "I hear people talk."

"Well, people exaggerate," Adrienne said. "Even me, if I was mad at him. You can't assume that everyone is telling the absolute truth."

"I know he wasn't good for you and the kids. I know that he left you high and dry, that he didn't even look after you when you were having a baby, just left you like that. No money. No home. Four little ones and a baby on the way, and he just left. Didn't bother coming back for two years!"

Adrienne looked at Erin, spots of color appearing in her

cheeks. "Bell. You need to watch what you say. You'll get me in big trouble."

Bella closed her mouth. She looked at Adrienne, then at her boss, then went back to cleaning up and prepping for the next day.

"Erin would never do anything to get you in trouble," she said. "I'm just blowing off steam. She wouldn't repeat it." Bella looked at Erin over her shoulder. "Would you?"

"No. But you do need to be careful what you say and who you say it around. Adrienne is going to have enough trouble with the police looking into Simon's death without either of us saying anything to anyone. And you..."

Erin looked at Bella, chewing on her lip. She didn't like to think that Bella might have lost her temper with Simon and done something she couldn't take back. But Bella was fiercely protective of Adrienne and the children. And sooner or later, the police would put everything together and come knocking at their door again.

"Just be careful, Bella. Be careful what you say and do. I wouldn't want you to get in any trouble."

CHAPTER 12

*I*t had been a long day, and Erin didn't feel much like making a meal, even just for herself. It was easy enough to prepare a sandwich or open a can of soup, but she didn't feel up to even just that. She suspected Terry would be engrossed in the Simon Simpson case and wouldn't be able to join her for dinner. She called him from her car after closing up.

"Erin, is everything okay?"

There had been enough drama in Erin's life, especially around untimely deaths in Bald Eagle Falls, that she supposed he could be excused for immediately worrying that something might be wrong. Had she found another body? Been threatened by someone? Heard something in the parking lot in the dark?

"Everything is fine," she assured him. "I just wanted to see if you wanted to go out to dinner. Can you take a break from your work?"

"I'm supposed to be off."

"I know. But are you actually going to put everything aside and come home?"

There was a pause while Terry considered this. Maybe he had been planning to go home but, looking at everything on his desk now, realized that there was no way he would be getting out of the office until late.

"Uh… you're probably right," he admitted. "I have a few things that still need to be done. Avenues of inquiry that need to be followed up on before the trail starts to go cold."

"Right," Erin agreed. "So, do you want to come home for supper or stop for something at the restaurant…?"

She hoped he would understand that her suggestion of a restaurant meant she didn't want to cook. He should know her at least that well.

"Uh… a restaurant is fine. I was probably just going to order something in."

If he ordered takeout, he wouldn't have to interrupt his work. He could just work at his desk. Or he and the rest of the police department would eat a pizza or two in the boardroom while discussing the case. It would mean that she wouldn't see him all night. Probably not before she went to bed. She had an early bedtime due to the need to rise early in the morning to bake before the opening of Auntie Clem's.

"Of course I'd love to see you," Terry said, his thoughts following these same lines. "I'm sorry. Yes. We can go to a restaurant."

"It will probably be good for you to get away from the office for a little while. Give you a new perspective."

"That's true," Terry agreed. "Sometimes stepping away from a case for a few minutes is just what you need to make a break-through."

"So you can take a few minutes for supper?"

"Sure. What are you in the mood for tonight?"

"I don't even know. I'm too tired to make a decision."

"Sure," Terry agreed. "I don't think you got enough sleep last night, and the gossip at Auntie Clem's probably has you all worn out."

"It's been quite the day," Erin admitted. She thought about Bella and Adrienne. With the right encouragement, she might learn more about the progress of the investigation from Terry. His investigation might be focused in another direction altogether. Maybe she didn't have to worry about the two young women.

"How about Chinese?" Terry suggested.

"Sure. Whatever you like is good for me. As long as all I have to do is sit there and eat it."

"Okay. Are you leaving now, or are you still closing up?"

"I'm in the car. I'll be there in five minutes."

"I'll see you there, then."

In a few minutes, they were seated at a table in the Chinese restaurant. Erin just motioned to Terry when he asked her what she wanted. He knew what she liked, and she was in no mood to have to choose. He ordered their favorite dishes.

"You shouldn't have gone in today," he said. "You really look worn out."

"I'll be fine. It was a long day, though. I sent Vic home early."

"You should have sent yourself home early."

"I like one of us always to be there, not just a couple of the part-time employees. Other than for the ladies' tea."

"A couple of hours in the afternoon wouldn't hurt."

"No… it wouldn't hurt," Erin admitted. It wasn't a rule that was set in stone. She didn't mind leaving Charley in charge, even though she wasn't the best baker, because she was the half-owner of the bakery. And she had sometimes left Bella in charge. Though in light of the current circumstances, she probably wouldn't do that again if she could help it.

Terry's head was cocked. Erin looked at him as if she were coming out of a dream. "Sorry, did you ask something else?"

"No. Just wondering where you are."

"Nowhere. Just tired." She didn't want him to read the truth in her eyes and averted her gaze. She had a sip of water. She was probably dehydrated. She had been talking a lot and had not thought much about taking care of herself. She was sure she had stopped for lunch but couldn't remember what she had eaten; it seemed like a long time ago. Her stomach ached with hunger.

"So, how is the investigation going?" she asked.

Terry paused to take a drink himself. He would have had a beer if he had been at home but, since he was still returning to the office, he had settled for an RC instead.

"I know that discussing the case over dinner is not ideal. And you're already tired, but…" He trailed off, watching her.

"What?"

"You saw the body. You saw the murder weapon."

Erin swallowed. She just nodded, not answering.

"I didn't ask you anything about it that day because I didn't realize it was special."

"There was something special about it?"

"I thought it was just a knife out of a block set, like you would get at the department store. Some kind of chef's set that any household might have."

Erin nodded. She hadn't said anything about it then, hoping that was the direction the police department would go. It was just a regular knife that anyone could have bought or had in their kitchen. Just an average, run-of-the-mill kitchen knife.

"But I'm told by the techs who were helping me to identify it that it is a cake knife."

Erin nodded. "Anyone could have a cake knife."

"But it isn't one that someone would have just picked up at the department store."

"A kitchen store would have them, though."

"It's a high-end knife. The type of thing that a bakery would have. High-quality materials and workmanship."

"But anyone could have one. It doesn't have to be a bakery."

"I suppose you have one at Auntie Clem's."

Erin nodded. "Sure. Of course."

"So you could show it to me."

Erin took a deep breath in and let it out again.

"You've checked to make sure that you still have yours at the bakery?" Terry pressed.

"I have more than one. I could show you."

He studied her as the waitress delivered their dishes, arranging them on the table.

"Then I guess the question is… are you missing any? Are they all the same brand and model?"

"I bought them at different times. They're not all identical."

"You didn't say whether you are missing any."

Erin sighed and rubbed her forehead, where a knot of tension was gathering.

"Just one," she sighed.

CHAPTER 13

*T*erry gazed at Erin steadily.

"I see. And how did your missing knife end up in Mr. Simon Simpson?"

"I certainly didn't put it there."

Terry chuckled, but he didn't sound amused. K9 looked up at him and readjusted his position, putting his head down on his paws.

"Who had access to the knife?"

"Anyone in the kitchen. Me, Vic, Charley, and any of the part-time employees. We don't allow the public into the kitchen, but sometimes there are other people… deliverymen, repairmen, people picking up day-old bread."

"Who does that include for the past week?"

Erin hadn't had any repairmen in. All of the employees had taken at least one shift. She didn't discuss who used the day-old bread program.

"I already gave Sheriff Wilmot the list of employees and their phone numbers. So he knows everyone who was on shift. I don't think… I can't remember anyone else that we've had in the kitchen in the days before Simon was killed. A few deliveries, but they're in and out pretty quickly."

"Adrienne?"

Erin shook her head. "Not in the week or so before Simon was killed."

"How long was the knife missing?"

"I'm not sure. Like I said, we have others, but Vic had noticed that one had gone astray around the middle or end of the week. It's hard to know when something isn't there anymore. You don't necessarily miss it right away. I figured it would turn up sooner or later. Sometimes people put things away in the wrong drawer or put it on top of the fridge or something silly like that while juggling things."

"You allow people to juggle knives in the kitchen?"

Erin rolled her eyes and gave a tired laugh at the way her words had come out.

Terry was still serious, and he also looked tired, but he was trying to lighten the mood and keep them from getting bogged down in the investigation. It was too easy for them to get tangled up in the immediate, in something that was pressing like a murder investigation, and to forget to take care of their relationship. They had not arranged to eat dinner together just to further the investigation. It was supposed to be their chance to connect.

"I know it looks bad," Erin said, "But couldn't it have been an outsider? A vagrant or someone who was passing through and argued with Simon? I mean, he didn't exactly steer clear of trouble. He liked to threaten."

"How did that person get your cake knife?"

Erin rubbed her forehead. She dished up a little food from each of the bowls. "I don't know. Maybe..." She tried to think of a scenario in which the cake knife had been taken from Auntie Clem's for an innocent reason, and then someone else had gotten their hands on it. Just one of those things, a bunch of things happening at the same time to cause the perfect storm. A murder that looked like it had been committed by an employee of Auntie Clem's when it had not. "I'll have to think about it," she admitted.

"I would be willing to entertain the possibility that it was someone else in Bald Eagle Falls or someone else from outside of Bald Eagle Falls," Terry said. "But we would have to be able to explain how a knife from your bakery was used as the murder weapon."

"I can't believe any of my employees could have done something like that. And if it was someone from the bakery, why would they leave the knife there? They had to know it would point right back at the bakery employees. Why not take it back into the bakery, clean it off, and put it in the drawer? No one would know the difference."

Terry shrugged. "Criminals are famous for doing some very stupid, self-incriminating things. If he was killed in the heat of the moment, I could easily see an unsophisticated killer leaving the weapon behind even though it pointed back at them. That's how we catch people. He—or she—panics and runs away, leaving it behind."

"But the body was there for two days. They could have returned to get it when no one else was around. If it was an employee, she would have a key and could let herself in when no one was around. Wash the knife off and put it away. Or put it on top of the fridge or in a place where it didn't belong so everyone would think it had just been misplaced for a few days. No one would connect it to the murder."

Terry's lips compressed together. "I think we would still have figured out that it was the murder weapon. There aren't a lot of knives around that fit the profile. That wide spade shape is pretty unique."

Erin shook her head. She ate some of the noodles on her plate, even though she felt more tired than hungry. "I just don't think it could have been anyone at Auntie Clem's."

"There's another possibility."

She looked at him hopefully.

"What if it was Simon who took it?" Terry suggested. "One of the dangers of arming yourself is that your weapon could be used against you. What if there was a struggle and someone else ended up with his weapon?"

"Yeah…" Erin liked that idea. She tried to figure out how Simon could have gotten his hands on the knife. He'd been in the bakery several times asking about Adrienne. He had come to the back once and his body had been found behind the bakery.

What if the back door had been left unlocked at some point? An employee going out to smoke and then forgetting to lock it again? A delivery man who brought in more than one load and had left the door propped for five minutes while he returned for his second load? Or what if an employee had used the knife in the front of the shop and had put it down on the counter where Simon could reach when he had been in?

She tried to picture each time she had talked to Simon. Had she kept her eyes on him the whole time? Watched every move that he made? She probably hadn't. She had tried to show him she wasn't interested in helping him by going on with her other work as if he hadn't been there. She had deliberately ignored him, hoping that would make him leave sooner.

"I guess it's possible," she said. "And if Simon was the one who stole it, then the killer could have been anyone. Not just an employee." She felt lighter at the possibility. The idea that the killer could be one of her employees had been tying her gut in knots.

Terry sighed. Having a larger pool to draw on was not necessarily good for him. It was much easier for the police department if they only had a few suspects. Or only one.

CHAPTER 14

*E*rin couldn't help smiling at his dismay. "Simon wasn't such a nice guy," she pointed out. "Did he have a lot of enemies?" Bella and Adrienne had implied that he was a gambler, swindler, or both. He had abandoned his family, which probably meant he'd had interests elsewhere. Maybe he was the type who had "a girl in every port" as he gambled his way around the country. For long-suffering Adrienne to say that she'd wanted to throttle Simon more than once, he must have really pushed the limits.

"We'll have more suspects than we know what to do with," Terry admitted, "if we don't find a way to narrow the pool."

"Well…" Erin ate a few more bites of her dinner, hungrier now as she considered unknown suspects instead of her friends and employees. If they could prove it was someone else, she wouldn't have to worry about Bella or Adrienne or anyone else. They could all go on as usual and forget that Simon had ever been a part of their lives. "What do you know about the time of death? Did you get anything from the medical examiner?"

"We're looking at Friday afternoon or evening, shortly after you kicked him out."

"After *you* kicked him out," Erin corrected.

"After *we* kicked him out."

Erin frowned.

"He had eaten part of the cinnamon roll he bought from you," Terry contributed, giving her more details. "He wouldn't have carried it around for several days."

"No," Erin agreed, nodding. He must have been killed within a couple of hours of leaving Auntie Clem's. Had he been interrupted after eating part of it? Had he gotten hungry after standing around watching for Adrienne and started picking at it, or had he met his fate within just a few minutes of leaving the bakery?

"Did the ME examine the stomach contents?" she asked. "They can pinpoint the time of death from that, can't they?"

"Only if they knew what time he ate the cinnamon roll. And it will keep dissolving in the stomach acids after death so, when the body has been there for two days already, it's pretty much useless. But..." he frowned and stopped himself. He shook his head. "Nothing."

"What?" Erin demanded.

Terry concentrated on a sweet and sour chicken wing. "These are really good."

Erin watched him, waiting. He wasn't doing a good job distracting her from the fact that he had nearly told her something and then taken it back. She knew that he was holding something back, and she was going to wait until she knew what it was.

Terry looked at her after a moment. "So how *was* the gossip at Auntie Clem's today? I assume everyone now knows everything there was to know about Mr. Simpson and how he was killed?"

"*But* what?"

He raised an eyebrow. "Hmm?"

"But what about the stomach contents? They found something else? He'd had pizza for lunch? Swallowed an SD card? Was muling drugs?"

Terry was shaking his head, but didn't fill in the facts. Erin stopped eating and sat back.

"I'm sorry," Terry said, "you know there are things I can't tell you. And that there are things that we hold back from the public."

Erin reviewed the conversation in her mind. He hadn't said that the ME had finished the autopsy yet or had examined or not examined the stomach contents. He had just made general statements about it. Statements that Erin figured would have been replaced with details if he had known them.

Yet there was still something about what Simon had eaten or not eaten or the time of death that Terry had been about to tell her and then had thought better of.

"This is something about what he ate?" she asked. "About the part of a cinnamon roll...?"

Terry gave no sign, positive or negative.

Erin didn't like to think about what she had seen in detail; she didn't want it to be lodged in her long-term memory. But she had seen Simon's body. She had stood near enough to smell it so clearly that she had been sick. The horrible smell of decaying meat, the offal, and the faint smell of... cheese?

Erin steadied herself on the table and took a quick drink, forcing the water down and hoping it would not bring anything else up.

No, not the smell of cheese. The smell of Parmesan cheese always made her think of vomit. She had looked it up once, curious as to why the two should be connected in her mind.

"Butyric acid," she said finally, her stomach back under control.

"What?" Terry was bewildered. He shook his head with no idea what she was talking about.

"It's what makes vomit and Parmesan cheese stink."

"Okay... and you're telling me this because..."

"Because I could smell it on Simon. Not very well, because

of… you know… the decomposition. But that means he had vomited, doesn't it?"

Terry closed his mouth and shook his head. But he wasn't denying it. He just couldn't believe that Erin had figured it out without his telling her.

"So…" Erin tried to follow the fact to its natural conclusions. "He didn't have anything in his stomach because he'd already thrown up? So stomach contents aren't going to help establish time of death."

Terry shrugged. "I didn't tell you any of this."

"Okay," Erin agreed. "I never heard anything from you. I figured it all out by myself."

Terry nodded his agreement. Erin continued to eat her dinner. She really shouldn't be talking about such things while she was eating. She got nauseated easily enough without trying to remember how Simon's remains looked and smelled. She wasn't the kind of person who could just shut off her body's natural reaction to such things. It was like a poison. Once exposed to the scene, there was no way to stop her body's reaction.

"Poison," Erin murmured. Looking across the table, she met Terry's eyes.

"What?" He broke eye contact, looking out the window beside the table.

"He threw up. Why? Do you think… he was poisoned?"

Terry cleared his throat. "There's no way to know that at this point. The ME needs to do an autopsy and lab tests have to be done. All of that will be determined eventually. For now, all we can do is speculate. It is… *suggestive* of poisoning."

"Someone poisoned him and then stabbed him?"

"It's been known to happen. Many times, poisoning doesn't work exactly how the killer expected, whether it is attempted suicide or murder. The victim gets sick and then recovers. The victim throws up, expelling the poison, or enough of it that he doesn't die. Or it is a long, lingering illness and the would-be killer gets impatient. He ups the dose, changes the poison, or changes the method. You find a lot of cases once you start looking."

"On TV shows or movies, they poison someone and they die. Or have a really close call and end up in the hospital with their stomach pumped and recover."

But Erin knew the details of more than one case of poisoning where death had not been immediate. Terry's words should not come as a surprise.

"Just like any method, there are many different ways it can go wrong," Terry said. "And it is usually a long-term method. Not the immediate frothing-at-the-mouth thing you see with cyanide poisoning shown in movies."

"So what killed him? The poison didn't work, so the killer switched methods and stabbed him?"

"We have to wait for the ME's findings. But that would be my guess. Or..."

Erin cocked her head and looked at him curiously, wondering whether he were going to tell her this time or try to keep it a secret again and make her guess.

"Or what?"

"Or it was two different people. One who poisoned him and one who stabbed him. Two different suspects, two different motives."

"What do you think the chances of that are?"

"I wouldn't want to guess. I'm assuming there was only one killer, but have to stay open to other possibilities, especially considering his reputation. Someone who has an alibi for the stabbing might not have one for the poisoning, and vice versa. Ditto access to the poison or the knife. We may have two killers."

CHAPTER 15

*E*rin enlarged the text on her computer and read the short obituary for Simon Simpson. The Bald Eagle Falls weekly would be out in two days and would probably contain a longer obituary and maybe an article or two on the murder. Still, she would have to make do with the bare-bones obituary that the funeral home had posted on their website until a more comprehensive version was published. Erin imagined that the funeral home had quickly put together a short-form biography to stave off the calls that they were getting until the family provided them with something else. And they would refer any inquiries about how he had died to the police.

There wasn't much to be gleaned from the obituary. Adrienne and the children were mentioned, although Erin noticed that not all of the children's names had been listed. Both baby Sarah and another of the children had been omitted, despite Adrienne's assertion that they were all Simon's.

But there was also a sister living in Bald Eagle Falls. If Simon's family were really multigenerational residents of Bald Eagle Falls and the surrounding area, it made sense that he would have some family around. Families were much smaller than they had been a few decades ago; it was not uncommon to have only one or two siblings now instead of six or eight. A lot of lines were dying out.

Simon's sister's name was Scarlett Simpson and, with a few quick searches, Erin managed to find her address. Erin had found that the residents of Bald Eagle Falls were not as concerned with protecting their addresses as city-dwellers were. People in Bald Eagle Falls went to school, church, and other community events together. They all knew where the other members of the community lived. There wasn't any way to keep it a secret.

She quickly arranged a plate of cookies, tarts, and dessert bars using what she had in the freezer. They would defrost quickly once she got into the car. By the time she arrived, they would be thawed through. That was one benefit of the Tennessee summer heat.

There were a few other cars in front of Scarlett Simpson's home. She'd probably had a pretty constant stream of visitors since the news of Simon's death had spread through the town.

It was an older house. A hundred years or more, Erin would guess. Older than Clementine's house, which Erin had inherited. It had, she assumed, housed several generations of Simpson family members. It appeared to be in pretty good shape. Carefully maintained rather than falling into disrepair after so long.

Erin walked up to the door and rang the bell. She knew that the proper etiquette was probably to knock or yoo-hoo and enter, allowing Scarlett to stay where she was instead of answering the door whenever another visitor arrived—no point in running her off her feet.

The door opened within a few seconds. It was an older woman, not someone Simon's age. Erin did a double-take and realized that it was Betty, an elderly woman who was a regular customer at Auntie Clem's.

"Oh, Erin," she greeted. "No need to ring the bell. Come on in."

Betty took Erin by the arm and escorted her first to a table piled with a mountain of casseroles and platters, exclaiming over the sweets, and then took her into the cool, dimly lit parlor where the mourners were gathered. There were murmured conversations, sniffles, and soft sobs.

"Scarlett, dear," Betty addressed a woman in her thirties at the center of the gathering. "I don't know whether you know Erin Price? She just brought a lovely plate of desserts. She runs Auntie Clem's Bakery. You know? Dear Clementine's great niece."

"Hi," the woman with long, sleek, dark-brown hair nodded. "Thank you so much. That was very thoughtful."

"I hope I'm not intruding," Erin said awkwardly. "I didn't really know Simon, but I'm very sorry for your loss and wanted to express my condolences."

"You're very kind. Why don't you come sit down and we'll tell you some of our stories about him?"

Betty nudged Erin toward an empty chair, and she sat down. Betty headed back toward the front door to man her post.

"She's so nice," Scarlett said. "And I happen to know she didn't even like Simon. I don't know exactly what he did to her when he was younger, but she's still holding on to a grudge. Or she was. I guess it's over now."

"Oh," Erin didn't know what to say to this revelation. "Well... I've always admired Betty. It's very nice of her to help you out."

"Some people just know what to do," Scarlett said, nodding.

Erin felt like she was the opposite. One of the people who never knew what to do. She always seemed to bumble through things until someone showed her the right way. She was grateful for Betty being at the door and helping her through what might otherwise have been awkward.

"I only met Simon when he got into town a couple of weeks ago. But I guess you guys grew up here?" she asked Scarlett.

"Yes. We lived here with our parents and grandparents. I stayed on. Simon... always had somewhere else to go. He had some big thing he had to try... some new venture or sure thing... he hated staying in one place."

"Wanderlust?" Erin suggested. "I moved around a lot from the time that I was young. Got used to it. This is the longest that I have ever stayed in one place."

"I guess some people are homebodies and some just have to be out adventuring. I always knew that Simon would be the one to leave. I thought he'd come back after a while, but..."

"I guess he must have returned a few times, with Adrienne being here," Erin suggested.

Scarlett rolled her eyes. "Adrienne is a lovely person," she said, "but I wish she and Simon had never met. He was always so... entangled with her. They were either all goo-goo eyes and making plans, or he'd had enough and was taking off."

And cleaning out the bank account before he left.

"And Adrienne wasn't from around here?"

"Not exactly. It would have been better if she had just stayed away."

CHAPTER 16

*D*o you think…" Rae Young, a woman Erin didn't know well, leaned forward in her seat, her voice low, "Was she the one who…?" Her meaning was clear, even if she didn't finish the question.

Scarlett rocked back in her seat.

"I can't see Adrienne doing something like that," she proclaimed, shaking her head. "She loved Simon. She was the only one who put up with all his crap." She continued to shake her head adamantly. "I can't see her doing anything to hurt him."

"But he wasn't faithful to her," Rae pointed out. "A woman scorned… even Adrienne couldn't ignore it when he took up with someone right under her nose."

Erin sat listening, eager to hear the gossip about who else might have a motive. She hoped that Scarlett was right and that Adrienne hadn't had anything to do with Simon's death, but she still had that worried knot in her stomach, that feeling of dread that at any moment, the whole world might come crashing down around her and Adrienne would be arrested for the murder.

If there were another woman, then that woman would have

just as much of a motive to kill Simon. Well, maybe not just as good as the woman struggling with raising his five—or three—children on her own and worrying that he would somehow get his hands on the money she had managed to get to build the house.

But still a good motive. People killed out of jealousy all the time. Maybe Simon had told the other woman that he was going back to Adrienne. That he wasn't going to divorce her as he had promised, but instead needed to take care of his children. When, of course, he just wanted to worm his way in to get the money.

"Who was he seeing in town?" Scarlett asked. She ran her fingers through her long hair, sweeping it back over her shoulders away from her face. "I thought… he was always pretty good about at least keeping his affairs out of town."

Rae shook her head. "Emily Johnson," she pronounced, drawing muffled gasps of shock—real or pretended, Erin wasn't sure which—from the other mourners.

"The schoolteacher?" Scarlett shook her head in disbelief. "She was here yesterday. Brought a casserole. She didn't say… are you sure? I don't think Simon had anything to do with her."

"Not after he was finished breaking her heart, maybe," the gossip said, "but I saw them together. There's no doubt. And if I saw them, then other people did, too. I'm sure Adrienne would have heard about it from some quarter."

"Did you tell her?" Scarlett asked.

"Me? I wouldn't do that!" The woman gave a little head shake. "I did ask her if she knew Emily. I thought that she should at least have her eyes open. Someone would tell her sooner or later, and she might as well be prepared for it."

"Simon and Emily Johnson? She's always been so quiet. When was this? Recently?"

"Last time he was in town. When was that? A year ago? Two?"

Scarlett didn't answer the question.

"Why would Adrienne do anything about it now?" Erin

asked, unable to keep quiet. "If it happened a year or two ago, and Adrienne wasn't getting back together with Simon, then why would it be an issue now?"

"Do you really think any of that matters?" Rae challenged, black eyes sparkling. "When you hear that your man has been messing around with another woman in town, right under your nose, does any of that come into it? I would be furious. They were still married. She was raising his children. And instead of stepping up and taking responsibility, she discovers he's catting around on her. He probably didn't even come back to see Adrienne. He probably planned to take up with Emily again."

"No," Erin disagreed. "It wasn't because of another woman that he came back here."

Everyone turned their eyes toward her, curious to find out what she knew.

"You don't know why Simon came home," Scarlett challenged. "He wanted to see his family. Me. His children. I know that Adrienne turned him out, but they were talking for a few days; there was the possibility of them getting back together up until Friday." She dabbed at the corners of her eyes. "Oh, if he could just have settled down. Maybe this wouldn't have happened if she had taken him back."

Erin didn't want to badmouth Simon before his sister and the other mourners and supporters. She had no intention of being unkind and hurting anyone.

"He wanted to see if he could work things out with Adrienne," she said, agreeing with Scarlett's statement. Simon had sought out Adrienne. He had been trying to work things out with her. Whether it was because he genuinely wanted to be with her and with his children or was just trying to get his hands on the money, Erin didn't know. But Simon had been trying to reconcile.

Her words hung in the air. Everyone was expecting more. To hear some dirt. Scarlett eyed her. Had Simon told Scarlett about the money and she was waiting to see if Erin would bring it up?

Or was she completely innocent as to the reason Simon had really come back?

"But I don't blame Adrienne for not taking him back," she asserted. "And I don't think that she had anything to do with his death. Adrienne couldn't do something like that. Even if she was in a jealous rage… she has the children to look after. She wasn't even in town that day."

"How do you know that?" Rae challenged.

"Simon was looking for her and she wasn't around. She was lying low, trying to avoid seeing him."

"Would have made more sense to just *off* him," Rae said. "Why sneak around and have to limit her life to avoid seeing him? Easier and cleaner to just get him out of the way. Not have to worry about him coming back to town again." She looked at Scarlett. "I don't mean it was justified. I'm just saying what *she* would have thought."

"Simon was a pretty bad husband," Scarlett admitted. "He was a good daddy, cared about his kids, but he wasn't a very good partner to Adrienne."

He was a good daddy? Erin didn't challenge the assertion out loud, but she couldn't help wondering where Scarlett was coming from. Maybe he loved his children. But abandoning them didn't show that love. It wasn't okay to be an attentive father for a day or two, buy the kids milkshakes, and then disappear again for a couple more years. With all the family's savings.

"Well, it isn't like Adrienne didn't do some… exploring of her own," one of the other women provided. "She was no innocent babe waiting for him to come back home to her."

Sly looks passed between some of the women. Erin shifted uncomfortably. She didn't know anything about Adrienne's private life. She had never seen Adrienne with a man. She was with her children, at work, or with Bella. It was rare for her to even be without the children. On the occasions when she had come to see Erin on her own, the children were playing in the park nearby, left alone for just a few minutes. When did she have time to have an affair?

"I didn't know that Adrienne was seeing anyone," she said as neutrally as she could, trying not to show her bias for Adrienne and against Simon. It wasn't really the place to show her antagonism for Simon.

"She's had her... relationships," Rae asserted. "Don't let her fool you."

"Is there something wrong with her having relationships with someone else when Simon was gone? It wasn't like he was off to war or something like that."

He had abandoned her. Why would anyone expect her to wait for his return and put her social life on hold indefinitely?

The women seemed shocked at the suggestion. A double standard. Fine for Simon to leave her behind and have a girl at every port. But not okay for Adrienne to find solace with someone else?

"She was a married woman," Scarlett insisted. "Any virtuous married woman would have waited for him to return. She wouldn't have sullied herself with other men."

Virtue. A concept Erin didn't know if she would ever understand. Why it was okay for a man to have whatever relationships he pleased and it was just brushed off as men having needs or boys being boys, yet for a woman to have a relationship before marriage or outside her failed marriage was somehow seen as a major character flaw and a disgrace.

"It's too bad that no one stepped forward to help her take care of those kids," Erin said. "Since Simon wasn't willing to do it."

There was silence in the room. Erin had done what she had just told herself she wouldn't do, pointing out the dead man's flaws. But it wasn't like everyone didn't already know them.

"He was such a scamp as a boy," Scarlett said, either changing the subject or turning those flaws into something boyish and silly instead of admitting her brother had some major character flaws and had been a deadbeat. "He was always getting into trouble one way or another. Schoolteachers, church, running around with other little hooligans around the neighborhood. How many times did they break Mr. Hanes's front window with a baseball? I'll bet that man regretted moving into a house across from the park!"

"Do you remember how they used to chase the little girls at school?" Rae asked. "Cooties! The boys and girls were always teasing each other. Funny the way that they fight all the way through the early grades, and then all that attention turns into… a different kind of attention in the teen years."

"It's all just practice," Scarlett agreed. "He never stopped chasing the girls. It was just that when he caught them…" She gave a high giggle.

"The only reason he liked Adrienne was because she was the new girl," Rae declared. "She was something different, novel. She wasn't someone he had known his whole life like the other girls. That was why he pursued her."

"And caught her," Scarlett pointed out.

There were indulgent chuckles from around the room. Erin closed her eyes, trying to remember something from months ago. Back when she had first met Adrienne.

"*Were* they married?" she asked Scarlett.

They had asserted that Adrienne was a married woman and that Simon was a poor husband, but Erin had lodged in her mind the idea that Adrienne was not, in fact, married. She was an independent person. She had fallen for Simon Simpson, but had they actually tied the knot? Or had Adrienne refused to be tied down to a man, just like she had refused to move to the city where there were homeless shelters available because she didn't want her children put in that atmosphere? She wanted them to be outside, running and playing in the fresh air, not cooped up in some program where they had to follow strict rules, go to school in a classroom, and be exposed to street people with TB, fleas, and lice.

Scarlett looked at the other women, hesitating. Erin knew that the church ladies would still consider it a sin if Adrienne had been with other men while unmarried. But maybe a little less than cheating on her husband while they were married.

"No," Scarlett admitted finally, "they were never actually officially married."

"Adrienne didn't want any part of it," Rae said flatly. "Maybe if she had tied the knot, Simon would have stayed home."

But Scarlett shook her head. She knew that it wouldn't have made any difference to her brother.

CHAPTER 17

There was a knock on the door and, a moment later, Betty escorted Mrs. Foster in with her two youngest children. She relieved the woman of a casserole dish and put it on the table with the rest of the offerings.

The Fosters were some of Erin's favorite customers. Peter, the oldest, was her special friend. He was a very serious and mature child and had celiac disease. He was delighted to be able to go to a bakery and pick out whatever he wanted, just like the other kids he went to school with, instead of being limited to whatever stale boxed cookies or bread sat languishing on the shelves of the Bald Eagle Falls grocery store. Before Auntie Clem's, one of his parents had occasionally made the drive out to the city and could pick up a specialty item, but that was rare. And Mrs. Foster did not have much time to bake special foods for him.

But it was a weekday and school had just started up again. With none of the bigger kids to help, Mrs. Foster had her hands full with Traci and baby Allan. Traci was a very active, very strong-willed preschooler, and Allan tended to be fussy and fretful. His disposition was improving as they identified what foods he reacted to and eliminated them from his diet. Erin would have been grumpy if her stomach hurt all the time too.

"You know Abigail Foster," Betty said to Scarlett, "and her children."

Mrs. Foster shook hands with Scarlett, and Betty helped to shuffle people around to make space for her and Traci. Allan was still small enough to cuddle in her lap if he would stay quiet. Mrs. Foster settled her diaper bag between her feet and pulled out a gluten-free teething biscuit from Auntie Clem's, tipping it toward Erin in a salute before giving it to Allan.

"I don't know what I would do without Auntie Clem's Bakery," she told Erin and the rest of the room. "You are such a lifesaver."

"How is Allan doing?"

"Not bad," Mrs. Foster said, "He's sleeping better, which is a great blessing."

Erin nodded. She could only imagine the difficulty of raising five active children on insufficient sleep.

Traci homed in on Erin and darted away from her mother before Mrs. Foster could grab her.

"Cook-kie!" Traci demanded, walking right up to Erin.

Erin laughed while Mrs. Foster tried to correct Traci and get her to come back to sit down, but Traci refused, repeating her demand for a cookie from the woman she knew to be the cookie lady. It was perfectly logical that Erin would have a cookie to give her, since she always had one when Traci came to Auntie Clem's with her mother. And Allan had a teething biscuit. Traci should get a treat too.

Erin gathered Traci to her to give her a hug. "Do you mind if Traci has a cookie from the table?" she asked Scarlett. "I brought some with me, and it looks like a few other people did, too."

Scarlett nodded. "Of course, help yourself."

Erin stood up, picking Traci up with her. "Is it okay?" she asked Mrs. Foster.

"Sure. Thank you. Traci, you tell Miss Erin 'thank you.'"

"Cook-kie," Traci insisted.

"I think she's going to wait until she has it in hand," Erin observed. She took Traci over to the table and let her choose from the available plates of cookies. "Which one would you like, sweetie?"

Traci considered, her lips in a pout as she considered her options carefully. Finally, she pointed. "Dat one."

Erin knew that if Traci didn't get the exact cookie she had identified, she would have a fit. It didn't matter if it were the same variety. She had to have the specific cookie she pointed at. Erin moved closer to make sure she knew which one Traci was pointing to and pulled back the plastic wrap to retrieve it.

"This one?"

Traci kicked excitedly. "Dat one! Dat one!"

"Let's get a little plate," Erin suggested. "We'll play tea party, okay?"

She put the cookie on a small plate and grabbed a couple of napkins as well. Traci was not a tidy eater; Erin knew from experience. She returned to her seat and sat Traci on her lap, whispering in her ear and setting the plate in her lap.

"Tell Miss Erin thank you," Miss Foster reminded.

"Tank you," Traci obliged this time.

Erin gave her a squeeze and wondered how Adrienne and her children were faring.

Erin had stayed at Scarlett Simpson's longer than she had planned to. But she had not wanted to leave Mrs. Foster alone to take care of both Allan and Traci, so she stuck around until Allan started to fuss and Mrs. Foster decided it was time to take him home. She thanked Erin for helping to keep Traci quiet and occupied as they stepped outside into the furnace-like heat of the summer.

"They are quite a handful, I'll tell you!" Mrs. Foster said. "It was one thing when Allan was happy being in the sling, but now that he is older, he wants to be moving around and more independent, and you know Traci…"

"They are a going concern," Erin laughed.

"They're going!" Mrs. Foster agreed.

Erin drove her car over to the mechanic. She had finally gotten around to setting up an oil change, which she knew she was late taking care of. Things got so busy with the bakery that sometimes other priorities slid.

But she couldn't let her car be one of them. She needed it to get her around reliably, both in town and out to the city. She knew how hard it was to manage without a car, even in a small town like Bald Eagle Falls.

She greeted Darryl Wilson, the quiet, unassuming mechanic who seemed to have a magical touch with cars. Erin had always pictured "car guys" as being burly, rough-and-tumble, constantly cussing men with pin-up girls in their lockers and grease under their nails.

But Darryl was soft-spoken and endlessly polite. Erin couldn't imagine him cussing over anything less than a car rolling over his foot and breaking his toe. His garage and the waiting room were spotless, and the coffee in the waiting room always fresh. He worked diligently to stay on time and under budget, and if he did go over, was always sincerely apologetic for it, even if it were due to someone else's emergency situation.

Erin pulled her car into the two-bay garage and slid out. She looked at the car in the next slot over.

"Is that Adrienne's car?" she asked curiously. She had only seen Adrienne drive a couple of times, but thought she recognized the rusting old station wagon. It was probably older than Adrienne.

Darryl looked at the car, color coming to his cheeks. He looked uncertain about whether to answer her. Erin didn't think there was such a thing as mechanic-client privilege but, like Erin, he probably wanted to protect Adrienne and make sure that no one could find or harass her.

"It's fine," she said. "I think it is Adrienne's car, but you don't have to say anything. Adrienne and I are friends. I'm not going to tell anyone that she's here. Or coming back here when you've had a chance to get her car fixed up."

Darryl nodded gratefully. "She's had enough to go through without more people coming after her."

"More people?" Erin repeated.

"Simon. And then the police. And unsavory-looking out-of-towners."

Erin frowned. "What out-of-towners?"

Darryl shook his head slowly. He didn't answer immediately, thinking about it and composing what he wanted to say. Erin had learned he was a very deliberate speaker and did not handle it well when he was hurried, so she waited for him.

"A couple of rough-looking guys were by asking where her place was, asking for directions to get there. They were quite upset when I wouldn't help them. Not the kind of guys I would want hanging around here." He looked worriedly at Adrienne's car. He clearly did not want it to be there when he knew that people were out looking for Adrienne and she couldn't be far away.

"Not mechanics?" Erin teased.

"No. Might know something about cars and bikes, but… not professionally. These guys were more the kind who are in the *collections* business."

Erin knew what that meant. She had been through enough lean times to know the allure of getting a loan from someone who offered to help and then the terror of being unable to pay it back by the deadline. Those guys could be scary. Of necessity, they *were* scary. Even if they didn't utter any threats and just politely informed her that they were there to collect and would take whatever she had that had any value. Which, unfortunately, was nothing. Erin had always lived close to the bone, perhaps with only one suitcase containing all her worldly goods. Maybe you couldn't squeeze blood from a stone, but Erin wouldn't put it past one of those guys to try it.

"Adrienne doesn't owe anyone any money," Erin told Darryl.

He looked grateful and nodded his agreement. "I know she doesn't," he agreed. "She won't borrow or overextend herself. She's very careful. But they wanted Simon and, since he's not around anymore…"

"They can't collect it from her," Erin said firmly. "She doesn't owe them anything."

"They can still come after her."

"Not legally. Not unless she signed for it."

"These folks don't always do *legal*."

"Did you warn her that they were around looking for her?"

He nodded. "Sent her a text after they were gone."

"Okay. Good. I'll let Terry know too, see if he can move them on their way."

"Thanks."

Erin started to walk to the customer waiting area. She could pull out her planner and work on Auntie Clem's upcoming campaigns.

"Miss Erin?" Darryl said.

She turned back to look at him.

"Adrienne is a good person. She didn't do this."

Erin took a deep breath in and let it out slowly.

"I don't think she did either. I hope not."

"She loved Simon. She knew that she couldn't live with him or let him back into her life again, but she still loved him. She wouldn't have done that."

Erin gave Darryl a long, thoughtful look before nodding and turning away.

CHAPTER 18

*E*rin was still in the waiting room when Adrienne returned for her car. Erin could hear her talking to Darryl in a low voice for a couple of minutes, probably just about the car and settling up, before Adrienne appeared in the doorway, peeking in at Erin.

Erin straightened in her seat and smiled. "It's just me," she promised. "How is it going? Did Darryl get your car all fixed up?" She kept her voice as light and cheerful as possible. Adrienne had enough negative drama going on in her life. She didn't need Erin dragging around like Simon's death was a huge tragedy that Adrienne might never recover from.

"Yes, it should run for a few more days now," Adrienne sighed.

Erin laughed. "That good, huh?"

"It seems like just when you fix one thing, something else breaks. I keep saying, 'This will be it; there isn't anything else to fix after this. Everything has been replaced.' And then something that I've never even heard of before breaks. If I didn't know how trustworthy Darryl is, I would think he was intentionally bringing me back here just so we could chat." Her smile seemed forced and plastic.

"I think he does have the tiniest crush on you," Erin teased, remembering how Darryl blushed when Erin asked him about Adrienne's car. Maybe it was true.

Adrienne swallowed and shook her head. "Be careful what you say," she warned. "Half the town already hates me. If they found out about Darryl and me, they'd never forgive me."

"You and Darryl…?" Erin repeated.

"We're just friends. Maybe. Now that Simon is gone, who knows? But you have to keep your mouth shut. They already think I'm some kind of… loose woman. You think I'm loose when I stayed with Simon for ten years? That's a long time."

"It is," Erin agreed. "And I don't care what anyone else says. I don't care who you were with. Or whether you were married. That's their hang-up," Erin made a motion waving them all away. "Not mine."

Adrienne looked at her for a moment, frozen like a rabbit that has been startled.

"You know what it's like," she told Erin finally. "They don't know. They've always had whatever they need, never had to hang on to someone just to survive. And then for him to take off, to take all that stability with him and leave me with nothing!" She spat. "He could be so aggravating. Come back here, treating me as sweet as honey and courting me. But I knew that it would all fade away again. As soon as he got the itch, he'd be out of town and probably all my money with him."

Adrienne went to the coffee station and looked down at the coffee supplies as if she didn't know what to do with them.

"I couldn't let him do that to me again. I couldn't let him take the one chance we had to make it. To build a place of our own, someplace that would be ours, that no one could take away from us. I could start to build a real life here instead of one where I have to keep moving every few months when someone chases us off."

"So you…" Erin was breathless, worried about what Adrienne was about to reveal. She did not want to know if Adrienne had killed Simon. She didn't want to have to cover for Adrienne. To lie to Terry. Her heart pounded hard and she felt nauseated.

"So I told him no," Adrienne finished sharply. "I told him he couldn't play daddy anymore. He couldn't take anything else from me. He couldn't hurt the kids. Make love to me and then take off. I wouldn't stand for it anymore."

Erin nodded. She sipped her cold, bitter coffee, hoping her relief was not too noticeable.

"That's good," she told Adrienne. "I wish that it had worked out differently. That he'd just gotten the message and… taken off."

"Me too." Adrienne scrubbed at her eyes. "Please… don't say anything to anyone about it. Or about Darryl. I just need… some time to figure things out. And to let people get used to the idea of Simon being gone. His sister, Scarlett…"

"I was over there today," Erin said. "Took some cookies from the freezer for her. I would come out and visit you too, but… I don't think you want anyone near your place."

"No," Adrienne agreed. "We need to stay out of sight. Especially when thugs are looking for someone to pay off Simon's debts." She shook her head. "Good for you for seeing Scarlett. I'm sure she needs the support just as much as anyone. But don't expect her to be warm toward me."

"I know. She's protecting the memory of her brother."

Adrienne laughed bitterly. "The memory of her brother. The way she wished he'd been, maybe. They never got along in life. She hated him as much as she hated me. Maybe I even got the warmer shoulder now and then. She was not a fan of Simon."

"Really?" Erin was shocked. "She kept going on about him. Childhood memories. All of the scrapes he used to get into. How *people* hadn't treated him fairly." Adrienne probably knew Erin meant that Adrienne had treated Simon badly, but she wouldn't say that to her face. "I thought they were close."

Adrienne shook her head, chuckling. "They could never get along. Fought like cats and dogs. I actually tried to get the two of them to reconcile. But Scarlett would have nothing to do with him. I think Simon would have made up with her and would have apologized for all of the stupid stuff he did to her growing up. But there was no way."

Maybe Scarlett was covering up her real feelings so that no one would think she had a motive to kill Simon. But would anyone kill over sibling rivalry? Erin thought not but, as soon as she thought it, she remembered Davis Plaint killing his brother Trenton over their inheritance. She reconsidered. Maybe Scarlett was a viable suspect.

But could she tell Terry or the sheriff that? She didn't feel like it was fair to accuse one of the chief mourners. Especially when she had no proof. Scarlett had said one thing and Adrienne another, and Erin was more inclined to believe Adrienne. But she didn't have any evidence either way. But it would be a lot harder for Adrienne to work around her five children to find a time to kill Simon without anyone finding out about it.

"Where *are* the children?" Erin asked abruptly, looking around.

"Playing in the park," Adrienne said, startled. They both studied each other. "Bella's watching them. She's good with them. Hope idolizes her."

Erin nodded. She sighed, thinking of Bella. She did *not* want to believe that Bella was mixed up in this, either in committing the act or enabling Adrienne to do it.

She couldn't let herself think that.

Adrienne fiddled with the coffee machine for a moment before saying anything.

"You've been a good friend, Erin," she said finally in a voice as whispery and unemotional as a dried reed. "I hope… you stay that way. Don't turn on me in the hardest time of my life."

Erin swallowed.

"I won't."

CHAPTER 19

*E*rin was relieved when Adrienne was gone and she was sitting by herself in the waiting room again. She was sure that Adrienne was innocent. How could she have killed Simon even if she wanted to? She couldn't leave her children alone and, if she left them with someone else, then they would know that she had been gone during the time that Simon had been murdered.

Of course, if that person were Bella, she would never tell Erin, the police, or anyone else that Adrienne had no alibi for the time of the murder. She would protect Adrienne to the bitter end. They were close friends despite the difference in their years. Erin thought that they were probably distantly related—all of the old mountain families were, to some extent—not just friends, but cousins of some kind. They had probably known each other since Bella had been a little girl. And neither was going to do anything to implicate the other.

Erin looked up at the sound of footsteps, surprised that Darryl could be done so quickly when he had just finished with Adrienne's car. Or maybe he wanted her authorization for some extra work that her car needed.

But it wasn't Darryl who appeared in the doorway. Nor was

it Adrienne, coming back to ask Erin again not to say anything that would bring any more attention to her as a suspect. It was Joshua Cox. Mary Lou's younger son, a friend of Bella's at high school, and intrepid investigative reporter, who had gotten himself into trouble with his investigations more than once. And had also rescued Erin from a dangerous situation when no one else had figured out where she was.

Erin knew that Mary Lou didn't like her talking to Josh or encouraging his investigations but, after all they had been through together, she couldn't just turn the boy away. She did her best not to "encourage" him, but how well she did that was a matter for discussion.

"Oh, hi Josh."

He smiled. "Miss Erin." He entered the room and took a seat near hers. "I didn't know you were here."

Erin shrugged. "Just getting an oil change."

He nodded. "Mom asked me to bring the car over for Darryl to have a look. It's making a noise."

"Well, he shouldn't be too long on mine. Adrienne just left, so he should be doing my oil change now."

Josh nodded. "How is she doing?"

"Adrienne?" Erin realized she probably shouldn't have mentioned Adrienne's name. The woman had just told her not to make things more difficult for her, so Erin promptly informed the investigative reporter that they had been talking? Not exactly the smartest way to honor Adrienne's request. "She's okay, I guess," Erin tried to brush the topic aside. "As well as can be expected under the circumstances."

"It must be tough for her." Joshua had been through his own trouble with suspicion falling on his family. Or with a family member being guilty of harming someone in Bald Eagle Falls. He knew what it was like to be the center of negative attention during a time of tragedy. He knew how the townspeople happily spent hours speculating on the goings-on in Bald Eagle Falls.

"Yeah," Erin agreed. "I think she'd rather not talk about it to anyone."

He raised an eyebrow at this. "I've already talked to her."

"Oh." So much for Erin discouraging him from talking to her. At least Adrienne couldn't hold her responsible for a call from Joshua that had happened before Adrienne had asked her not to interfere or draw any attention to her. "Well, that's good. You're out ahead of this story. I guess the paper probably needed more information from her for the obituary."

Joshua looked at her for a moment, then nodded. "Yeah. That and other articles."

"The obituary put out by the funeral home doesn't even have all the children on it."

"Maybe there is a reason for that."

Maybe Simon wasn't the father of all the children, he meant. Erin shook her head.

"I don't think now is the time to be airing dirty laundry in public."

He gave a little smile at that. "Is there ever a good time to air dirty laundry in public?"

"Well… no, I guess not," Erin admitted. The whole point of the saying was that private matters should be kept private.

Joshua pulled out his reporter's notepad and settled more comfortably into his chair. Erin took her planner binder from her oversized purse and pretended to be hard at work planning the following week. She really should be working on it. But she was finding it difficult to focus on the things that she needed to. With everything that was going on in Bald Eagle Falls, she didn't know how she could be expected to stay focused. Yet work went on. If she didn't stay on top of business at the bakery, who would?

"So, what did you think of Simon Simpson?" Joshua asked after they had both flipped pages for a few minutes in silence.

"I don't think anything of him now. He's dead and gone, and good riddance."

"So you didn't like him."

Erin shook her head. "I didn't know the man, other than knowing that he was trying to separate Adrienne from her money. I didn't find that endearing."

"I guess not. What made you think that it was about money?"

"His timing. He has five kids with Adrienne, and I'd never even seen him in town before! Then she gets a settlement—" Erin didn't know how much, if anything, Joshua knew about the settlement with Fontainbleau's estate. "—and he shows up in town looking for her? It was obvious that he was only here to try to get his hands on that money."

"How did he know about it?"

CHAPTER 20

*T*hat gave Erin pause. The payout hadn't exactly been public record. Certainly, there was nothing on the records of the estate or with the probate court. Neither Adrienne nor the woman who had effected the payment would be spreading the news.

"I don't know." The only thing that made any sense was that Adrienne had told him. But why would she? Had she wanted to draw him home, but then had decided after his arrival that she couldn't take the chance on letting him into her life and the lives of the children again? Had she discovered something else about him that made her change her mind?

"If you came into money and knew someone like that, would you have told them?" Josh asked.

"No. I probably would have left town. Gone somewhere that no one knew me, and he wouldn't be able to find me."

Just like Erin hadn't told her ex-boyfriend about moving to Bald Eagle Falls. But he had still had his ways of finding out where she had gone. And eventually, he had caught up to her. Simon hadn't had to figure out where Adrienne was. He had known that she was somewhere around town and would show up there sooner or later, even if he couldn't find the campsite out in the wilds.

"If she told him about the money and asked him to come back, then why would she kill him?" Erin challenged. "That doesn't make any sense."

"I didn't say she did. I'm just making observations."

"Adrienne did not kill her husband. Simon, I mean. It was… probably some stranger from out of town. Someone we've never even heard of before."

"Why?"

"I don't know. Simon's past caught up with him. His gambling debts or a jealous woman. Who knows what else he was into? He didn't exactly look like the most reputable-looking guy."

"You can't judge a book by its cover," Joshua reminded her. He was probably thinking about Willie, who had always looked like a dirty, homeless man when he was really one of the most industrious members of the town. Or Beaver, who was involved somehow with Joshua's brother Cam and was an undercover federal agent. Neither one was what they looked like.

But Erin hadn't judged Simon by his looks. He could have been a perfectly respectable man and still looked like a thug. But Simon's behavior had told Erin much more about him.

"He was asking after Adrienne when she didn't want to be found. Came here looking for money that wasn't his, but was the only way to guarantee his children's future. Made threats. And the things I'm hearing about him from around town do not indicate that he was a *respectable* man," Erin insisted.

Joshua wrote down a few notes. Erin needed to be more careful what she said to Josh rather than giving him more ammunition.

"It wasn't Adrienne," Erin asserted again.

"Of course not," Joshua agreed.

"Have you looked into Simon's sister? Apparently, there was no love lost between the two of them."

"What did you hear?"

"No specifics. Just that he was a hellion when they were growing up and the two of them never got along very well."

"He was a prankster," Joshua said.

"Apparently. Although 'prankster' implies that it was just silly little pranks. And that's not what it sounded like to me. It sounded to me like he was cruel."

"What specifically did he do to her?"

Erin had to shake her head. "I don't know. I didn't hear any specifics. Adri—I just heard that they didn't get along, and Scarlett could never forgive Simon for how he had treated her. That sounds pretty serious to me."

"So you think that she's a suspect."

"I guess…" Erin shrugged. "But she's not the only one. If that is the kind of person he was, and he grew up in Bald Eagle Falls, then there are probably a lot of people with grudges against him. I mean, even Betty Thompson. She's such a nice old lady and I've never heard her say an unkind word about anyone, but Scarlett was surprised that she showed up at the house, because she had never forgiven Simon for something that happened when he was younger."

"Betty Thompson?"

Erin nodded. "You know her? She's an older lady, friends with my neighbor Mrs. Peach?"

Joshua nodded. "Yes, I know who she is."

"And there are ex-girlfriends. I guess Simon gambled. There were people looking for him that he owed money to. That are still hanging around thinking they can get money from Adrienne."

Joshua bit his lip as he scribbled down some notes. "How do you know that?"

"Da—someone told me. Sounds to me like he must have owed a lot."

"Must be, if they are chasing him around the state for it or across the country…" Joshua agreed. "If they're willing to spend money looking for him." He made a couple of notes. "Do you know who they are? Where I could find them?"

"I don't know. Out-of-towners. I don't know where they are staying, if anywhere. Just that they're asking around after Adrienne."

"I hope they don't find her."

Erin cleared her throat and nodded. Adrienne was tough. Despite her attraction toward him, she'd been able to stand up to Simon. But could she stand up to thugs? Could she protect herself and her children if they got violent or made threats?

Had she stood up to Simon's threats?

"And you think Simon had affairs?" Joshua asked Erin. "I know he ran around a lot... but he wouldn't get together with someone here in town, would he?"

"From what I hear, yes."

"Do you have names?"

"I think I should probably leave that to the police."

"Come on," Joshua coaxed. "The great Erin Price is going to leave it up to the police department? You know they won't hear all of the gossip you do. They're going to be three steps behind."

"I'm not a detective. Just a baker. It's up to the police." Erin pushed aside the misgivings she had about the police department and the number of times that she had scooped him on a murder investigation because they were just a little too far behind. It had put her in danger more than once. And not because she was a meddling, interfering snoop. No matter how hard she tried to stay out of an investigation, it came to her.

CHAPTER 21

If Erin wanted the police to investigate people other than Adrienne and to know what things she had encountered about Simon so far, then maybe she should talk to them. It wasn't like she didn't know anyone inside the police department.

She stopped by Auntie Clem's to make sure that everything was going smoothly. It was getting close to closing, so she grabbed a selection of the sweets that remained in the display case before heading over to Town Hall, where the police department offices were.

Clara, the receptionist, had apparently left for the day. Erin could see through the glass doors that no one was handling the reception desk, and the glass doors were locked. Erin knocked on the door, hoping that someone would still be there and would hear her.

There was no immediate answer. Erin juggled out her phone to call Terry. Then she saw someone emerge from the hallway to see who was at the door.

Stayner.

Of all the law enforcement officers who worked in Bald

Eagle Falls, he was Erin's least favorite. She sighed, the knot in her stomach tying even tighter.

Stayner, a square-jawed rookie with limited people skills, opened the door and looked at her inquiringly. Erin proffered the box of treats. "I just brought some baking by. I was hoping that I could talk to someone. Terry's not here?"

He took the box of treats from her. "No, he's out on a call."

The crime rate in Bald Eagle Falls was pretty low. It always surprised Erin when Terry was actually out on a call. She hoped that it was something minor—nothing involving weapons or domestic violence.

"Oh, okay."

"Did you have some information to share?" he asked, surprising Erin. She had thought that he would just put her off. Let Terry take care of it when he got back to the office.

"Well… there are a few things that have come to my attention. I don't want to take you away from something important, but…"

He opened the door the rest of the way. "Come in."

Erin's mouth was dry and her stomach was doing all kinds of acrobatics. Stayner led her, not to the small office he and Terry shared, but to one of the interview rooms. That was probably just because the office was so small, Erin assured herself. He wanted to have more space, not be cooped up in a tiny office with avalanches of stacked files and papers all around them. Terry didn't mind getting cozy with her, but Stayner was another story.

Stayner motioned for Erin to take a seat. He opened the box of treats on the table within reach and invited her with a gesture to help herself. Erin didn't. Stayner fell into one of the sturdy chairs with a grunt. He rubbed the back of his neck and rolled his shoulders. Too much time sitting in front of the computer.

"How is the Simon Simpson case going?" she asked him tentatively, knowing he would not share anything with her.

Stayner shrugged. "Lots of avenues to investigate. Did you have some information on it?"

"I heard there were some rough-looking men in town looking for Adrienne, his wife—domestic partner. I guess Simon owed them some money and they were hoping to recover it from her."

Stayner frowned. "We don't like people like that hanging around town."

Erin nodded. "I was hoping that you would be able to... encourage them to move on."

He wrote it down in his notebook. "I'll have someone look into it," he agreed.

Erin glanced around. She didn't like being cooped up alone with Stayner in the interview room. The door was still open, but she felt anxious. "Are you the only one around tonight?"

"Right now, yes. Terry's still on duty, as you know. If he finishes with any active calls, he will come back here."

Erin tried to turn her attention back to the matter at hand.

"Right. Of course. I wondered about... other suspects in the Simpson case. Whether you are investigating other avenues..."

He would just brush the question aside, she knew. He wouldn't share anything with her about an active investigation.

Stayner studied Erin. "Suspects other than you?"

CHAPTER 22

*E*rin caught her breath. She swallowed, mouth drier than ever, and looked around for a bottle or glass of water. Even cold coffee would be better than nothing. But Stayner didn't offer her anything. He sat there, staring at her, analyzing every movement or change in her expression.

"I'm not a suspect... am I?" Erin asked, her voice squeaking and barely louder than a whisper.

"Let's see." He looked up at the ceiling as if trying to remember a long list. "There is the murder weapon. That's yours. And he was found outside of Auntie Clem's Bakery, your business. By you. You had hoped that someone else would discover him before he had decomposed too much, but you couldn't stand the smell anymore, so you called it in. *And then* we find out that he was also poisoned."

"Terry mentioned that," Erin said in a tiny voice.

"Poisoned by a cinnamon roll from your bakery," Stayner said. "So... everything points to the baker."

"It wasn't me," Erin said, "That's ridiculous. Why would I kill him? What motive did I have?"

"He was harassing you. Showing up at your place of business. Maybe at your home. You wanted to protect your friend.

101

To keep them apart. Eventually, you decided to do something about it."

Erin shook her head. "No, nothing like that. The last time I saw him, when he wouldn't leave the bakery when I asked him to, I called Terry to send him on his way. I didn't need to resort to violence."

"But he came back after that. When no one else was around. When you didn't have time to get to your phone before he came after you. You grabbed the nearest knife and you stabbed him."

"But first I poisoned him," Erin said sarcastically.

"Everybody saw you sell him the poisoned cinnamon roll. You had done that earlier in the day. You hoped that it would do the job for you. Women prefer poison, death from a distance instead of having to do it face-to-face. But he threw up. Ejected most of the poison out of his system. So that didn't work. He came after you, whether because he realized what you had tried to do or he was trying to bully the information he wanted out of you."

"No. That's ridiculous. Why would I open the door to him?"

"He came in while it was unlocked. You had been out to put the garbage in the bin. Or he ambushed you while you were still outside. He knew that if he waited out there, you would come sooner or later."

"And I took the garbage out with the cake knife in my hand?" Erin demanded. "Trust me, I don't arm myself for an ambush when I take out the garbage!"

"Then he followed you back in. You grabbed the knife from the counter to confront him. And presto, Simon Simpson is dead, and you are responsible."

Erin looked around again for a drink of water, but none had materialized.

"No way," she said. "Never happened. And if it had, I would have called the police."

"You drag the body out behind the dumpster—"

"Do you know how much strength it takes to drag a dead body?"

He gave her a little smile. "Do you?"

Erin felt a chill. She shook her head. "You know I didn't do this. Why would I kill him? I would just call Terry again. He hadn't been physical with me."

"There's nothing to say that he didn't escalate to violence. I'm sure if I talked to Mrs. Simpson, she would tell me of a time or two that he had gotten physical with her. I know how guys like that operate. I have no doubt he would have put hands on you if he thought that would give him what he wanted."

Stayner was probably right about that. But Erin wasn't going to let him treat her as a suspect. As his primary suspect, from the sounds of it. He had already had her in mind because of the knife and the location of the murder. It seemed clear that it had been an employee of the bakery, or else someone who wanted to implicate them. But as soon as Stayner had seen the results of the autopsy and knew that Simon had been poisoned, he had decided that it was Erin. She was the baker and proprietor. She was the one who was responsible for whatever went into the baking.

Her stomach lurched at the thought of her baking being used to poison someone. She had been accused of poisoning before but, of course, she had been exonerated. It wasn't her fault if someone used her baking to kill someone who was allergic to the ingredients.

She looked daggers at Stayner and didn't tell him he might just be at the top of her hit list. She had come to the police department offices to help with the investigation, to offer her insights, and to see where they were on the investigation. She had even brought cookies.

As if hearing her thoughts, Stayner's eyes strayed over to the box of baked goods.

Oh good grief.

Did he really think that she would try to poison the police department as well? Or even just him?

She admitted that it was a tempting thought. Just Stayner. After hours. When they were alone in the interview room. There would be no record that Erin had been there. No one would know.

Except that the poison would be in his stomach and they would know what he had eaten. She wouldn't get away with anything.

Erin reached over and selected a classic chocolate chip oatmeal cookie. Stayner watched her take it out and bite into it.

"If this is your version of a cyanide capsule, I'm going to be very disappointed," he told her.

"Disappointed? Why?"

He shrugged. "I'm always interested in your... *unique* take on a case. No one can question your solve rate."

He folded his arms and sat back in his chair, watching her. Was he waiting to see if she would drop dead from eating a poison-laced treat? If so, he was going to be waiting for a long time.

She pondered on what he had said. If he really thought that she had poisoned someone, then he wouldn't be concerned with her solve rate or *unique* view on this murder case or any other.

"You don't think that I did it."

He gave a slight smile. "It seems a little heavy-handed," he admitted. "The cake knife. Behind the bakery. Poisoned baked goods. The baker as the victim of Simpson's harassment and protective of her friend."

"You think everything was intended to point to me? That I was targeted and framed?"

"It would certainly appear so, don't you think?"

Erin blew out her breath in a long, slow stream, relieved. "Yeah. It does," she agreed. "But why would anyone target me?"

He held his hand, palm up, and moved it toward her as if handing the problem back to her. "Why do you think?"

"I don't know…" Erin thought about it, closing her eyes and picturing the different people that might have had motive to kill Simon, but also to frame her. What could they have against her? She was a baker. She tried to be kind and fair to everyone. As far as she knew, she hadn't stepped on any toes lately, and any that she had stepped on previously were healed and she was forgiven.

Several people in the state penitentiary might have a grievance against her, but they were locked up. They were not running around Bald Eagle Falls planting clues.

"I don't know… maybe someone got the idea because I've helped out with other murder cases in the past. They associated me with murder, and just…"

"An unconscious association? I don't think so."

"Maybe… they were afraid that I would figure out who did it, so they wanted me out of the way?"

He considered. "Possibly," he grunted. But he didn't seem too excited about the idea.

"I don't know of anyone who would want to put me in prison for murder. Not anyone who could be in Bald Eagle Falls."

Stayner reached over and selected a white chocolate chip brownie. "Melissa always steals all of these."

Erin's stomach and chest muscles relaxed. Stayner would not eat the brownie if he thought that she was involved in a poisoning. In trying to decide whether she was really considered a suspect, that brownie tipped the balance. He did *not* consider her a viable suspect.

CHAPTER 23

"I hear you were by the office to see me this evening," Terry said casually as he and Erin started to work on dinner, Terry setting the table and Erin starting some soup stock simmering while she cut up vegetables.

Orange Blossom came yowling into the kitchen, loudly complaining about how Erin had neglected him and hadn't given him anything to eat today. Erin got the can of kitty treats out of the pantry and skimmed a couple along the tile floor for him to chase and devour.

K9, lying beside the table waiting patiently, looked up with interest. Erin got out one of his gluten-free doggie biscuits and offered it to him. Unlike his feline rival, K9 was the perfect gentleman, never harassing her for food or snatching it away. He took it from her with his lips, and then lay down again with it between his front paws to munch on.

Hearing the other animals getting treats, Marshmallow lolloped into the kitchen with long ears pricked up and looked at Erin for his share. Erin took a handful of the ends of the vegetables she was cutting and offered them to the soft brown and white rabbit. Marshmallow munched happily.

"So…?" Terry prompted.

Erin looked at him. "What?"

"I missed you at the office this afternoon. I was out on a call."

"Oh, yeah." Erin looked sideways at Terry, wondering how much of the conversation Stayner had relayed to him. "I left you some brownies."

"Yes, they were as good as always. I tried to leave enough for the rest of the staff when they arrive in the morning, though it was a hardship."

"You can always come by Auntie Clem's for more if they run out."

After adding the chopped vegetables to the simmering stock, Erin glanced over her shoulder at Terry. He was smiling, the dimple in his cheek prominent.

"Make sure you ask for the ones that aren't poisoned," she told him.

Terry chuckled. "I was going to talk to you about the poison tonight. But Rod beat me to the punch."

"He had me believing I was the prime suspect. Again."

"You have to admit that on paper, you look good for it. If we didn't know you as well as we do, there might have been reason for concern. Even now… we're being very careful and trying to document everything. Explain why we did not believe you were a viable suspect. There's no guarantee that whoever acts for the defense in the case won't present you as the suspect in an alternative theory of the murder and demand to know why you were not arrested."

Erin wasn't as worried about that. It was still concerning but, at that point, it would mean that they had the actual killer in custody, and she was sure that they would be able to dig up enough evidence to convict him—or her—and Erin wouldn't end up fighting charges herself.

"Do you know what kind of poison it was?" Erin asked. "Rat poison? Something that had to be ordered on the internet?"

Terry shook his head. "Mushrooms."

Erin was taken aback. "Mushrooms? Poisonous mushrooms?"

He nodded. "Apparently… death cap mushrooms."

Erin thought of the pictures she had seen of the innocuous-looking white mushroom. "Do they… grow around here?"

Terry nodded. "Yes. They are native. Untraceable."

"Anyone could have picked them…" She frowned and shook her head as she stirred the soup. "But mushrooms in a cinnamon roll? Someone would notice if there were pieces of mushroom in a cinnamon roll."

"Apparently, it is pretty easy to prepare a liquid extract."

Erin shivered in the summer heat of the kitchen. Someone could be walking around right now with a vial of death cap poison in his pocket. It would not take very much to poison a person. The mild mushroom flavor could be covered up with the intense sugar and cinnamon spice of the cinnamon rolls. Topped with cream cheese icing, of course. A little of the slightly nutty-tasting death caps would be undetectable.

Simon was lucky that he had thrown up the death cap toxin. Maybe he would have survived if it hadn't been for being stabbed in the chest with a cake knife.

"How could someone have poisoned him? Do you think it was in the cinnamon roll or something else? I don't see how anyone could have poisoned the cinnamon roll between me giving it to him and him eating it."

"Someone must have had access to it at some point," Terry said. He grimaced. "I know you didn't poison it. Of course not. But if you could think about what was happening at the bakery when he bought it… who handled it, who was near it? Whether anyone could have contaminated it before he left the bakery."

Erin was shaking her head. She tried to remember who had been in Auntie Clem's at the same time as Simon. She was sure that she was the one who had handled the cinnamon roll, taking it out of the display case and sliding it into a sleeve for him. And then… had she put it on the counter next to the till? Who had rung it up? Had Simon picked it up or had someone handed it to him? And then there was the cream cheese. Erin couldn't remember who had handled the little condiment cup full of icing.

"I don't know." She rubbed her forehead. "I'll have to think about it."

Terry nodded. "We'll ask the others that we know were in Auntie Clem's at the time. I'm afraid I had a bit of tunnel vision —I really didn't look at anyone other than Simon."

She was glad that Terry's recollection wasn't any better than hers. It would have been embarrassing if she could remember nothing and he could reel off the names of everyone who had been in the bakery and every move they had made. Terry was trained to notice things, and if he had missed whatever opportunities anyone had had to poison him, then Erin didn't have to feel inferior for not being able to either.

"If it wasn't poisoned at Auntie Clem's, then he must have met someone else between the time he left the bakery and when he ate the cinnamon roll," Terry said, "We're trying to trace all of his movements during that time. If someone saw him with his killer... Any meeting between them probably looked completely innocuous. If Simon let himself be poisoned, then he wasn't suspicious of the person who killed him. It might have been a friend or casual acquaintance, but not someone he was worried about."

Erin pictured Simon meeting with a friend in a cafe or on a park bench. Somewhere, Simon had felt comfortable sitting down, spreading the icing on the cinnamon roll, and eating a portion while he sat and visited with some unknown person.

He had been completely unworried about the person having access to his food. Like the woman who left her trusted friend to watch that no one mickied her drink while she went to the ladies' room, giving him the opportunity to dose it with his date rape drug of choice.

"It couldn't be anyone at the bakery," Erin said. "No one

knew that he would be there or would decide to buy a cinnamon roll. I pushed him to buy something or move on, or he wouldn't have."

Her face warmed.

"I suppose that makes me look like the killer, but I didn't put anything in it. I would never poison my own baked goods. It's like… desecration. My whole goal is to provide people with baking that they can eat without it making them sick. Besides—it would be stupid."

Terry nodded.

"But it couldn't have been any of the employees," Erin reiterated. "No one knew ahead of time Simon was going to order it. They wouldn't have had time to poison it. And someone else in the bakery…" She shook her head. "You think someone was following him around with a vial of poison just waiting for the opportunity to poison him? And that they would have time to poison the roll before he picked it up? It must have been done later."

Terry scratched K9's ears. "I can't completely eliminate the possibility that it was dosed while he was at Auntie Clem's. But you're right… it seems unlikely."

Erin couldn't help thinking about Bella. She took the soup off the burner and left the pot in the center of the stove while she got out the soup bowls and ladle. She tried to fix in her mind where Bella had been each moment Simon had been in the bakery. She had been in the kitchen. She had been behind the counter. She had argued with Simon about his right to know where his wife—or domestic partner—was. And then…? Erin didn't think she had been close enough to tamper with the roll or the cream cheese, but she couldn't swear to it. After Simon had left, Bella had clocked out. She had needed to study for a test.

"Stayner thinks that someone wanted to frame me or someone at Auntie Clem's. He thought that it was…" She tried to remember the words he had used. "That it was heavy-handed. An obvious frame job."

She looked at Terry expectantly as she placed the soup bowls on the table.

"We are all in agreement," he admitted. "We know you and the other employees at Auntie Clem's. And you're not stupid. You've been involved in enough murder investigations." He shook his head. "Using a knife from the bakery and leaving it in the body? Calling the discovery of the body in yourself and *still* leaving the knife in the body? Poisoning your own baking? Yes, heavy-handed is a good word for it. Based on that evidence, it might seem like you or your employees are good suspects. But I can't see you leaving that much of a trail. And the same applies to your employees."

Erin sat down. While her stomach was still tight, she felt like she could manage the soup and the biscuits she had already set on the table. She wasn't that worried about herself or about Terry or the other law enforcement officers, assuming that she was the one who had poisoned and stabbed Simon.

But she was still worried about Bella and Adrienne. More worried than she would like to admit.

CHAPTER 24

*A*drienne was still the main suspect in Simon's murder, and she and Erin both knew it. Erin kept telling herself that there was no way that Adrienne could have left her children to kill Simon, but she knew she was looking for reasons to exclude Adrienne as a suspect. She hadn't dared to ask Adrienne about her alibi.

"I know I don't have any right to ask," Adrienne told Erin over the phone. "You helped me out when Mr. Fontainbleau was killed… and I just… I don't know who killed Simon, but it wasn't me."

Erin made noises of agreement, though she wasn't sure what to say to Adrienne. It would make sense to say that she believed Adrienne and knew she hadn't had anything to do with Simon's murder. But she didn't think she could make her tongue form those words.

"What can I help you with?" she asked finally, after fumbling about for some response.

"I just thought you might be able to help me figure out who did it. Maybe… it was probably something to do with something he did when he was out of town. I know that Simon was no saint," she admitted. "If he thought he could make a buck without too much work… he was always running one scam or another. Maybe someone wanted to get back at him."

"Maybe," Erin agreed.

"He was crook… I didn't want to know what he was involved in. I never wanted to know what he was up to, how he was bringing in the money when he did. And it wasn't very often he actually brought something for me and the kids. When he did, I knew it was best not to ask where it came from."

"I'm not sure how I can help," Erin protested, when Adrienne trailed off.

"When I finish work this afternoon, I'll be over at Prosts'. Cindy said I could use her computer, but I'm crap when it comes to computers. I thought maybe you could help me to… see if we can figure out some stuff about Simon's past while Cindy watches the kids. If there are—were—people looking for Simon… it might explain what happened."

Erin wasn't the best on computers herself, though she had grown more proficient in the time she had been in Bald Eagle Falls.

"I shouldn't ask," Adrienne said again. "I know you're busy with other things. But if you could help me…"

"Okay," Erin agreed. "Of course. I'm not sure I'll be able to do much, but we can try."

She got the details from Adrienne as to what time she would be at the farm and agreed to meet her there.

Erin had been to the Prost farm before, off in "the sticks" outside Bald Eagle Falls. It was a goat farm. They circulated the goats through a couple of pastures, and Erin didn't see any of them close to the house or old barn. They were probably in the upper pasture or the newer barn.

After pulling into the driveway, she stayed in the car, looking for the guard dog. Adrienne came out of the house a minute later and motioned her in.

"Dog's tied up behind the house," she said, noticing Erin looking around for it. "He won't bother you."

Erin could hear the shouts of the children as they played, and hoped they knew enough not to get too close to the dog. But maybe he knew them well enough now that they could approach him and could talk and play with him without any danger.

"Thanks for coming," Adrienne told Erin. "Can I get you some tea?"

Erin nodded. "Sure. That would be nice."

They would ease into the computer searches. It would be best to get more background from Adrienne before they started so Erin had a better idea of what to look for. Adrienne probably knew more about Simon's past than she was willing to share initially.

Adrienne took her into the kitchen and Erin sat at the table while she watched Adrienne put the kettle on to boil and put a little basket of tea bags on the table for Erin to sort through. She picked out a ginger peach tea. She smelled the tea bag before putting it in front of her. It smelled like summertimes with Clementine. She could remember her great-aunt making them iced ginger peach tea as a special treat on hot summer days.

"How long did you and Simon know each other?" she asked.

Adrienne considered. "About… ten years, I guess. We met each other in high school when my family moved into town. I was… I didn't make friends easily. I was kind of an outsider. But Simon was nice to me. He would talk to me and didn't make fun of me for being from away. I guess… I fell for him because he was one of the few people who accepted me."

"That's nice. I'm glad he was welcoming."

"Simon was always eager to meet the new girl," Adrienne said, unsmiling. "I'm not sure it was a demonstration of his good character."

CHAPTER 25

*A*drienne brought the teapot over to the table. She poured for Erin and then herself, selecting a green tea.

"But the two of you stayed together," Erin observed. "A lot of couples don't."

"I probably shouldn't have. I should have just dumped him and gone on with my life. But I kept taking him back when he showed up again. Pretending that it was going to be different. That I believed he was going to be different every time. That this time, he would stay, and help to support the children. Help raise them so it wasn't just me all by myself."

Adrienne sighed and swept her thin, straight hair back over her ears and behind her shoulders. She looked not just exhausted after a busy workday, but world-weary. She was younger than Erin, yet had been through so many trials with her children and Simon. Erin had been through her own tough times, but at least she'd only had herself to look after. She couldn't imagine going through it all with young children to look after as well. Putting a roof over their heads and food in their mouths. Trying to take care of them or arrange for childcare. Erin didn't know how she had managed it.

"What did he do when he was away? Do you have any idea?"

Adrienne sipped her tea, frown lines between her eyebrows. "He would go off, saying he'd heard of an opportunity. Or saying that he had a job interview or had gotten hired for something. But I knew that most of the time, he didn't have a new job. He just had… an idea of something else he could do. A new scheme. Or scam. I always wanted to believe him. But after a while, I knew it was just… him getting tired of the quiet life and chasing rainbows. He loved the kids, and I'd like to think he loved me too, in his own way. You always want to believe that a man really loves you, don't you?"

"Yes," Erin admitted. She too had dealt with that longing. That wish or pretense that the man she was with really loved her, was devoted to her, and would do anything for her. She hoped that she'd found that with Terry, but she often found herself doubting either his devotion or that, this time, she had found something different, and she and Terry were in it for the long haul. It had lasted longer than most of her relationships, and Terry really was a good guy. But sometimes she worried she was just lying to herself.

"I know that there were other women," Adrienne said. "I knew that when he went off somewhere for weeks or months, that he wasn't keeping himself for me. He would come back and sometimes I would be able to smell her on his clothing, until everything had been washed a few times. It wasn't just hotel soap."

She sniffled and wiped her nose with a tissue tucked in her pocket.

"When he was with me, I wanted to believe that he'd realized the error of his ways and had come back to me for good. But after a while… I realized how bad that was for the kids. And I tried to change. To be tough and not just take him back. Sometimes that made him mad and he would take off again. Others… he would try to prove himself. Try to show me how much he had changed."

"But it didn't last."

"It never did. If it lasted longer than the time before, I would get to thinking that it might stick this time. But it never did."

Erin wished she could hug Adrienne and make her feel better. But Adrienne was not a touchy-feely person. She kept herself aloof most of the time. Even asking Erin to help with the computer work and have tea together was very unusual. And Erin found shows of affection awkward enough without trying to judge whether Adrienne would accept her ministrations. She wished she had someone like Betty Thompson there to tell her what to do next.

Adrienne took another sip of her tea and looked at her watch. "We'd better get started. I want to be done by the time Bella gets home."

Erin waited for a more thorough explanation, but Adrienne didn't clarify. Maybe Bella would need the computer for homework when she got home.

Adrienne brought her cup with her and motioned for Erin to do the same. They climbed the stairs to the small bedrooms, and Adrienne led her to a tiny computer station wedged into one corner of the master bedroom.

"Internet here is pretty slow," Adrienne warned. "Someday maybe they'll get that satellite connection here but, right now, it's just over the phone lines."

They sat down, Erin taking the computer chair and Adrienne perching on the corner of the bed, close enough for her to see most of what Erin was doing on the computer.

"So I'm not sure exactly what you want," Erin said tentatively. She typed Simon's name into the search bar, and most of the results on the screen were obviously for other people. Erin scrolled through them, looking for Simon's face. She found him on one of the social networks and clicked his name to pull up his profile. She and Adrienne skimmed through the last few entries he had made before his death.

"I guess…" Adrienne leaned forward, looking at the details. "Does it say where he has been? Who his friends are? That kind of thing. Then maybe there will be something on their social media… maybe some pictures of him or things he was involved with."

Erin looked through the pictures and entries on his timeline. She opened a new document and started noting the places and people with their profile links. Simon's timeline was pretty innocuous. Only a few posts a year. There was a picture of him with Adrienne and some of the children crowding into the frame. Erin looked at the date. Two and a half years previous. That might have been the last time he'd been home with them. Erin could see the joy in Adrienne's eyes at the family being together.

And then he had left.

She followed the links to some of his friends. Some of them posted more actively than Simon. Others had profiles that were completely locked down so that only their few close friends would be able to access anything.

They were generally a rough lot. Erin glanced at Adrienne's face to see if she recognized any of them. Were any of them the men who were looking for Simon, who wanted to collect his debts from Adrienne?

Adrienne just shook her head. "No one from around here."

Drinking pictures. Pictures of them with barely clad girl-friends. Trucks and motorcycles. Off-roading holidays.

Erin went back to the initial search that she had done and started clicking on some of the results that didn't have pictures beside them. Some of them were obviously not him. Erin accidentally clicked on another profile on the social network she had found him on and hovered the mouse cursor over the back button.

"Wait," Adrienne held up her hand. They both watched the page load over the slow internet connection. It was Simon's picture, but it was not the same profile as they had already looked at. Erin looked at the details along the left side of the page. "Arizona," she pointed out, shaking her head. "Maybe it's one of those fake profiles? He got hacked?"

A picture appeared on his timeline. Simon holding a couple of children on his knee. Towheaded twins about two years old. The comment posted with the photo said that he was grateful for his family and professed his love for them. Erin scrolled down a little to look at other comments, puzzled. She glanced over at Adrienne, who was staring at the screen, her face white.

A picture of Simon with a short-haired blond woman with an angelic face in a flowery cotton dress.

A picture of two red-skinned twins in a hospital bassinet.

CHAPTER 26

$\mathcal{E}$rin swallowed. She copied his girlfriend's profile to her document and glanced through the few posts for any friend mentions. She pressed the back button and the pictures disappeared.

"He has another family," Adrienne said hollowly. "A newer one."

Erin shook her head in disgust. "That's really dirty," she said sharply. "That's really unfair. If he's going to go off and start another family, what's he doing coming back here and trying to work things out with you?"

Adrienne shook her head. "He wouldn't stay. He never did before. He just wanted the money." She took a couple of large gulps of her tea. "I kept telling myself that it wasn't about the money. But look at her. She's not going to be satisfied squatting or living out of her car or some shelter. And those babies…" Adrienne's voice broke.

"Oh, Adrienne." Erin wished there was something she could say. She had nothing to offer to comfort her. Adrienne had been taken by a scoundrel. Taken in by him over and over again. She had trusted him even though she knew what kind of a person he was. She had allowed him back in and he had just kept taking from her, someone who had nothing. Meanwhile, he had started another family somewhere else.

Erin typed Simon's name into the social media search bar and clicked the search button. The profiles with matching names were listed on the screen. Simon Simpson was not uncommon, and there were a number of them scattered across the world. Erin narrowed the results to just the United States. Simon wasn't a jet setter. He hadn't been traveling to other parts of the world. Just the United States. There were still a lot of profiles. She started scrolling down the list, looking at the profile pictures. Some of them had only avatars. Some of the photos were not clear at thumbnail size. Erin clicked on one and, again, Simon's face appeared on her screen.

Erin wished she could take it back. What was she thinking, searching for him again? She had already discovered the first two profiles. What need was there to find any more?

Adrienne swore under her breath.

This time, the woman Simon was with was a redhead. She was tagged as Tate Banks. Erin wrote down the name. She scrolled down the timeline. As with the other profiles, Simon hadn't posted very often. Once or twice a year and, sometimes, it wasn't even a picture or explanation of what he was doing. Some were just memes or Christmas graphics that said nothing about him.

But there he was, several days' growth of beard, cheek pressed against Tate's, and a little boy below their chins. Maybe a five- or six-year-old. Black hair. Darling little dimples as he grinned up at his parents. Erin felt sick.

"No, no, no," Adrienne murmured, looking at the little boy. She shook her head. "How many more are there?"

Erin shook her head. "I don't know. And there is no saying how many he might have never created profiles for. He might have told them he didn't like social media, and these are just the ones who talked him into it. There's no way of knowing."

"I knew there were women. I didn't think... I never knew

that there were children. And so many of them... I thought there was another woman. Maybe two regulars. And the others were just... one-night stands. Just... satisfying a physical need. But this..." She closed her eyes to block it out and shook her head.

"It's too much," she told Erin, waving it away with one hand. "I don't want to see any more. Now I know what he was doing... fine. He was a worse kind of dog than I ever imagined."

Was it worse to establish multiple families than it was to pursue one-night stands? Erin supposed it was the children who made the difference. Not the length of the relationship. Adrienne had always thought that her children were the only ones. That he would always come back to her because she had the children.

"I don't want to see any more of that," Adrienne insisted. "You can give that to the police. Have them chase every one of these women down and talk to them. See if they have alibis. If any of them knew about me. Maybe one of them followed him here."

"Okay. Is that it, then?" Erin glanced around for a printer to send her document to.

Adrienne shook her head. "I want to know what else he was doing. I know the police are going to come after me. Who else is a better suspect? They know I had a motive. And he would have met me anywhere if I called him or sent him a message. I was the one who could get close to him, who had something that he wanted. So they're going to come after me."

Erin didn't deny it. But she still wasn't sure what Adrienne wanted her to do next.

"All of those different places," Adrienne said, motioning to the list Erin had typed up. "All of those friends. I want to know what else he was doing. If he was involved in something." She hesitated. "I never wanted to know what he was doing. I didn't want to know where the money came from. It was better if I didn't know, if I didn't have anything to do with it. I know there is no way that he would have given me all of his money, but sometimes it was thousands of dollars. We had credit cards that had to be paid off, vehicle loans with back payments due. He had bookies and loan sharks. A couple of times, we had houses where back rent was due. He would sweep in, pay everyone off, and leave me with a little spending money. It was never enough. But it was something. And I knew how much other stuff he had to pay off. I never believed it was one big win. I think… it was something else."

"Some other scheme or scam," Erin repeated what Adrienne had told her earlier.

"Yeah. There was always something. Another way to make it big. And sometimes… it paid off. But I didn't want to know what."

"And now you do." Erin stared at the computer monitor. "I have no idea how to find anything. It isn't like he would post about it online if it was some scam or something illegal."

"But people do," Adrienne insisted. "The police catch them —drug dealers, fraudsters, murderers—because they post about it. Brag about it. They want everyone to know what they did."

"Well… when was the last time he came home with a lot of money?"

Adrienne thought about it and gave her an approximate date two years earlier. Erin wrote it down.

"Don't look," she told Adrienne.

Adrienne looked bemused but obeyed, looking away from the computer screen. Erin searched for posts by Simon around that date. Which profile had he posted on?

She found one close to the date that Adrienne had provided, professing love to his family in Ohio. She double-checked that the picture on the profile was Simon's. A charming smile, photo taken while he played with a train set on the floor, a child's feet extending into the picture beside him.

"Okay. Ohio," Erin said. She clicked away from the social

profile and returned to the search engine. Adrienne looked back at the screen.

"Ohio?"

"Yeah. Did he ever say anything to you about Ohio?"

"I remember him saying that he had a job out there. I forget what nonsense he told me about it. But he had money when he came back. Samuel Andrew was sick in the hospital and we couldn't afford the treatment he needed."

"Well, I don't know if I can find anything, but…"

Erin tried a few different searches. First with Simon's name and then broader searches. Combining "police" with the town name. Trying different words like "scam," "fraud," "drugs," and "cash."

A few different possibilities floated to the top. Erin clicked on the various stories. Most of them led to arrests by the police, but no pictures or names to indicate that Simon had been one of those involved. She clicked on a report on a bank robbery. It wasn't the kind of thing that she thought Simon would be involved in. He was a small-time crook. Someone who had not, as far as she knew, done any hard time.

She looked at the detailed news reports. Four armed gunmen had held up a bank in a town in Ohio close to the one Simon lived in with girlfriend number four. Or were they up to five or six? They had gotten away with thousands of dollars but, in the process, they had killed a bank security guard when he had opened fire on them. Both he and one of the four gunmen had been killed in the exchange, but three of the gunmen had gotten away cleanly with their haul.

And then Simon had shown up in Tennessee to see Adrienne, money in hand.

Adrienne swore as Erin read the details out to her. "Tell me you wouldn't have done anything so stupid, Simon," she said softly. "Tell me that wasn't you."

"There's no way to know," Erin told her. "They don't have pictures of the robbers. They were wearing masks."

"Maybe I don't want to know this," Adrienne said. "I thought I did, but…. if he was involved in stuff like that, I don't think I can face it." She cleared her throat. "There's a reason I never demanded to know where the money had come from. There's a reason I never wanted any details."

"Did you suspect something like this?"

"I don't know what I thought it was. I hoped it was just gambling. But the guys he met with sometimes, the men he hung out with… I never trusted any of them. And I never wanted to know what Simon was doing with them."

There was a sketch of the robber who had been killed. Erin guessed that an actual photograph of the dead man would have been too gory to print in the paper or post on the internet. The sketch was softer and would not give children nightmares. Erin displayed it full size on the screen and showed it to Adrienne.

"Did you ever see him with this man?"

CHAPTER 27

*A*drienne could not get any paler. Her expression was pinched. If she weren't already sitting down, Erin would have taken her to a seat. She felt guilty for uncovering what she had. She felt like she should have stayed out of it. Not looked so hard. Just reassured Adrienne that yes, all Simon had ever done was gamble. The only person he had hurt was himself. And Adrienne and the children.

But now Adrienne knew he had been involved in much worse than that. At least once. Erin tried to convince herself that it had only been a one-time occurrence. She had only found one heist, so maybe that was the only time Simon had done anything like that. It hadn't turned out well, so he had never attempted such a thing again.

But Adrienne said that he had shown up other times with thousands of dollars to pay off his growing debts. What were the chances that all of those times, it had just been gambling winnings and he had only ever pulled off a robbery at gunpoint once?

There might be dozens of other incidents that Erin hadn't found yet. Now that she knew what to look for, she might find more. But there might be a lot of robberies that were smaller and never made it to the news as well—a convenience store, a home invasion, a gas station—there were a lot of crimes that were too commonplace to make it to the papers.

Adrienne stared at the sketch. She shook her head.

"Simon, oh Simon…" Her voice was soft and rough. Not only had the man she loved died, but her perception of who he was had been killed too, violently struck down by Erin.

"You knew him?" she asked Adrienne unnecessarily.

"Reggie. I met him a few times… he would pick Simon up and they would go out for a 'guys' night.' Go to a bar and watch the game. Just the boys hanging out for the evening…"

Planning a heist or maybe even breaking into a closed business or invading someone's home. While Adrienne had thought that he was having a good time with his buddies, they had been committing violent criminal acts.

Unless the bank heist was a one-off. An ill-thought-out job that they had regretted afterward and never attempted again.

But Erin suspected that was not the case. And Adrienne didn't think so either, judging by her expression and the tone of her voice.

"What do I do?" Adrienne asked in barely more than a whisper. "Do I tell the police about this? Give them someone else to look at? A different avenue to pursue? I don't want anyone to know this. I want to bury it and not have anyone know… what kind of a man I took up with."

"He was from Bald Eagle Falls stock," Erin pointed out. "If they admit he was bad, they're putting a black mark against the community. They're more likely to romanticize him. You know how everyone likes a bad boy."

Adrienne nodded, sniffling.

"Scarlett was already doing that when I went to see her," Erin said, "Talking about the scrapes he got into as a kid. Laughing about what a troublemaker he was. Even though you told me how much they fought and that she wouldn't forgive him. He's dead now, and they'll pretend he was just... high-spirited."

Adrienne grimaced, attempting to force a smile to cover the mask of grief.

"I wish I could say that. I wish I could just pretend. To the town, the children, myself... I wish he could just be..." She sniffled and rubbed the corners of her eyes. "Like a pirate. Not the modern kind from Somalia or in the South China Sea. But you know, the ones in Disney movies."

Erin nodded her understanding.

"What if they don't romanticize him?" Adrienne demanded. "What if they say that I made him into a criminal? That it was because of something I did? Because I entrapped him and he had to find a way to provide for his family. Or that my out-of-town friends pulled him into something?"

Erin looked back at the pencil sketch. A guy friend of Simon's or an old friend Adrienne had introduced him to?

She didn't want to ask.

"I think... you should give this information to the police," she said. "It might take the focus off you. You need to be able to concentrate on the children and not worry that the police could be coming after you at any time. That's why you wanted me to find this."

"But... I didn't think it would be so bad. I thought we might find some unsavory people... out-of-towners that we could point at to keep the focus off me. But I didn't think it would be something like this. They killed one of the bank employees. They killed someone, Erin! That bullet could have come from Simon's gun."

Erin nodded in agreement. She couldn't deny it. But she felt so bad for Adrienne.

"Well, we don't have any proof that he was actually there or ever pulled the trigger of a gun. It's only a guess based on where he was and who he associated with. The police in Ohio will know more. They might have suspects or be able to eliminate

Simon. This is just a news article and only has a few of the details. They'll know a lot more than that."

Adrienne nodded. "I suppose. He might have just been involved in the planning. Or not involved at all and those were just gambling winnings. Just because he knew Reggie, that doesn't mean that he was involved in the bank heist. *I* knew Reggie, and I wasn't involved." She gave a wild laugh.

Downstairs, the front door banged. Adrienne and Erin froze, listening. Erin expected the voices of one or more of Adrienne's kids. Maybe one of them had skinned a knee and needed a kiss from his mother. Or they were hungry for a snack.

"Anyone home?" Bella's voice floated up the stairs.

Adrienne looked at the computer. She shook her head at Erin.

"I'll be right down," she called to Bella, hoping that she wouldn't come upstairs to see what Adrienne was doing.

"I'll email these links to myself," Erin said, copying the information she had jotted down and switching to the email app. "Do you want me to give it to Terry? Or do you want to think about it? I won't do anything until you say."

Adrienne bit her lip. "Give it to him," she said recklessly. "If Simon did this… if this is the kind of thing he was up to, then there are other suspects. People who are much more likely to be violent than me."

"Are you sure?"

Adrienne nodded. "Yes. Do it."

"Okay. I will." Erin pressed Send to route the links to her own inbox and closed all the windows that she'd had open.

CHAPTER 28

*E*rin wasn't in a rush to tell Terry everything that they had found. She wanted to give Adrienne a chance to change her mind. Adrienne had made the decision in a hurry and might regret it afterward. Erin couldn't do anything about it if she had already passed the information on to the police. But if she held back, then, if Adrienne changed her mind, there was no harm done and she and Adrienne would be the only ones who knew what she had found.

So she didn't tell Terry when she returned home. She let Adrienne sleep on it and didn't go over to the police department offices until after her early shift at Auntie Clem's.

She hoped Terry would be in the office and not out patrolling. Her hopes were rewarded by Clara's nod.

"Yes, he's here. Let me see whether he is free to see you."

Erin knew that he would be. Clara liked to play the gatekeeper and bar Erin from entry, but Terry never refused Erin unless he was right in the middle of a call or interview.

Once upon a time, Erin would have just gone in, waving at Clara as she passed or leaving her a box of treats to keep her busy for a few minutes. But after a couple of unfortunate incidents where Erin had been caught snooping where she shouldn't have been, Clara was now charged not to let her past without an escort.

But Erin wasn't there to snoop; she had legitimate information to pass on to Terry to aid him in his investigation.

"He will see you," Clara said in a slightly disapproving voice as she hung up the phone, which meant that Erin could walk over to Terry's office. It was a worse mess than usual—maybe the investigation into Simon's death was producing a lot of paperwork—and the tiny office, made for one person and occupied by two desks, was claustrophobic.

"Uh, let's grab a meeting room," Terry suggested as he came out from behind his desk and stepped around a couple of stacks of paper on the floor. There was no more room on his desk or credenza.

Erin looked curiously at the paper but was too far away to make anything out. Terry took her to the same interview room that she and Stayner had occupied while he told her about Simon's poisoning and all the clues that pointed to an employee of Auntie Clem's Bakery, Erin in particular.

"Coffee?" Terry offered.

"No. I'm good."

"What can we do for you today?"

Erin had printed out a few of the web pages that she had found while working with Adrienne.

"I have some additional information for you about Simon Simpson."

"Oh, really? Where did this information come from?"

"Public internet search. Nothing confidential. Nothing shady."

He nodded and leaned forward, keen to see what she had.

Erin first showed him the social profiles. All of Simon's little families. Or all the ones that she had found. She didn't doubt that she might have missed some additional social profiles, maybe ones where he used a different name or an avatar rather than his own picture, and kept the security settings locked down so that pictures of the children could only be seen by close friends or family members.

Terry gave a snort of disgust. "Unbelievable. What a jerk. He can't make a clean break with Adrienne. Or any of these women, apparently. Just keeps stringing them each along, making her think she is the only one."

Erin nodded.

"Well, it certainly widens the pool of suspects." Terry's eyes flicked from one picture to the next. "We'll have to see whether there were any strange women seen around town before Simon was killed."

"You've probably already been on the lookout... but men more than women."

"True. The men you reported looking for Adrienne seem to have either left town or gone quiet. None of us have been able to catch sight of them. Which is both good and bad."

"Good because maybe they're gone, but bad because you don't know for sure?"

"And if they are still here, we don't know where they are or when they might pop up again. Or who they were or if they had something to do with Simon's death. I'm glad that Adrienne is out of town where she is safer... but if she's isolated and someone with bad intentions figures out exactly where she is, she is vulnerable."

Erin too worried about Adrienne being alone. She knew that the Prosts kept an eye on her, but they weren't with her all the time and, if something happened to her, either an accident or an attack by someone who wanted her out of the way, they might not know anything was wrong until hours later.

"Oh, there's Tom. Tom!" Terry called out to Tom Banks, who was walking by in the hallway.

Tom stopped in the doorway of the interview room and nodded to them. "Hey. What's up?"

"You see any sign of the out-of-towners who were looking for Adrienne?"

"Nope. No luck there. I talked to Darryl to get detailed descriptions, but I haven't been able to find them or where they are staying. I suspect they're probably staying in the city until they can get a better lead on Adrienne's location."

Terry nodded his agreement. Tom's eyes flicked over the papers on the table. "What's this?" He stepped into the room for a look, though he paused for a second before approaching to see if Terry would shoo him away.

"Some more background on Simon. All the women he was stringing along. Lots of little Simons running around out there now."

Tom made a noise of disgust. "Always hated that guy. What's amazing is that he wasn't killed sooner. By one of these women when they found out about his philandering ways. Or a brother or other family member that found out what he was up to." Tom's eyes blazed.

"That's not the worst of it," Erin advised. "I was just about to show Terry… this." Erin took a breath before she placed the article about the bank heist in front of Terry. "This went down in Ohio shortly before Simon showed back up in town with thousands of dollars to pay off his debts. This man…" she pointed to the sketch of the dead bank robber, "was a known associate of Simon's. Adrienne says they hung out and did things together. Went for 'guys' night out' when she thought they were watching TV at a bar."

Terry skimmed through the article, his face serious. He swore under his breath. "I knew Simon was a lowlife, but I never envisioned him being involved in something like this. They never caught any of the other robbers?"

"Not that I could find. But if you talked to law enforcement in Ohio, they could probably tell you more. Stuff that wasn't released to the papers."

"Yeah. They'll at least have approximate heights and builds. Maybe a recording of their voices. This is serious stuff. Not just penny ante misdemeanors. I never would have picked Simon for something like this."

"Adrienne is sick about it all."

"She didn't know at the time?"

"She didn't know anything until I found this yesterday. She thought the money was gambling winnings."

"And the other women? Did she know about that?"

"She thought that there were other women, but she thought they were just one-night stands. Didn't realize that he had families sprinkled all over the country."

Tom, standing beside them, was red-faced with fury. "How could this be going on and her not know about it? She must have had some inkling."

Erin shook her head. "He would leave for months at a time. How was she supposed to know what he was doing when he was halfway across the country? She had children to take care of. She had to eke out her own living. It hasn't been easy for her, you know."

"I know, I know. But Adrienne should have known. He comes home with thousands of dollars and she doesn't ask where it came from? Doesn't question him more closely to see if he is telling the truth? If she knew he was cheating on her, why did she keep taking him back? I guess she liked the convenience of that money every now and then."

Erin had never known Tom Banks to be anything but kind and compassionate. His sudden accusations surprised her.

"The person who is at fault here is Simon. Not Adrienne," she told him firmly.

Tom clenched his jaw.

Terry gave a little nod. "We know that, Erin. It's sometimes hard for a cop to see how citizens ignore what's right in front of their own faces. Law enforcement would be much easier if people told us what they saw or suspected and didn't try to protect family members or friends who break the law. But it's easy to say that you should report everything you know. It's another to actually do it."

His eyes met hers. This wasn't the first time that Erin had been a suspect in an investigation he had a part in conducting. She could only imagine how hard it was for him to be open and honest with his team, even if what he said implicated Erin in some way.

At least the fact that he hadn't been kicked off the case meant that she wasn't a serious suspect in Simon's murder. If they believed that Erin had done it, Terry would not have been able to take part in the investigation.

The problem with Simon's murder wasn't a lack of suspects. It was that there were too many of them. And Erin had just widened the pool further.

CHAPTER 29

*E*rin headed over to Auntie Clem's after she was finished at the police department offices. She knew that it would be closed and locked up tight. But she wanted to make sure that everything had been properly prepared for the next day and to get something put together for her advertisements in the next week's newspaper. She was always either preparing for a new sales campaign or analyzing the last one. When she'd decided to open a bakery, she'd had no idea how much administrative work would be involved. She had just pictured herself going in to bake bread every day. All other parts of the business would somehow sustain themselves.

But that wasn't the way it worked.

Erin reached for the burglar alarm panel when she stepped in the door, but saw that the green light was on rather than the red, indicating that the alarm had not been armed. She frowned at that. The employees were normally very good about ensuring the bakery was properly secured when they left at the end of the day. Of course, it was still possible to lose track of things and for an employee to think she had armed the alarm when she had not, but the failure was a major breach that she would have to talk to everyone about.

She reached for the light switch instead and flicked on the three switches for the kitchen.

She stopped, a scream stuck in her throat and her heart racing. She stepped back out the door into the parking lot, scrabbling for her phone in her purse. It should have been in her hand. She shouldn't ever go in the door of Auntie Clem's without the phone in her hand, ready to make a call if something were wrong.

She swiped and tapped frantically, but the screen rewrites were slow, and she kept hitting the wrong buttons. A call went through to Vic when she had meant to call Terry. Erin wanted to hang up and try again, but Vic would see the missed call and wonder what was happening. And Erin wasn't confident that she would be able to hit Terry's name on her second attempt either. It was like one of those nightmares she had when everything went wrong, and the more she struggled to right them, the worse and more confusing it became.

Maybe it was a dream. Had she gone home and gone to bed? What day was it? If she could wake herself up, she could go to the bathroom or silence her alarm—whatever it was that had disrupted her sleep and brought her into that panicked dream state.

"Hello? Erin?" Vic's voice was tinny and far away. Erin drew the phone up to her ear with great effort, as if it weighed a hundred pounds.

"Vic?"

"Are you okay? You sound funny."

"Call the police, Vic. Call Terry. I need him."

"Where are you?" Vic demanded, her voice forceful.

"Auntie Clem's."

"Are you okay? I'm going to hang up and call him right now."

"Yes."

"Okay, stay put. He'll be right there."

There were two beeps as the call ended. Erin let her arm fall back to her side again, the phone still heavy in her hand. But she didn't drop it. Once her arm was back at her side, she couldn't even feel it anymore. Erin felt like she was drifting, lost in space somewhere.

There was a siren far away, carried by the cooling breeze. Goosebumps prickled on Erin's arms. She was rarely cold in Tennessee, but she was now. She started to shiver deep down in her stomach, the muscles quivering uncontrollably.

Terry's truck pulled into the parking lot and skidded to a stop a few feet away from her. He jumped out of the car and hurried toward her, one hand on his hip, head swiveling to look for any danger. K9 was at his heel, ears pricked forward, nose scenting the breeze.

"Erin." He didn't touch her, didn't immediately sweep her into his arms. "What is it? What happened?" He turned his attention to the open door.

They'd been there before. Erin had a strong feeling of Déjà vu as he stepped over the threshold of the bakery door, drawing his gun.

The lights were still on, so he could immediately see what she had seen. He stayed in the doorway, gun drawn, frozen like a statue. Erin wondered why he didn't go in. But she knew why. He was waiting for additional law enforcement officers to arrive. He knew better than to rush into a dangerous situation without backup. They all knew what could happen. It wasn't TV, where everything would turn out well in the end. An officer who ran into a building without backup might never come back out alive. No amount of sharpshooter or ninja skills would protect him from an ambush by a criminal or criminals with multiple weapons.

Erin tried to control her breathing. She could hear it rasping in the dark, like a bad horror movie. But she couldn't feel it or control it. Two squad cars pulled into the parking lot, and the sheriff and Stayner jumped out.

"Rod, go around front," Terry ordered. "See if the front is locked and keep an eye on it. We'll wait until you're in place."

Stayner hurried down the block. The stores were interconnected, so he couldn't just go around Auntie Clem's, but had to go down to the end of the block and around. In a few minutes, Erin heard his voice crackle over the radio.

"Erin, I need you out of the way," Terry told her. "Can you go stand behind my truck?"

She didn't move. She was fastened to the concrete.

"Erin." He took her arm and gave her a little tug. Erin's feet followed. "Over behind my truck."

She had trouble getting her feet to obey but, eventually, she was on the other side of his truck. She couldn't see clearly as he and Sheriff Wilmot entered the bakery through the back door and searched it for intruders. He was back at her side a few minutes later.

"There's no one there," he assured her. "You are safe. Whoever was there is gone."

Erin nodded.

"Why wasn't the burglar alarm armed?" Terry exploded. "What is the point of us putting an alarm in there if no one arms it? This is exactly the kind of thing that we are trying to prevent from happening!"

"I didn't close today. But we always arm it. Every night."

"Was it armed when you got here? Did you disarm it?"

"No." Erin shook her head. "It was green."

"So whoever closed didn't arm it. Who was on this afternoon?"

Erin tried to remember. Her brain moved as slowly as a rusty bike chain.

"Bella. And Charley."

He shook his head. "They both know better," he growled. He turned to Sheriff Wilmot. "Can you get them both back here? I want to know what happened tonight."

Wilmot nodded agreeably. Even though he was in charge, he

wasn't offended by Terry taking over and giving the orders. He worked in partnership with his officers, confident in letting each play to their strengths. And anywhere Erin was concerned, that was Terry's wheelhouse. Unless she was a suspect.

"I can go in?" Erin asked, wrapping her arms around her body in a hug, shuddering with cold.

"You can go in, but you can't touch anything," Terry warned her. "Hold on." He went to the truck and pulled a blanket out of the back seat. It had collected a lot of dog hair. He unfolded it, shook it, and wrapped it around her so that the dog hair was on the outside. "You wait inside," he told her. "Just don't touch anything."

"I won't," she assured him.

She walked inside and through the kitchen with her eyes half-closed, determined not to see anything in the kitchen. She would sit at her desk in her office. There wouldn't be anything disturbing in there.

The first thing she checked when she entered her office was that her computer was still there. Then the backup drives in her drawer. She had another backup drive at home that she rotated out every week so that no one could ever make off with all the data vital to the bakery's running—once burned, twice shy.

She closed her eyes, cuddled in the blanket and pretended that she was at home on the couch, warm and cozy, and everything was right with the world.

She wasn't sure how long it was before Vic was allowed in. She brought Erin a thermos of hot tea.

"Be careful," she warned. "Don't burn yourself."

Erin sipped it. Hot and sweet, like Vic's mother would have told her. Southern first aid.

"Are you okay?" Vic asked.

Erin nodded. "Yes." Her voice came out as a whisper at first. She cleared her throat and tried again. "Yeah, I'm fine."

"Why did you call me?" Vic asked curiously. "Why didn't you call Terry directly?"

"Stupid phone refreshed the screen and my fat fingers hit the wrong number." Erin shook her head. "I meant to call him. Thanks. For everything."

"Of course," Vic said. She rubbed Erin's shoulder. "What happened? How did someone get in? Was it left unlocked?"

"No. I don't know. Terry is calling Charley and Bella back in. They closed."

"I can't see either of them forgetting to close properly. They're usually great at following procedures."

"I know."

It wasn't long before Erin heard Charley's strident tone as she objected to answering any questions and insisted on being allowed inside to see Erin. Terry apparently did not bar her entry, and Erin heard Charley swear as she saw the state of the kitchen and walked through to Erin's office. Vic moved out of the way. There wasn't enough room in the office for two people, let alone three.

"Erin? Are you okay?" Charley demanded. She swore again. "What happened?"

"I don't know. Did you lock up?"

"Of course I locked up," Charley said irritably. "I don't know how to lock a door?"

"Someone... got back in."

"Yeah, obviously." Charley was growling. Her eyes flashed. She looked back toward the kitchen and then returned to Erin. She was looking for someone to attack. Someone to blame. She was action oriented. She didn't want to talk about the crime. She wanted to do something about it. Retaliate or catch the culprit.

Erin shook her head. "I don't know how. I just came in to do some work and..."

"Was the alarm set?"

"No."

Charley huffed. "Then someone disarmed it. We set it when we left."

"Who did? You or Bella?"

"Bella. She was right behind me."

Bella. Erin sighed.

"Where is she?" Charley demanded. "Why isn't she here?"

"She was probably all the way home. It takes a while for her to drive in."

"She should be here," Charley grumbled.

There was another voice in the kitchen, but it wasn't Bella's. It was a calm, drawling voice that Erin recognized. Beaver. Rohilda Beaven was an agent with some federal agency, though Erin wasn't sure which one. Beaver always seemed to show up when something interesting was going down, whether she had a professional interest in it or not. She and Vic's youngest brother, Jeremy, were a couple. Beaver didn't live in Bald Eagle Falls. But she was at Jeremy's often enough.

Erin stood up, pulling the blanket more tightly around her and taking the thermos of hot tea with her. She didn't want to be cooped up in the tiny office any longer and felt strong enough to be in the kitchen again. She watched Beaver come into the kitchen through the outside door. Beaver took in all the knives stabbed into the drywall, the red gel icing dripping down the walls and smeared into a messy message.

MURDERER

Beaver stared for much longer than Erin expected her to. What was she thinking? Did she see things that Erin didn't? Did she recognize the vandalism as someone's signature? Did she know why it had been done? Was she profiling the person who would have done such a thing?

Eventually, Beaver turned to Erin, her jaw working hard at the omnipresent wad of gum.

"You do seem to attract interesting characters," she said casually.

CHAPTER 30

*E*rin shook her head helplessly. "I can't understand who would do something like this!" she told Beaver, trying to keep her voice from cracking with her overflowing emotions. "This... why would someone target the bakery? Target me? Do they really think that I did this? Is this the person framing me for the murder? Or someone who believes that the evidence all points at me? Why would anyone believe I would do something like this after all that has happened?"

Beaver nodded slowly. "Lots of questions to be answered yet. First and foremost, how did they get into the bakery?"

"Terry said that the alarm must not have been armed. Charley said that it was. We're waiting for Bella to get back. She was the last one to leave the bakery. Charley said Bella was the one who armed it. If Bella says that she did... I don't know where that leaves us."

She couldn't imagine Bella intentionally leaving the bakery unlocked. It didn't make sense that she'd want anyone to get in while they were gone. Bella was just as much a suspect as Erin. The "murderer" accusation might just as easily be intended for her as for Erin.

But had she been so distracted by everything going on that she had accidentally left without arming the alarm?

Or locking the door? Surely the door hadn't been left unlocked too. Charley would have been watching to ensure everything was properly secured.

"Someone must have broken in," Vic said firmly. "This wasn't anyone's fault."

"It's possible," Beaver agreed, looking at the burglar alarm panel. "These systems aren't completely foolproof. An experienced burglar could find their way past it pretty quickly."

"Terry said it was a good system."

"It is. Adequate for most places like this. You just want a deterrent. Thieves will go for the easy targets. If a good security system is in place, they'll go on to the next store. But that doesn't mean that it can't be defeated. Nothing is that secure."

"Nothing?"

"You don't have armed guards here. Guard dogs. Biometrics. Just a security alarm with a six-digit passcode. I could probably get around it given enough time, and burglary is not my specialty."

"But why would someone even want to?" Erin gestured at the damage to the wall. "Why break in here to accuse me of being a murderer? I didn't kill Simon Simpson. The police don't even think so."

"The Bald Eagle Falls residents know enough to make you a viable suspect. Most of the people who know you won't believe you had anything to do with it, but those who are just gossips and don't know you... it's fun to speculate."

Erin didn't consider it much fun.

"But people who are just gossiping about who killed Simon and whether I'm a good suspect are not going to be skilled enough to get by the burglar alarm."

Beaver chewed for a few minutes. "Then maybe the burglar alarm wasn't set and the door wasn't locked."

"It was locked," Charley insisted. "I watched Bella lock it.

Everything was secure. I don't care what you think; you're wrong." Charley looked at Erin. "We all know that there have been break-ins at Auntie Clem's before. That's why the security system is in place. We're super careful to arm the alarm and lock the door every time we close. We didn't want anything to happen."

"And all of the tunnels were blocked off?" Beaver asked.

It had been a long time since Erin had thought about the old tunnel system beneath a number of the Bald Eagle Falls businesses that they had discovered was being used for drug trafficking shortly before they had moved Auntie Clem's Bakery to its new location. Erin had been sure to wall everything off securely so that the tunnels could no longer be used to access the bakery basement.

"Of course," she told Beaver. "What's the point in putting locks on the doors if you allow free access through another entrance? We didn't want anyone to be able to get in here that way."

Beaver shrugged. "Sometimes people ignore the obvious. Barricade the front door and leave the back insecure."

"Maybe we should have Terry look at it anyway," Charley told Erin. "Or maybe someone like Willie. He might be able to see if someone has messed around with anything down there. Maybe someone reopened the tunnel and hid a door you don't know about…"

Erin remembered the one that had been hidden behind a stock shelf before. None of them had been able to see it until the release button was pushed. "Or K9. He was the one who found it when…" She looked over at Vic and didn't finish. *When Vic had been on the other side of that door.*

Vic didn't seem to be disturbed by the allusion to her kidnapping or Erin's deliberate avoidance of mentioning it directly. "I'll get Terry and K9 to recheck it," she offered, and headed back outside.

CHAPTER 31

*S*heriff Wilmot came in. He looked at them. "Sorry ladies, I need you to clear out so we can take pictures and gather evidence. Terry and Rod can take your statements if you are ready."

Erin and Charley headed back outside to the parking lot. Beaver trailed them out, though Wilmot would probably have allowed her to stay. Bella was pulling into the parking lot and stopped behind the police vehicles. She got out of her car quickly.

"What happened?" She demanded. "There was a break-in?"

Erin nodded. "Yeah. Someone got in after you and Charley left. I just came by to do some desk work, and…"

"What did they do?"

Erin looked toward the bakery door. If the sheriff hadn't just kicked them out, she would have told Bella just to go in and have a look. But that was out of the question while they were documenting the vandalism.

"They… stabbed all of the sharp knives into the drywall and used food coloring to… write a message."

Bella shook her head. "Why would anyone do that? I'm so sorry, Erin."

"The burglar alarm must not have armed properly when you left," Erin said, blaming the system rather than on Bella herself.

Bella shook her head. "It did! I always make sure that it beeps and turns red. Sometimes it takes twice if you do it too fast and it doesn't register the first time. I always wait for the confirmation that it is armed."

"Maybe this one time, it didn't work."

"And the one time it isn't armed properly is the one time it gets broken into?" Bella asked. "Just coincidentally, it happens not to be armed and someone comes along and tries the door?"

Erin considered this. Bella was right; it was a pretty big coincidence if the one time they forgot to arm the alarm was the one time someone had broken in to vandalize the place. Maybe Beaver's scenario was the right one. Someone who knew what they were doing had defeated the alarm.

But how many people in Bald Eagle Falls could do such a thing? Maybe Beaver, by her own admission. Maybe Willie. He knew a thing or two about security systems and electronics. There couldn't be too many more in a town the size of Bald Eagle Falls. And what had they gotten out of vandalizing the bakery? Why would someone break in to do that? Was it someone who really thought that she was a murderer or just someone who wanted to make trouble? Why go to all the work to break into the bakery? That made it seem like it must be something important to them.

Erin watched Terry go back into Auntie Clem's after talking to Vic. K9 heeled sharply. He was very well-trained and, even when off-duty, he rarely did anything silly or naughty. Did she want him to find something in the basement or not? Erin would welcome the knowledge that the vandal had not defeated the security system. But she didn't want to worry that even if they blocked off the tunnels, someone could still get through them again and attack from an unexpected direction.

And the burglar would still have had to override the system to unlock the back door. The password was needed to disarm it.

If the vandal had just come and gone through a tunnel entrance, the alarm would still be armed. But it had been disarmed and the outside door accessed. Whether he had entered through a tunnel or not was immaterial. He had still cracked the alarm system.

"I promise I armed the alarm and locked the door," Bella reiterated. "Charley was there. She knows."

Charley nodded. "I told Erin that already."

Bella looked at Erin, her eyes worried. "I'm always careful," she insisted. "I never wanted something like this to happen."

Erin closed her eyes and shook her head. "I'm sorry they made you come back here. There isn't really anything you can do."

"Erin?"

Bella's voice was insistent. Erin opened her eyes and looked at her again. She recognized how young Bella was for the first time in a long time. Erin always considered Bella an equal; she had such a good business mind and was so responsible. Erin accommodated Bella's high school schedule and knew that Bella had plans to go to college and to start her own business, but she still somehow forgot how young she really was. Bella looked at Erin with big, tear-filled eyes, looking for reassurance.

"I believe you, Bella," Erin told her. "Like I said… I'm sorry they called you back. You should be at home relaxing or doing your homework."

"I want to help."

"Nothing you can do right now. Once you've talked to the police, just go home. I don't want to be in trouble with your mom for keeping you from studying!"

"I can help clean up." Her eyes darted toward the bakery. "How bad is it?"

"It's manageable. No permanent damage. Nothing stolen. At least, not that I've noticed yet. The computer and everything important are still there. I didn't count the knives or anything."

Bella looked down at her feet, her face getting red. Erin's

heart sank. She knew which of her employees had taken the cake knife.

Why would Bella do such a thing? Had she taken it for protection because Simon was threatening her or one of Adrienne's kids? Had she been the one to stab him? Was she the poisoner too, or had that been someone else?

Originally Erin had thought it would be a weird coincidence if two people had been trying to kill Simon using two different methods. It would have to be the same person. She had just changed methods because poisoning was taking too long or because she was afraid that Simon had thrown up all the poison.

But now that she knew more about Simon, she wasn't so sure. Erin did not doubt that he could have a dozen people trying to kill him. There were undoubtedly more than that who had good reason to want him dead.

"Is there anything you want to tell me?" she asked Bella.

Bella shook her head. She forced a smile. "I'm just tired. And worried about Auntie Clem's. I hate to think of anyone doing anything to harm it."

Erin nodded. "Of course."

Charley looked at Erin, frowning. Erin didn't know whether she would tell Charley about Bella having taken the cake knife from Auntie Clem's once they were alone. Charley was Erin's partner in the business, and she liked to know what was going on. She might not work as hard as Erin thought she should, sleeping in too late to be able to take anything before the afternoon shift, always wanting to try new things before waiting to see how the last campaign or change had turned out, not showing the customers the deference Erin thought she should.

But she was still a good partner. She let Erin have the final say on things they had a different opinion on, since Erin was the original owner and the one who ran all the day-to-day operations. And Charley did work hard when she was there and could take over management in a pinch. Erin had the feeling that Charley would have grown even more in the management of

Auntie Clem's if Erin hadn't kept such a tight grip on the reins. As it was, she was like a smothering mother who wouldn't give her kids enough freedom to explore and make mistakes on their own. Because it was her business, she didn't want anyone experimenting and making mistakes with it. Other than herself.

Erin would tell Charley about Bella and the missing cake knife. Eventually. When they were alone. Charley should know what was going on.

CHAPTER 32

*E*rin had done the best she could to get in enough sleep before her next shift at Auntie Clem's. She knew that it wouldn't be easy. She had wanted to wait until the police were finished with the kitchen and get it cleaned up, but Terry wouldn't let her.

"You'll be too exhausted to work tomorrow, but you'll get up for it anyway. You don't want to make yourself sick or make mistakes at work. I will clean up when we are done. You go home, have a cup of sleepy tea and go to bed. I'll be home later."

Erin knew that it wasn't the job of the investigating officers to clean up a crime scene, even the stuff they had done themselves, like smudges of fingerprint powder. There were companies a person could hire for crime scene cleanup. At least, in the city there were. There weren't any such companies in Bald Eagle Falls. Though she could hire a regular maid service and handyman to clean up and repair the vandalism. Terry shouldn't have to do it after putting in a full shift.

Of course, Erin had put in a full shift too, getting up a few hours before he had, and she was exhausted, physically and emotionally wrung out after the discovery of the burglary and vandalism.

She finally obeyed Terry's order to go home, take care of herself, and leave him to do the cleanup. She had her cup of sleepy tea with Vic, who would also take an Ambien to ensure she could sleep and be ready for work in the morning. She was lucky enough not to get groggy and hung over from sleeping pills. Erin would prefer being regular-tired from not getting enough sleep to the fogginess and nausea she felt the morning after taking a sleep aid.

The next morning, even though Erin knew that Terry had cleaned up the kitchen for her, she still dreaded opening the door and seeing what it looked like. Would there still be red stains? Would the word "murderer" still be visible? She knew that Terry would have removed all the knives from the wall, maybe even keeping some of them for evidence, but the handles of the knives protruding from the walls were imprinted in her brain and she didn't really believe that they would be gone.

Vic gave Erin a sympathetic look when she stalled at the back door of the bakery, her hand on the handle, afraid to open it.

"Let me go first," Vic offered.

Coward that she was, Erin stepped back and let Vic go ahead. Vic opened the door, disarmed the alarm, and turned on the light in rapid, efficient movements. Erin waited to see what her reaction would be.

"They did a really good job," Vic told her, motioning her in.

Erin reluctantly entered the kitchen.

She exhaled as she looked at the clean, white walls. The red gel coloring had not permanently stained the paint. From a distance, Erin could not even tell where the knives had been stabbed deeply into the wall. She stepped closer to examine the surface.

Terry—and the other members of the police department, if Erin was not mistaken—had carefully applied drywall filler to the cuts from the kitchen knives. The surface was smooth, but the filler could be seen on close examination. It would need to be sanded and painted. They hadn't been able to do that during the night because it needed time to dry and cure. Erin made a mental note to give Terry a call when he was up to thank him for taking such good care of Auntie Clem's for her.

"You're right, it's a nice job," she told Vic.

"We'll sand it and paint it on the weekend," Vic said. "You won't be able to tell anything ever happened."

Erin nodded. There was a lump in her throat that made it difficult to speak or swallow. Vic gave her one pat on the back and then got to work. Erin was glad to jump into the routine and distract herself from the break-in and Simon's murder. If she just focused on her baking, nothing else existed.

Erin hadn't told anyone about the break-in at the bakery but, of course, everyone knew about it the next day anyway. Even if no one had seen the arrival of the police cars, Melissa Lee was eager to spread the news to everyone she could, dramatizing it as much as possible while pulling a tragic expression so it didn't look like she was enjoying herself too much.

Erin caught several people craning their necks to see into the kitchen to catch sight of the knives and garish red letters that were no longer there.

All the interest and activity was good for sales, but mentally exhausting.

Business had slowed after the lunch rush. Vic was in the kitchen taking care of a few sheets of cookies. Erin smiled at the next customer and found it was someone she didn't know. She held the smile firmly in place.

"Welcome to Auntie Clem's Bakery. I don't think you've been here before…?"

The young woman didn't respond at first. She looked around. "I was actually here once before, but someone else was on."

"Oh, okay. So you already know that everything is gluten-free. If you have any allergies or sensitivities, please let me know and I can help you to pick out baked goods that are safe for you."

"I had the cinnamon roll with cream cheese icing. It was really good."

Erin smiled. "They're so decadent, aren't they? I just love making them."

"Just perfect," the customer agreed.

"I didn't catch your name?"

"It's Juliet."

"Juliet. Glad to meet you. I'm Erin Price."

"You're the baker?"

"We all bake, but yes, I'm the proprietor and head baker."

"The other girl I talked to couldn't tell me... I'm looking for Adrienne. Do you know how I could reach her?"

"Oh. Sorry, no. I can't help you there. I could give her your name if she comes by. Will she know how to reach you?"

"Uh, no..." Juliet hesitated. "She doesn't actually know me. We have... mutual friends. I was hoping to be able to connect."

Erin's senses were all on alert. Juliet didn't know Adrienne but wanted to meet her? Was she a reporter? A curiosity seeker? Someone who wanted to see the dead man's widow and possible murderer?

"What did you want to talk to her about?"

"That's... sort of personal," the woman said.

Erin studied her. The woman's mane of red hair flowed down to her shoulders. She was slim—not as skinny as Adrienne—with big blue eyes. They were similar in age. After looking at the pictures on Simon's various social profiles, Erin should know whether he had a "type" and whether Juliet fit it. But she wasn't sure if he preferred a certain look or was indiscriminate in his affairs. Maybe any pretty face would do.

"Were you and Simon involved?" Erin asked.

The woman's eyes widened. Her mouth dropped open. She

didn't look quite as cute and innocent with her mouth hanging open like that. "What?"

"I know that Simon was seeing other women. Are you one of them?"

The redhead just looked at Erin. She was probably trying to figure out whether it would be to her advantage to admit it or to protest. Would she have a better chance of getting Erin's help if she were one of those unfortunate women? Or should she pretend to have some other relationship or reason to be looking for Adrienne?

"You are, aren't you?" Erin prompted. She shook her head. "Why would you come here looking for her? Why don't you just leave her alone? Don't you think she's been through enough without you coming around here?"

She couldn't imagine what the woman hoped to accomplish. Did she think that she would be friends with Adrienne because of what they had each suffered? Did she want to throw her relationship into Adrienne's face and claim he loved her more? Maybe she had a child or two and hoped to beg money from Adrienne, thinking that a portion of what Adrienne had should be hers. She probably had no idea where that money came from. It had nothing to do with Simon.

"I just wanted to talk to her," Juliet said.

"About Simon?"

"About... things that happened."

"If you want to leave me your number, I can have her call you the next time she's around. But I'm not just sending you to her. She deserves her privacy. She needs time to grieve."

"She doesn't know what kind of a person he was," Juliet said darkly. "No one here knows what he was."

"We're starting to get a pretty good idea. But it's not Adrienne's fault. He scammed her too. Took all her money more than once. So you're not getting to see her unless she says."

"She deserves to know about him. Why... things happened the way they did."

"Just go home to your kids," Erin suggested gently. "Go be with them and forget about Simon."

Juliet closed her eyes and shook her head slowly. "I don't have any kids." She opened them again, the blue irises burning brightly. "He took everything."

"I'm sorry." Erin couldn't think of anything else to say to this. She still wasn't going to put Juliet in touch with Adrienne. "Would you like another cinnamon roll? On the house?"

Juliet looked into the display case, a slight smile on her face. "With cream cheese?"

"Of course. I'll even warm it in the microwave for you. Make it nice and drippy and syrupy."

"*Mmm.*" Juliet groaned. "Okay, you've got a deal. And you'll give my number to Adrienne; tell her to call me?"

"I won't tell her to call you. She can decide whether to call you herself."

"Deal."

Erin got out a big cinnamon roll while Juliet wrote her phone number on a scrap of paper.

Vic looked up as Erin entered the kitchen to warm up the cinnamon roll.

"Everything okay?"

"Just warming up a roll."

"Who is out there? I didn't recognize the voice."

"Someone named Juliet. Out-of-towner looking for Adrienne."

"Everyone is looking for Adrienne. I wish they would all just leave her alone."

Erin nodded her agreement. "I understand people wanting to connect with her because of what happened. But these folks from out of town… seems like all they want is money. And it isn't like Adrienne even has that much. She has what she needs to build her house and give the kids somewhere to live. To have a little security. And that money doesn't have anything to do with Simon."

"I know," Vic agreed.

The microwaved beeped and Erin removed the warmed roll. It was just the right temperature to remain soft and fluffy like it had just come out of the oven and to melt the cream cheese icing so that it seeped into the spiral of dough.

"Those smell so good," Vic said. "It should be illegal."

CHAPTER 33

*T*erry wandered into Auntie Clem's about the time they were getting ready to close. Coincidence? Erin thought not. There were a lot of good reasons for stopping by the bakery as it closed. One was that it was a good time to get a free handout as they cleared the display case and put the left-overs in the freezer for the day-old bread program.

Or Terry might want to get to work on the next step of the wall repair and sand the spots he had filled the previous night so that they could be painted over without showing any sign of the repair job. Or he might want to supervise the closing so that he could be sure that Erin was on her way home and the bakery was locked up tight and properly monitored by the security alarm.

But both guesses, though good ones, appeared not to be the case. Terry's expression was grim.

"Is everything okay?" Erin inquired.

"I wish I could say it was. There have been developments in Simon's murder case, and I don't like the direction they are going."

Erin swallowed, wondering if they were once again pointing the finger at her. Maybe the police department had decided it wasn't just an attempt to make Erin look guilty, but that she actually was.

"What's wrong?"

"Do you know where Bella is?"

"She wasn't on today. It was her day off."

"So would she be at home now? Or does she study in town or have late after-school activities?"

"At home. She helps with the farm work. And helps with Adrienne's kids when they're there." Erin glanced around, ensuring no one was within earshot. She was getting paranoid about everyone wanting to know where to find Adrienne.

Terry nodded. He stood there with his thumbs in his belt loops, watching Erin clear out the display case.

"Why? What's happened?" Erin asked. She handed him an apple tart, one of his favorites. He took it with a nod of thanks.

He didn't answer immediately, and Erin began to marshal her arguments for why he should tell her what was going on. She would find out anyway once it went public. Or when Melissa leaked it. She could help him to brainstorm and think of whether there were any other explanation for the new evidence. Clearly, he wasn't happy with whatever it was or how he interpreted it.

"Bella's fingerprints were on the murder weapon," Terry said abruptly, eliminating the need for her arguments.

Erin shook her head. She rubbed the back of her neck.

"It couldn't be Bella," she said. "It just isn't her nature. And if it was… it would have to be something like self-defense or trying to protect one of the kids. She is not a murderer."

"I agree that she isn't the typical killer. But who is? We have had plenty of unlikely killers. Just because she's young and because she seems to be nice, that doesn't mean she is innocent."

"If the cake knife came from here, then any of our fingerprints could be on it. We all handled them."

"Of course. I'm not saying that it's proof she did it… but there have been… other things."

Erin avoided saying anything. She didn't want to agree that there were things that pointed to Bella, or protest and make herself sound overly defensive.

Terry looked at her, waiting.

"What other things?" Vic asked from the doorway to the kitchen, obviously having overheard the conversation.

Erin should probably have asked that too, and Terry was wondering why she hadn't.

"Bella and Cindy are very close to Adrienne, physically and emotionally. They are very protective of her and her kids. Bella has been known to be confrontational with Simon or others who might have threatened Adrienne. We know that threats were made."

"She's a teenager," Erin dismissed. "Teenagers say things they shouldn't. So do plenty of adults, for that matter. It doesn't mean they plan to do anything to hurt anyone."

"I can't see her doing anything violent," Vic agreed.

"I still need to talk to her about it. An alibi would go a long way to eliminating her from suspicion."

Erin wondered fleetingly if there were anything she could say to alibi Bella. Say that she had seen Bella somewhere else around the time of the murder. Say that they had been together. That Bella had gone straight from Auntie Clem's to… where?

She would need to talk to Bella before Terry to find out the details and ensure they had a story that would hold up under examination and persistent questioning.

Vic and Terry were both looking at Erin with an expression that told her that her thoughts were an open book to them. She turned her face away, heat blossoming in her cheeks.

"I'm sure Bella will be able to tell you where she was and what she was doing around the time of the murder," Erin assured Terry. "She is *not* a killer."

"I'm sure she will," he agreed. "So you figure she is probably on the farm?"

"I'm sure. She doesn't spend much time in town other than to go to school or work."

He nodded and ate the apple tart with his fingers. "Do me a favor and don't call her to tell her I'm on my way."

CHAPTER 34

*A*fter Terry was gone, Erin looked at the clock and then at Vic.

"I'll be in my office. I have some phone calls to make."

Vic looked at her doubtfully. Erin never shut herself in her office to make phone calls. She sometimes made calls on her cell phone on Bluetooth while she and Vic closed. Or sometimes she sat at her desk to make calls to suppliers or her accountant while she sat in front of the computer and could see her orders or numbers while she talked. But she didn't shut her door.

"Personal calls," Erin said.

As if that explained anything. She and Vic talked about everything. Erin often bounced ideas off Vic or discussed her problems or troublesome thoughts. Vic generally knew what was going on in her life—even more than Terry.

Not that Erin didn't have her secrets. She liked to keep the past in the past. But that was different. Everyone deserved their privacy about some things.

"Terry knows what he's doing," Vic said slowly. "You know he's not going to railroad Bella."

Erin smiled, though the expression felt strange on her face and she was worried it would look more like a grimace of pain.

"Terry is good at his job," she agreed pleasantly. "I'm sure that he will do everything he can for Bella. But... that also means that he needs to follow certain policies and procedures and, if he or Sheriff Wilmot feel like there is enough evidence pointing to Bella killing Simon, they will have to act on it." She paused, trying to decide whether to say more to Vic about it. "Sometimes, the law needs a little help toward the right outcome."

"You don't want to get in trouble for interfering with an investigation. And you don't want... Terry told you not to tell Bella he was going out there to talk to her."

"Which is more important? Keeping Bella out of prison or keeping Terry happy?"

She didn't relish the idea of his being angry with her. And he would be, even though he was the one who had come to her in the first place.

"I'm not going to tell Bella he's on his way out there," Erin assured Vic. "But why would he come here and tell me that her fingerprints are on the murder weapon and that she needs an alibi if he didn't want me to do something about it?"

Vic's mouth worked for a minute, opening to speak and then discarding what she had been about to say before the words finally came out. "He told you that because he felt bad about what he had to do. Because he's worried about Bella. Not because he wanted you to interfere and... invent an alibi."

"I'm not inventing anything." Erin stepped into her office and reached for the door. "I just have some business calls to make."

She ignored the look of concern on Vic's face and shut the door before she could make any other arguments. She sat down at her desk, picked up the phone, and looked at it for a moment, trying to figure out what she would say to Bella. She wasn't sure how to initiate the conversation or tell her what was going on in a way that she could defend in the future. Because she was pretty sure she would have to defend her actions very soon.

She forced herself just to dial Bella's number and trust that she would be able to come up with something on the fly. It was one of those times when, no matter how much thought she put into it ahead of time, she wouldn't come up with the perfect script. And the longer she took to initiate the call, the harder it would be. She didn't want to end up just sitting there staring at the phone for an hour. She needed to talk to Bella before Terry arrived at the farm, which only gave her a limited amount of time.

"Hi, Erin," Bella answered the phone. Her tone was calm, but tentative. She probably had an idea of what was going to happen. They had both been fighting against Bella being identified as a serious suspect for some time. Ever since Erin had discovered Simon's body. "What's up?"

"I just wanted to see how you were doing. I know… things have been pretty crazy lately. Since Friday…"

"Friday?"

"Friday was when Simon came to Auntie Clem's that last time. I guess you remember that."

"Of course," Bella agreed, sounding confused about why Erin was calling her.

"And you remember what you were doing after that," Erin suggested. "How you spent the rest of the time you were in Bald Eagle Falls."

"Umm…"

"You know where you were and what you were doing."

There was a long pause. Erin looked at her phone, trying to reassure herself that Bella was still there.

"Erin, you know that I wouldn't—"

"Of course I do," Erin cut across Bella's protest and anything she might not want to hear. "You and I were…"

"No." It was Bella who cut Erin off this time. "I wasn't with you. I was with Josh."

Erin breathed out. "Joshua Cox?"

She didn't know of any other Josh. She just needed to reassure herself that Bella understood and would be protected.

"Sure. We were studying," Bella said. "We've got a big test and needed to prep for it."

"So you were studying… in the library? Or at the school?"

"No, just… like, in the park, out of the way. Enjoying some fresh air."

Not in the library or school where the other students might have seen or not seen them. Erin swallowed, nodding to herself.

As long as Bella had Joshua to back up her alibi, she would be fine. As far as Erin knew, the two of them were not romantically involved, so the police couldn't accuse him of just covering for his girlfriend. He was more objective—a better, more reliable witness.

"Okay, good," she told Bella. "And as far as the equipment at Auntie Clem's goes… it would be perfectly natural for your fingerprints to be found on anything. You work there. You wash and put cutlery away in the drawers. Why wouldn't your fingerprints be on them?"

"Well… yeah," Bella agreed. Her voice sounded choked and Erin wondered if she had pushed it too far. She didn't want Bella to shut down before Terry got there. If Terry arrived to find her hysterical or defensive before he even said anything to her, it would look a little suspicious. Bella needed to be strong and confident. She couldn't be tentative about her alibi or her explanation of why her fingerprints were on the murder weapon.

"You use all of the tools at Auntie Clem's," Erin told her firmly. "You do the washing up and put stuff away."

"Yeah. I do. Almost everything will have my fingerprints on it," Bella said faintly.

"It's perfectly natural," Erin reiterated.

"Sure," Bella's voice gained strength. "That's right."

"Good. I guess I'd better get off the phone. You might have some calls of your own to make. Soon."

"Yeah," Bella agreed. "Thanks for calling… I guess I'll see you tomorrow."

"See you then. Take care."

Bella murmured something and ended the call.

Erin pushed her breath out slowly, trying to remain calm and in control of her emotions. She didn't need to worry about Bella. Bella understood and would have a good alibi for Terry. Terry would accept it and report back to Sheriff Wilmot and the other law enforcement officers that Bella could not be the killer despite any other evidence of her involvement.

CHAPTER 35

*W*hen Erin hung up the phone, she could hear voices in the kitchen on the other side of the door. Vic and a male voice. Had Terry come back for some reason? It was a good thing she had shut the door to talk to Bella. Erin stood up and returned to the kitchen.

It wasn't Terry, but Tom Banks, another member of the police department. For a moment, Erin let her anxiety take over. Was he there to execute a search warrant? Was there some other piece of evidence they hoped to find in the bakery implicating Bella or someone else?

She couldn't think of what else might be a problem.

Tom smiled and lifted his hand, showing her a can of paint.

"Just stopped by to put a coat of paint over those patches," he explained.

"Oh, you don't have to do that!"

They had already gone way above and beyond what an ordinary police department would have done. A coat or two of paint and the wall would look perfect. There would be nothing to remind Erin of the vandalism.

"We take care of our own," Tom assured her.

"You guys have been so good about all of this." Erin's eyes

burned with tears. "You could have made things really difficult for me with the cake knife and the cinnamon roll and everything." She rolled her eyes to the ceiling, trying to keep the tears from escaping. "And I know you don't have to do all of this, but you've all done such a nice job."

Tom smiled. "Why should you have to suffer because some lunatic decides to target your bakery? You've had enough trouble here. You don't need that. Don't worry." He waved this aside. "We'll take care of this."

Erin helped Vic get the last few jobs of the day done.

"Do you want me to stay here?" Vic asked, glancing over at Tom. "Wait until everything is done?"

"No, you go ahead. I'll stay a bit longer. This won't take long."

Tom looked at them. "I can lock up after I'm done, if you like. You don't have to stay to supervise."

"I've still got a few things to do," Erin said. "It's fine."

Vic nodded. "Okay, well, if you've got this covered, I'll see how Willie's day has been. Call me if you decide you need anything."

"Go ahead. You've done your duty today. You still need to give Willie some time and attention."

"Yeah," Vic massaged her neck and shoulders. "I hope he's not too negative tonight, or I might have to take drastic measures." She shot a look at Tom. "You didn't hear that."

He chuckled. "You do what you gotta do."

Vic and Erin laughed, and Vic left.

"It's a good thing someone finally took care of Simon Simpson," Tom said as he started to slowly roll paint over the sanded patches.

Erin was working on the schedules laid out on the whiteboard on one wall of the kitchen. "I thought that as a law enforcement officer, you would be against any kind of violence."

"Normally, yes. But I can't say I feel bad when a lowlife

scumbag like Simon is removed from circulation. Some people just don't deserve to be a part of decent society."

She probably shouldn't have been surprised. She'd heard him mutter a few things about Simon when he'd found out about all the different women that Simon was stringing along in what they thought was a long-term committed relationship. And he'd been there when Erin had shown Terry the information she'd found about the bank robbery that went bad. Tom knew as well as anyone what "lowlife scum" Simon was.

He might appear to the women he was stringing along to be a decent family man but it was far from the truth. He would have kept taking everything he could from them. And she didn't believe that the bank heist was the first violent robbery he had committed. That didn't just come out of nowhere. Someone didn't just wake up one day and decide to rob a bank at gunpoint with three accomplices. It had all been set up ahead of time. And there had undoubtedly been smaller crimes leading up to it and other jobs that followed.

That hadn't been the only time Simon had gone home to Adrienne flashing plenty of cash and making good on his mountainous debts.

"I feel bad for the girlfriends especially," Erin said. "Or the wives, if he was actually married to any of them. I can't believe that he just kept stringing women along, having babies with them, taking their money, and they kept taking him back."

"He got them so twisted around, they thought it was their fault if he didn't come home. Or he convinced them he was off on a job that paid well and would get them out of the hole. But of course it never did."

Erin frowned at Tom. She kept working on the schedule while he painted, and she turned his words over in her mind, trying to get a handle on what was bothering her.

"How well did you know him when he lived here? It sounds like you knew him pretty well… or is this all just from your investigation of his death?"

Tom wasn't of the same generation as Simon. He was an older man. Old enough that he could have retired from the police force, but he kept serving part-time because they needed him, and he enjoyed still having his hand in and knowing what was going on in the town.

Tom considered, a long pause between Erin's question and his answer.

"He took up with my niece," he said finally. "I told her to stay away from him. But when did warning a young lady about a scoundrel ever produce the desired results? They have to find out for themselves. They think that you're an old fogy and don't know the way the world works anymore. They think that things are different now and they're more sophisticated."

He *tsked* while he continued to roll the paint in long, slow strokes that didn't cause any drips and covered the wall evenly.

"Oh, I'm sorry," Erin said. "I didn't know."

She vaguely recalled one of Simon's social networking profiles with a Banks. What had her name been? It had also started with a T. A funny sort of name. Tara? Something more masculine.

"Tate," Erin remembered, "Tate Banks."

Tom turned his head to look at her over his shoulder, sheepish. His face turned slightly pink.

"I saw it that day when you had them all on the table for Terry." He stopped painting for a moment, thinking about it. "Up until then… I thought he was just two-timing her. Splitting his time between Adrienne and Tate. Maybe some time on his own as a swinging bachelor. I had no idea that there were so many of them." He shook his head. "Unbelievable. Why did they all do it? I never could see what Tate could see in him. He was a troublemaker from early on. It wasn't like he appeared to be a nice, law-abiding guy. Why are women attracted to that type?"

Erin didn't know if Tom had ever been married or had a long-term relationship. He hadn't been for as long as Erin had been around, but that had only been a couple of years. Men naturally slowed down as their testosterone flagged.

"Some girls are just attracted to bad boys," she admitted. "I don't know if it is a rebellious thing or what... but it's not uncommon."

"Did she think she was going to reform him? That he was going to turn around and become an outstanding citizen?"

"Women marry men to fix them," Erin said, quoting a foster mother. "But you can't change someone else."

Tom nodded, grunting his agreement.

Erin tried to remember what she could about Tate Banks from Simon's posts.

"Was she a redhead?"

Tom nodded. "Yeah. Carrot top. We always teased her when she was little."

He didn't say what had happened to her after that. She had left for other climes. Had she run away with Simon? Gone away to school or to a job? Had she felt she wasn't taken seriously or respected by her family members and wanted to show that she could stand on her own two feet?

"And she has a little girl? No, a little boy. Do they ever visit?"

"No, not very much. Her mother, my sister, lives in the city, so sometimes Tate makes it there. But not back to Bald Eagle Falls." He sighed. "Too many memories, I guess. Her mother was never happy here either. Small-town life isn't for everyone." He shook his head. "I wouldn't give it up for anything. You think I want to live in the city where no one knows your name unless it's to give you a bill? No thank you, ma'am. Here, where I'm known, if anything was to happen to me everyone would know about it. The community pulls together when something bad happens. You've seen it with Adrienne. With Simon's sister, Scarlett, even though people hated him. They still draw in to comfort her."

"She didn't... Tate didn't come here for Simon's memorial, did she? Or to see Adrienne or you?"

"No. I don't think she'd come here to see him off after everything he did to her. And I'm not going to be the one to tell her that he's dead. She's better off if he just disappears from her life."

"She doesn't know that he's dead?"

"I haven't told her. Maybe one of her old school friends will tell her, but I won't."

Erin thought about the woman who had come to the bakery. She had been a redhead. She had as much as admitted that she was one of Simon's women. Had that been Tate? That wasn't the name she had given and she said she didn't have any kids, but what if she hadn't wanted to tip off Tom or other old acquaintances that she was in town? What if she knew Adrienne wouldn't see her if she gave her real name? Did they know each other? Did they know about each other? Or had they before Adrienne had seen Tate's picture on Simon's other profile?

"So... you haven't seen her lately? She doesn't come to Bald Eagle Falls?"

Tom shook his head. "What's here for her, other than her old Uncle Tom? She didn't have the best experiences growing up in Bald Eagle Falls. Why would she come back here? Especially if anyone else knows that she left with Simon? Or that she was still with him? And Adrienne here with five children of his?"

Or three, if the obituary were to be believed. Who had given them the information? Scarlett? It couldn't have been Adrienne because she would have included all the children's names. Did Simon have anyone else in town? That schoolteacher, Emily, or another woman? His mother?

Erin put the finishing touches on the schedule and pondered whether to leave Tom on his own to lock up or to stay until he was finished. He only had a few more minutes to go and he would be finished with the repair job on the wall.

CHAPTER 36

*I*t had almost been a week since Erin's discovery of Simon's body back behind the bakery dumpster, and things were starting to quiet down again. There had been a full spread in the Bald Eagle Falls weekly newspaper, with articles contributed by several different reporters or civic leaders. Joshua had put together a "crime beat" article listing the facts of the case and the clues that he thought important. He didn't say who his suspects were. Obviously, he didn't think that Bella had done it since he had been with her at the time. And Erin hoped that he knew it hadn't been her, either. The clues pointing toward the bakery were too heavy-handed and the vandalism of the kitchen hadn't exactly been subtle.

Erin smiled at Mrs. Foster as she entered the bakery with her little crew. The children swarmed around other customers to look in the display case and began to debate which cookies they should get. As the older girls' debate got louder, Traci started banging on the glass, shouting "cook-kie, cook-kie, cook-kie!" at the top of her lungs. Peter bent over her, trying to convince her to quiet down, and pointed out to the little girls that the louder they got, the louder Traci was getting. Eventually, he got them to settle down and shot a look at Mrs. Foster, who smiled tiredly and nodded at him.

"Thank you," she mouthed.

Peter grinned and looked proud. Erin gave him a thumbs-up. He was such a good big brother.

She served the next couple of customers and then smiled down at the little girls as Mrs. Foster took her place at the counter.

"Have you girls chosen what you want for the kids' club yet?"

Traci pounded the glass again, with her usual demand of, "dat one!"

"Please," Mrs. Foster prompted tiredly. "Be polite, Traci. Say 'please.'"

Traci pounded harder, "Please, dat one, please!"

Peering at Traci from the back of the display case, Erin tried to determine which exact cookie she wanted and put it in a sleeve for her. The other children were easier to deal with. Allan was still working on teething cookies and not old enough to choose his own treat from the display case.

Once everyone was happily munching on their cookies, Mrs. Foster could select the baking she would need for the rest of the weekend and the beginning of the following week.

"I heard you had some trouble," she murmured as Charley rang up the purchases at the till, indicating the kitchen with a slight jerk of her head.

"Yes," Erin admitted. "But nothing serious. It has all been taken care of."

"I can't understand why anyone would do anything like that," Mrs. Foster said, shaking her head. "What's wrong with people who have to be so destructive? And the violence..." She was always careful not to mention murder or specific examples of violence in Bald Eagle Falls in front of the children. "We live in such a fallen world."

Erin wasn't entirely sure what that meant, but she nodded sagely, deferring to Mrs. Foster's judgment.

"You can't make other people's choices," she said. "All you can do is choose not to do things like that."

"You're so right," Mrs. Foster said emphatically. "All we can do is make our own righteous choices."

The conversation was more religious than Erin was comfortable with, and she was glad when Mrs. Foster paid and motioned for the children to follow her to the next store. Peter helped to herd them along, waving goodbye to Erin.

"That one's a little…" Charley grimaced and didn't specify whether she thought Mrs. Foster crazy, overly concerned, or too religious. "Doesn't she know you're an atheist?"

"Yes, she knows. But people forget. Or they think everyone still has the same Christian values even if they aren't Christian."

Charley snorted. She'd been raised by strict Christians and was still a little rebellious about it.

"But she's right about there being too much senseless violence," Erin offered. "Trying to make sense of it is…"

"A lost cause."

Erin nodded. She looked at Charley curiously to see if she had any comments about violence in the world. Charley had been part of one of the organized crime families before meeting Erin. While she wasn't part of that scene anymore, Erin imagined she had some very different ideas about the acceptable use of violence.

But Charley kept her mouth shut and didn't offer anything in front of the customers waiting to be served.

One of the next customers was Mary Lou. She looked her usual unflappable self with a helmet of gray hair that was never out of place and a professional-looking skirt suit that showed not a single wrinkle.

"Hi, Mary Lou," Erin greeted. "I don't think I've seen you since… what, last Friday? You must have had a busy week."

Mary Lou nodded. "When I left here, Roger's aide called to

say that he was having a meltdown, so I had to go straight home to try to settle him down."

Roger was Mary Lou's husband, not a fractious toddler. He had some challenges following his near strangulation several years earlier. He was home again now, but he needed to have someone there to watch him any time that Mary Lou or Josh couldn't. Their lives revolved around his home care schedule.

"Oh, I'm sorry. Was everything okay?"

Mary Lou shook her head. "He was really agitated. I could not get him settled down. I had to call Josh home. Sometimes, he can distract Roger with talk of fishing or some other father-son thing. And he's stronger than I am if Roger tries to leave."

Erin winced. She didn't like the sound of that. Roger was strong and could do a lot of damage if he were out of control. They had him on medications that usually kept him calm, but it sounded like something had really triggered him.

"Neither of us slept," Mary Lou confessed. "Saturday, we took him into the city to the hospital. It turned out he had an infection. Apparently, that can really throw people off. Cause a lot of psychiatric complications."

"It really can," Erin agreed. She had done home care for elderly people herself, those whose families wanted them cared for at home and not at a nursing home. They didn't always pay well, but offered room and board, which reduced her other living costs. "I've seen that with elderly people and UTIs. If someone suddenly starts hallucinating… lots of times, it's a UTI, not a stroke or drug overdose."

Mary Lou shook her head. "You learn something new every day. So that was our weekend, and we've been recovering from it since. Roger is finally back to normal, so I thought I'd better sneak out while I could and get some supplies."

Erin assembled the baking Mary Lou requested and wrapped everything up for her. "There. Charley will ring it up for you. You take care and don't try to do too much. You think you should be able to jump right back into everything, but you probably need recovery time just as much as he did. Especially if he's been keeping you up nights."

"We've been alternating nights, Josh and I, but it will be good to get caught up again. I won't deny that."

Charley took care of Mary Lou's purchase, and Erin looked at the next customer.

It wasn't until later that she realized the real impact of Mary Lou's words.

CHAPTER 37

*B*ella looked critically at the wall that had previously been defaced. She nodded her approval. "It looks really good. Even knowing that's where it was all messed up, I can't see any sign of the vandalism. Terry fixed it?"

"All of the police had a hand in it, I think," Erin said. "Tom Banks was by last night to put a coat of paint on it." Erin studied it. "I don't think it's going to need another coat."

"No. It looks really good."

"New schedule is up," Erin told her, pointing to the whiteboard. "Let me know if there are any problems with it."

Bella looked it over and took a picture with her phone. "Looks good. And, um…" Her voice faltered at first, then strengthened. "Thanks for the call yesterday. Officer Piper came by, but we were prepared for him."

"Good." Erin was glad that disaster had been averted. She didn't need one of her best employees being arrested for something Erin was pretty sure she hadn't done. "I'm glad you had someone to back up where you…" Erin stopped.

Bella turned around and looked at her after a minute. "Erin? What?"

Erin pressed her knuckle to the front of her forehead. She

had as much as offered Bella an alibi, but Bella had said that she had been studying with Josh. And that was presumably what she had told Terry when he had visited her.

And Terry had been satisfied with their alibi. He'd probably talked to Josh to confirm it and been happy to eliminate Bella as a suspect. Her fingerprints on the weapon could be explained and she hadn't been anywhere near Simon at the time of his death.

But if he talked to Mary Lou to confirm Joshua's story, then Mary Lou would tell him what she had told Erin that morning.

That Roger had suffered a crisis and they had been with him all afternoon and night and had spent the following day at the hospital. Joshua had not been with Bella. He'd been helping take care of his father.

Bella took in Erin's look of dismay. Her face turned white. "What?" she demanded. "Why are you looking at me like that?"

"You lied about your alibi."

Bella shook her head. "I needed to study for a test. Joshua and I—"

"You weren't with him."

"We were by ourselves. You weren't there. You couldn't know."

"I know where Joshua really was."

Bella looked uncertain about this. "What do you mean where he really was? We were together. That's what he told Officer Piper. He believed him. I have an alibi. He knows I didn't do it."

"Until he talks to Mary Lou."

Bella shook her head. "What? What did Mary Lou say?"

"She said that there was a problem with Josh's father, and Josh was helping her. Simon was here, at the bakery and, when he left, Mary Lou got called home to see to Roger. And she had Joshua come home to help her too, because he was so agitated and she hoped that Josh could get him calmed down."

"Maybe it was after that… or she got her days mixed up."

"They were with him all night and took him to the hospital Saturday morning. And then they were at the hospital all day. So Josh can't give you an alibi for any of the time of death window."

Bella shook her head. "But… why didn't Josh tell me that?"

Erin held up her hands palms-up, at a loss. "I don't know. He's short on sleep. Maybe he got his days mixed up. If you put him on the spot, maybe he didn't remember. Maybe he looked at his calendar and there wasn't anything there, so he thought he was safe saying he was with you."

Bella pulled at her hair, distressed. "Or maybe he just thought that he could get away with it. I mean, so far, it has worked. I don't think that Officer Piper… I think he wanted me to have an alibi. I don't think he cared what it was."

Erin had gotten the same feeling from Terry. That he knew that Bella wasn't the one who had killed Simon and wanted to be able to pursue other avenues to find the real killer. Even if all the clues pointed toward it being a bakery employee, and now Bella in particular due to her fingerprints being found on the murder weapon, he knew that it wasn't one of them.

To think that Bella could have killed Simon was ridiculous. Bella was cool-headed and smart. She wasn't someone who was likely to be provoked into doing something violent and stupid, even by Simon. Even if she had been angry at him and threatened him, that had just been words. It wasn't the same as physical violence. Erin had never seen Bella be physically violent toward anyone. Not even a push or a playful slap.

But Bella *was* guilty of something.

Erin breathed out slowly. "Tell me about the cake knife."

Bella shrugged. "It was just the same as the other cake knives."

"Why did you take it?"

"I didn't!" Bella protested. Then her eyes met Erin's, and she dropped them to the floor. "I'm… I'm sorry. It wasn't like that."

"Wasn't like what? I didn't say anything. I asked why you took it."

"How did you know it was me?"

"The way you've been acting. I thought it was you right from the start. But I couldn't figure out why. I still can't figure out why. So you need to tell me what's going on. I can't keep covering for you without knowing why."

"I didn't even mean to take it."

Erin tried to imagine it just falling into Bella's school bag as she cleaned up at the end of a shift. *Oops.* It just fell in there and she didn't realize it until she got home.

But then how had it ended up in Simon's chest?

CHAPTER 38

I would have said something to you," Bella's voice was tearful. "I would have told you; things were just crazy here and I didn't get the chance. I was just borrowing it and I would have brought it back here and put it back in the drawer on Monday."

But by that time, it had already been in the decomposing body.

"It was my Home Ec teacher, Mrs. Parker. We were talking about different kinds of kitchen knives in class, about the different shapes and what they were used for, and how to recognize them. But she had never seen a cake knife like that. She had only seen the long skinny ones, with a rounded or blunt end."

Erin nodded, following Bella and suspecting she knew where Bella was going with the explanation.

"She hadn't ever seen the spade-shaped one that can be used as a lifter as well as cutting with it," Erin contributed.

"It's so handy," Bella agreed. "A really sharp tip for piercing or starting a cut, the blade edge, and the wedge shape to serve the slices. It's like three tools in one."

And it was apparently nice and sharp and sturdy enough to be used as a weapon, too.

"So you took it to show to Mrs. Parker."

"Yes. I was just borrowing it. I didn't mean to *take* it, and it wasn't a secret. I just wanted to show her. When she asked the class what a cake knife looked like, and I said it was wedge-shaped, she said I was wrong, and everyone laughed because I work in a bakery, and I should know. So I was going to show her." Bella finished lamely. "I just wanted to show her."

Erin nodded. "And then what happened?"

She probably shouldn't ask. She knew she should probably encourage Bella to confess to the police what had happened and stay out of it herself. But Erin couldn't help feeling protective of Bella. She needed to help Bella sort it out and ensure that she would be okay.

Bella bit her lip and didn't answer.

"Did he come after you?" Erin asked. "How did you end up…"

"It wasn't like that. That isn't what happened."

"What, then?"

"Simon *did* come at me again, demanding to know where Adrienne was and saying I had to take him to her. Saying that money was his just as much his as it was hers. He'd given her lots of money in the past, and this was his chance to finally get something back from her."

Bella wiped at her nose.

"He was just so… awful. All he cared about was himself, and he had no idea what Adrienne and the kids had been through. Because of *him*. He acted like he'd given her this wonderful life, always giving her whatever money he had, and she just spent it all. But I know what it was like. All of Adrienne's money went into caring for the kids and herself. She didn't spend it on stupid stuff. Simon was the gambler."

"He wasn't very nice," Erin agreed. "So what happened when he went after you demanding to know where Adrienne was so he could get the money from her?"

Tears spilled down Bella's cheeks. Erin tried not to be

affected by them. Guilty people still cried. Even if someone didn't feel sorry for the person she had hurt or bad for what he had done, she still cried about getting caught, and how a conviction would mess up her life. Bella swiped at the tears.

"He was threatening. He was pushing me around and threatening me... and I remembered the knife in my bag. I held the bag between us to try to block him, and then I felt it through the bag and remembered it was there. I took it out and..."

Bella gulped and tried to get her tears under control. It took all of Erin's self-control not to take Bella in a protective hug and tell her that everything would be okay. She needed to hear the story. She needed to know exactly what had happened to formulate a plan.

"Just tell me what happened."

"I didn't stab him," Bella insisted. "I got the knife out to show him I could protect myself and he needed to leave me alone. I just wanted him to leave me alone."

Erin nodded. "And?"

"I wish I'd had what it took to actually stab him. But I've never done anything like that. I've never hurt anyone or threatened anyone with a weapon. He just laughed. He tried to grab it from me. I pulled back... I stepped back from him. He pushed me up against the wall. He grabbed my wrist and pinned it." Bella shook her head in disgust. "I wish I could say I was a ninja, but I'm not. He got it off me."

"He took the knife away?"

Bella nodded. Her eyes were swimming in tears. "Just like taking candy from a baby. I couldn't do anything to stop him. I outweighed him. I'm not some helpless little girl... but I was. I wanted to fight him. Not to stab him, but to hold him off... to show him that I had some teeth and he couldn't just push me around like that."

Erin thought about that.

Then Simon had been the one with the knife. Had someone wrestled it away from him and stabbed him with it? Or had he trusted his attacker and handed him or her the knife willingly? Had he attacked someone and had the knife turned back on him?

"You're going to need to tell Terry or one of the other law enforcement officers the truth."

"No, Erin…"

"They're going to figure it out. It's better to come forward and tell them what happened willingly. Say that you panicked and told a lie, but you realize they need to know the truth to investigate this killing properly. If they catch you in a lie… it's not good. It's going to make them more suspicious. And you don't want to get Josh in trouble too. You guys are young. Just tell him that you made a stupid mistake."

"If they know I took the knife from here, they're going to think that I murdered Simon."

"They already know that you had it in your hand. That you were one of the last people to hold it."

"I thought you said that you would help me."

"Well, it's too late for me to give you an alibi. They need to know that Simon himself had the knife. It changes things. Someone didn't go after him with the intent to kill him. He started something. Or he got into a heated argument and pulled it out."

"What does that matter?"

"It puts a completely different spin on who killed him. It might have been an accident or manslaughter or self-defense. It wasn't necessarily a premeditated murder."

The death cap toxin kind of argued against that viewpoint. But maybe there were two killers, one who planned things out and one who was opportunistic or who had killed him in self-defense.

*J*t was not unusual for Erin to show up at the police
department offices with a box of treats in hand.
Sometimes it was because she wanted something, and sometimes
it was just to pamper them or to thank them for some action
they had taken. Between Erin's deliveries and the muffins or
other treats that Bella picked up, the police department usually
had treats from Auntie Clem's once or twice a week.

It was unusual for Bella to show up with Erin, however.
Clara looked at the two of them over the top of her glasses rims
as she wrote something out on a yellow legal pad.

"Yes...?"

"Is Terry in?"

"No one is in at the moment." Clara looked at her watch.
"Terry will be off soon. I don't think he'll be back here before he
heads home."

Erin wasn't sure what to do. Take Bella home with her? It
would be more comfortable for them to have a living room
conversation than sitting on the hard chairs in an interview room.
But would Terry agree to that? Or would Sheriff Wilmot insist
that the interview had to occur at the station with cameras rolling?

Clara was waiting for her response. Erin handed her the box of cookies while thinking about it.

"Bella needs to talk to someone... if no one is in, then I guess we may as well go home..."

"You could see someone tomorrow. Is it urgent?"

"Well..." Erin looked at Bella, who looked miserable. She did not want to be there. And making her wait until morning the next day? Making her stew overnight and then drive back in on a Saturday? At least she didn't have school to get through before she could talk to someone.

Bella had already been holding on to her story for a week, bearing that burden alone. It was too much for a teenager, especially someone as sensitive as Bella.

"Do you want to come over for supper?" she asked Bella, at a loss for what else to do.

"I don't think I can eat," Bella protested, one hand over her stomach.

"Would you rather talk to Terry tonight or tomorrow?"

"Can't I just... I don't know. Next week, sometime. Maybe. When I run into him."

"No." Erin was firm. Bella couldn't keep putting it off. That wouldn't help her, and the police would just be that much more suspicious when they realized that she had lied. "Tonight or tomorrow morning?"

Bella moaned, hand over her stomach.

"Erin..."

Clara looked sympathetic, but didn't say anything to interrupt the decision-making process. She set a couple of cookies on a napkin beside her keyboard and took a bite of the first one before she began typing.

"I guess tonight," Bella finally conceded. "I'd better call my mom and tell her I'll be late getting home. She won't be happy about it," she warned Erin, as if that might make her change her mind.

"The other option is tomorrow morning," Erin reminded her. "Maybe that would work better for Cindy."

"No," Bella sighed. "I have chores to do in the morning. I was supposed to help take care of the kids tonight."

"Well, maybe you'll still get to, and it won't take long to talk to Terry."

But they both knew that wasn't very likely. Police interviews took a lot of time. They always made her repeat the whole story at least three times. Erin knew it was a way of checking details, making sure that the interviewee was not lying, and teasing out any more information that the witness or suspect might have.

Bella just shook her head.

"Thanks, Clara," Erin told her. "Sorry to leave you with all of those cookies." She winked. "Take them home to your family or give them to the boys tomorrow."

"Will do," Clara agreed, taking another bite.

After getting back in the car, Erin texted Terry to warn him they would have company, but she didn't say why.

Although Bella and Erin were home before Terry, he arrived home not much later. He greeted Bella pleasantly without realizing she was there to see him, and went to shower and change into street clothes before dinner. Erin thought it best if he were nice and relaxed and didn't see it as an interrogation. She hoped that would help to put Bella more at ease. But Bella didn't look very comfortable.

"Sorry," Erin said. "Won't be much longer."

Bella gave her a look that told Erin she was looking forward to the conversation about as much as a firing squad. Sooner was not necessarily better.

Erin cooked and Bella paced around the kitchen and helped with a few small jobs like setting the table. She enjoyed giving the animals their treats but was not distracted from the reason for being there for very long.

Eventually, Terry joined them in the kitchen. "Should I come in?" he asked. "Or do you need more time to get ready?" He would happily go through his news and social media feeds if she weren't ready for him.

"We're ready. Come on in."

Terry sat down in his usual chair at the table. Erin brought the hot dishes over and motioned for Bella to sit down. She didn't dish anything up. Terry looked up after a moment, noticing that no one else was dishing up or eating.

"What's up?"

"Bella needs to talk to you."

Terry looked at Bella. He chewed and swallowed. "Okay. What can I help you with, Bella?"

He flashed a look in Erin's direction that told her he was not happy about being ambushed with the interview. Though he had no way of knowing yet what it was about.

Bella folded her arms. She rubbed her forehead. Placed her elbows on the table and her hands over her eyes.

"Bella might want to revise her statement on what happened Friday afternoon."

"Oh?" Terry looked at Bella, his expression serious. "Okay."

He pushed himself back from the table and patted his chest where he normally had a notepad in his shirt pocket. He settled on finding his phone in his pants pocket and putting it on the table. He tapped the screen a few times to start recording. Bella stared at it dubiously.

"What happened on Friday afternoon?" Terry prompted. "After Simon had left the bakery and you left for the end of the day."

CHAPTER 40

*B*ella rubbed her face. "I… do I have to start there? Can I start with what happened before that?"

"Sure. Of course."

"Before I left Auntie Clem's… I put a cake knife in my school bag."

"I see. Why did you do that?"

"I just… was going to take it to school to show to one of the teachers. Because it is a unique kind of knife that she hadn't seen before."

"And how did that come up?"

"It was my Home Ec teacher. We were talking about different kinds of knives in class, and she knew about the long kind of cake knives, but not those ones. The wedge-shaped kind."

Terry nodded. That was something he could check. "Okay. So you put it in your bag to show her."

"Yeah. Erin didn't know about it," she told him. "I was just borrowing it, but things were so busy at the bakery that I didn't ask. I just assumed it would be okay."

Erin appreciated Bella's effort to let Terry know that she hadn't been holding this knowledge back from him.

"Sure," Terry agreed in a neutral voice. "You were just taking it for a short time to show someone, and then you were going to return it."

"But… well, that's not what happened."

The tears started again. Erin had been hoping that Bella would find it easier to tell the second time around or that talking to Terry would make her calmer and more objective. Erin stood up to get a box of tissues from the living room and put it on the table. Bella nodded her thanks and wiped her eyes and nose.

"Simon came after me. He knew I was Adrienne's friend and someone had told him I knew where she was or could give him her phone number. So he insisted that I stop blocking him and help him get in touch with Adrienne. He said they were family and I had to help him get what was his."

"What was his?"

"Her money. Simon had given her money in the past, so he figured that now that she had money, she owed him part of it to pay him back. Never mind the fact that he had stolen all her money half a dozen times." Bella's eyes snapped and her words were clipped and hard.

Terry nodded. "So he came after you. He was angry. Making demands."

"Pushing me around. Threatening." Bella's eyes shifted toward Erin. "Smacked me a couple of times."

Did she add that for Terry's benefit because she wanted to make Simon look more violent? Or did she not tell Erin that part because she hadn't wanted Erin to see her as a victim of violence?

Erin kept her mouth shut. It was Bella's story. Bella's witness testimony. Erin had not been there and could not say what was true and what wasn't.

Terry waited for Bella to go on.

"I pulled the knife out of my bag. I wanted to make him stop. To scare him away."

"And how did he react to that?"

Bella shook her head, fresh tears spilling from her eyes. "He just laughed. He grabbed it from me and threatened me. Said that he could kill me if he wanted to. I didn't... I didn't know what to do. I couldn't do anything. So I... I just ran away when he let me. Left him there, with the knife, laughing and shouting after me."

"I don't know how Simon attracted so many women," Erin said. "He was such a nasty guy."

"I'm sure he wasn't that way when he came on to a woman," Terry answered. "He might have let some of his 'bad boy' edge show, but he would be sweet, making her think she could see his vulnerable side. Talk about how no one had ever really given him a chance. And then he would reel her in."

Bella stared at Terry, her eyes widening. Had she been taken by Simon, too? Had he been nice to her to begin with? But then, when she refused to help him talk to Adrienne, he had shown his true colors, threatening and scaring her.

"Where was Simon when you ran away?" Terry asked.

"Kind of back behind the general store."

Not far from Auntie Clem's, but not where Erin had found him. Something or someone had brought him closer to Auntie Clem's.

"And what time was that?"

"I don't know. Six-thirty, seven. Not any later than that."

"And then what did you do?"

"Went to the store. Got something to eat. Went home."

"And was your mother at home?"

"No."

"Adrienne? Anyone?"

"No. Mom took them into the city." Bella's eyes were averted. Another lie? Or just embarrassed by her previous lie and her inability to fight Simon?

"What did you get at the store?"

"What? Oh. Chocolate. A frozen dinner. I knew Mom wouldn't be home and I didn't want to make anything."

"Who did you see there?"

"I don't know. Don't remember."

"You remember who was at the checkout?"

"No."

"Stop to talk to anyone?"

"No."

"How about outside? Was there anyone around when you were arguing with Simon? Did you see anyone after that? Anyone who would have seen him alive after your fight?"

"I didn't kill him."

"Answer my question."

"I don't remember seeing anyone else. I don't know. There wasn't anyone around when we were fighting, or he wouldn't have touched me. And I wouldn't have pulled the knife on him."

Erin believed that. Simon would have behaved in front of witnesses. And Bella would have gotten away on her own or shouted for help. But they had been alone for the confrontation. No one to stop Simon from abusing Bella. No one to vouch for the fact that she hadn't killed him.

"Did you call anyone?" Terry asked. "Tell anyone that this had happened? Adrienne? A girlfriend? Erin?"

He didn't look at Erin when he asked the question.

"She didn't tell me," Erin said. "Not until today, when I told her she needed to come to you."

Terry kept his eyes on Bella. "Anyone, Bella?"

"No. I didn't want to tell anyone. I just wanted to forget about it. Pretend it never happened."

She'd bought chocolate and dinner and gone home to lick her wounds and put it all behind her. It sounded just like what Erin would have done.

"So when you left Simon, he was alone. There was no one else around. And he had in his possession the knife that would kill him."

Bella nodded. "Yeah."

"And you have no idea who was around. Who he might have talked to after you were gone."

"No."

Erin watched Terry, waiting to see what he had to say. Whether he was going to get aggressive with Bella and tell her that she was a suspect unless she could give him more information that pointed to someone else. Threaten to arrest her and send her to prison for life for killing Simon in a premeditated attack. Somebody had killed him, and she was the last one to admit to seeing him alive.

But Terry remained calm and relaxed as if he were still off duty rather than taking a witness statement. Maybe this was the story he had expected to hear from Bella all along. He had just been waiting for it. He took a couple of bites of his dinner, chewing slowly.

"You know that if you killed him in self-defense, that is different than murder," Terry suggested. "There *is* justifiable homicide."

"I didn't do it. I swear I didn't."

"I will need to get your statement transcribed, and then you need to come in and sign it."

Bella nodded. "Okay."

"Is there anything else you want to tell me?"

"No."

"Anything that you want to revise? That might not have been quite true?"

"No. It's all true. That's really what happened."

"Why did you lie to me about it before?"

"I… I didn't want you or Erin to know I had taken the knife. I knew that he was killed with it after I took it… I knew it would look like I killed him. So I just wanted… I didn't want anyone to know about it."

"Even when you knew we had found your fingerprints on the knife."

Bella nodded, her face getting pink. "I just thought… it was natural that my prints would be on it anyway." She looked at Erin. "I handle all the implements at Auntie Clem's. I help to wash up and put stuff away. You can't do that without getting your fingerprints on them. So I just thought… it didn't prove anything."

"And you called Joshua Cox to give you a fake alibi."

"Well… I know. I shouldn't have done that. I was scared when I knew you were coming over, and I knew I needed to cover myself because I didn't have a good alibi for that evening. I was just… with Simon and then by myself."

Erin avoided looking at Terry when Bella indicated that she knew that Terry had been on his way over to talk to her. Hopefully, that would just go over his head. Or he would accept the fact that, yes, if one of Erin's employees or friends were in trouble, of course she would do whatever she could to help.

Whether he liked it or not.

Erin was intensely loyal. Maybe that was why she felt so betrayed by Bella lying to her. Bella should have told her the truth from the beginning. She should have asked to take the knife to school. She should have gone to Erin as soon as she had problems with Simon. She should have come forward and let Erin know of what had happened as soon as she knew about Simon's body being found. But despite all the time they had spent together, all the confidences, everything Erin had done to protect Adrienne in the past, Bella still hadn't trusted her.

CHAPTER 41

*E*ventually, Terry sent Bella home, reminding her that she would need to come in to sign her statement, but not threatening her with anything. He thanked her for coming forward with the information she had provided. Bella's shoulders were slumped, finally relaxed after a week of walking around expecting the whole world to blow up around her.

Erin knew what that felt like. Holding back information that she hoped no one would ever find out about, but knowing that in the end, it would somehow come out. Dreading what people would say. What they would think. No matter how she tried to protect herself, the secrets seemed to eventually come out.

She hoped that she was stronger because of it. But that was probably just empty words, something people said to make themselves feel better. People were not better because of the trials they had gone through. They were just more beaten up. Tireder.

"She's just a kid," Terry said.

Erin tried to push her dark thoughts to the back of her mind and to focus on Terry, sitting on the couch next to her and yet far, far away. She hadn't paid any attention to him all night. When they were together, she should give him her full attention.

If she ignored their relationship, it would fall apart. Partners needed to spend time together. To be seen and heard.

"What?"

"Bella is still a teenager. You can't expect her to behave like a responsible adult. I know that most of the time she does, making it hard to see her for what she is. But she is still a kid. Her brain isn't fully developed. She hasn't had the experience you and I have."

Even with all of Erin's experience, she had still done the same thing as Bella and tried to hide the things that she had done in the past. Even during murder investigations, she had tried not to let Terry or the other law enforcement officers or Bald Eagle Falls citizenry in general know all that had happened, even when it was far in the past. She couldn't very well fault a teenager for doing the same.

"I know. I just feel... betrayed that Bella didn't trust me. That I had to figure it out myself; she just lied to me and tried to keep me from finding it all out."

"It's hard, isn't it?" He didn't rub her nose in it, but Erin still felt the sting. It *was* hard when someone she loved lied to her like that.

"I'm sorry," she said with a little laugh. "All the stuff I've done and haven't told you about. Kept a secret from you. I'm sorry."

Terry put his arm lightly over her shoulders and, when Erin snuggled into him, he tightened his grip and held her close.

"I know. It's fine. We've gotten past all of that, haven't we?"

Erin thought about it. How many more secrets did she feel she needed to keep from him? Could she just let them go, talk to him about her life before they met, her growing up years and her lonely adult years? She had started fresh when she had moved to Bald Eagle Falls, and she thought she could put all of that behind her. Would the past ever truly be behind her?

～

Sunday afternoons were one of the few times that Erin could be sure to have time to rest and recover from her week. With Auntie Clem's closed for Sunday, only opening for a couple of hours to serve the after-church ladies' tea, Erin could focus on herself and whatever other things the week required. She tried not to fill it up with planning marketing campaigns or any other bakery-related business, though sometimes things popped up that she had to deal with anyway. It was usually a nice, quiet time when she could daydream, spend time with Terry, or read through Clementine's family history books and files. She didn't get much "me time."

Sitting on the couch with her planner binder and tablet, Erin tried to relax and let the week's trials fade behind her. It was not a huge surprise that her mind kept returning to Simon Simpson and his murder. It seemed like it had been ages since she had discovered his remains. But it hadn't been. It had been just a week. So much had happened since then. She thought the police should have enough evidence to figure out who the killer had been. Yes, Simon had a lot of enemies, but it was someone who had to be in Bald Eagle Falls recently, and it wasn't that easy to sneak in and out of town without being seen by anyone.

Had it been one of the men who had been looking for Simon or Adrienne, people he owed money to? A Bald Eagle Falls resident, maybe even someone Erin thought she knew well, who had a grudge against Simon for something that had happened long ago or because of one of the women he had taken up with? Even sweet Betty Thompson had nursed a grudge against him for many years. While Erin didn't think an old woman could have driven the cake knife into Simon's chest, Betty was just one example of the resentment many Bald Eagle Falls residents probably nursed against him despite the intervening decades.

Not Betty. Simon would just have taken the knife away from her, as he had from Bella. Though maybe at that point, he had been suffering from the poisoning and had been weak or disoriented. Erin couldn't eliminate someone he would have easily been able to fight before being poisoned. She had no idea how disabled he might have been by the death cap mushrooms.

Something stirred at the back of Erin's mind. Something that she had thought of before and had wanted to look up. But life was so busy that it had been driven from her mind and overtaken by other, more immediate concerns.

What had it been?

She thought that she had been at Auntie Clem's at the time. That was a time when thoughts often came to her and fled just as quickly when she had to deal with customers and didn't have time to stop and write down an idea while it was still fresh in her mind.

Had it been something that Mary Lou had said? Erin was pretty sure not. Mary Lou had given away that Joshua had not been with Bella during the window of time that Simon had been killed. But Erin didn't think there was anything else.

Other than that she should check in with Mary Lou to see how Roger was doing and if there was anything else the family needed. She worried about the hospital bills that they would have incurred. The Coxes didn't have extra money. Mary Lou counted every penny and was very frugal. They had lost their life savings and home before Roger's hypoxic brain injury. And who knew how many other debts Mary Lou was trying to pay off while taking care of herself and Joshua. And Roger, since he was home again. Erin hoped that the paper was paying Josh well for the articles he was writing for the newspaper, but suspected not. Josh was still very new to investigative journalism and, even though he had written some excellent articles on breaking news or developing situations within Bald Eagle Falls, the paper probably didn't have the budget to pay him very well.

Erin should drop a care package off for Mary Lou. A box of baking from the freezer that would last her for a few weeks so that she didn't have to worry so much about the grocery bills. It might not be a lot, but it was something she could do to help.

It came to her as Erin jotted a note to herself in her planner. It hadn't been Mary Lou she had been talking to. It had been Tom Banks. When he had been talking about his niece. What was her name?

CHAPTER 42

$\mathcal{E}$rin tapped the screen of the tablet and searched her email for the notes she had made while doing the research with Adrienne. She had jotted down the various names associated with the social profiles Simon had created for himself.

There was a lot of stuff in her inbox that she needed to deal with. Why did it seem like the more she did, the more emails appeared in her inbox?

She found the email and skimmed over it.

Tate. Tate Banks.

Was that the woman who had shown up at the bakery asking after Adrienne? Tom had said that she had not been in town, but he could have been covering for her. Or he might not have had any idea that she had been in town. If she were there for nefarious purposes, she wouldn't exactly call her uncle the part-time cop to tell him about it, would she?

Erin searched for the woman's profile. It took her a few minutes to dig down and find the right one. She would not have thought there would be so many people named Tate Banks on one social network. She eventually found the one that was associated with one of the Simon Simpson profiles. She clicked through and looked at the pictures of the woman on the profile avatar and timeline. She breathed out a sigh of relief. It was not the woman who had introduced herself as Juliet. She was a redhead, but not the same woman.

At the same time, she was disappointed. She didn't want someone that Tom knew and loved to be a killer, but she also wished she could move the case forward and help identify the real culprit. It would be a big relief to Adrienne and everyone else if they arrested someone. The rumors would die down and Erin, Bella, and Adrienne could go on with their lives without whispered accusations following them everywhere.

She went painstakingly through each of the other Simon Simpson profiles she had found with Simon's picture on them, and then searched for more, trying to make sure that she had all of Simon's identities. He was a busy man. Lots of girl-friends with children scattered across the country. But she couldn't find the red-haired woman who had come to the bakery.

But some profiles were locked down so that all the pictures and friends were hidden from Erin. Women who were more careful of their online security or who didn't even use social media. Any one of them could be the redhead who had shown up at Auntie Clem's.

Erin hadn't seen her since then. She hadn't continued to come by, asking for Adrienne's information. Did that mean she had gotten it or given up?

Eventually, Erin had to concede that the social networks were a dead end.

What about other crimes? She had found the bank heist. Maybe she could find other criminal acts that Simon had been involved in. Looking at the various posts he had made, she tried to match the cities he had been in with police activity reports. But she didn't have much success. She'd been lucky the first time. But then, Adrienne had given her the timing of Simon showing up with money to help pay the hospital bills. If she hadn't known when he had come into money, she wouldn't have been able to match it up with a successful bank robbery or other heist in the area.

Maybe that bank heist had been his only one. That would explain why things had gone so badly. Maybe it wasn't his area of expertise, just a one-time job. And then he hadn't done it since because he'd lost a man in the process.

Erin searched for reports on the bank heist and read through them, looking for the name of the robber who had been killed. Maybe she could find out who his online friends were and then see if any of them had been arrested for anything else. Chances were, it wasn't the first crime he had participated in.

A few minutes later, she was plugging the name Denny Martin into her search field. Again, there were far more of them than she would have expected. But none of the faces on the social profiles she could find matched the sketch that had been published. But as she was scrolling through search results, she found a recent obituary.

Would his family publish an obituary when he was killed in the crossfire at a bank heist? Erin had assumed they would not want to draw attention to the family members and would not publish anything.

But the picture of the smiling man beside the obituary was a match for the sketch of the robber who had been killed. Erin focused on the small, dense text next to the picture and tried to work her way through the description of how he had grown up in Ohio and the long list of family relationships. Reading was not her strong suit, but it probably helped that she had been going through Clementine's family history files, which included a lot of dusty and faded obituaries, some much smaller than the type on the screen.

She zoomed in on the text, but it became too wide for the screen and she had to scroll back and forth to see it all. Then she lost her place when she pinched it to make it smaller again. She skimmed over the words, trying to find her place.

Juliet Marsh.

The woman who had come to the bakery had said that her name was Juliet.

Erin read the words again.

Survived by his spouse, Juliet Marsh.

Juliet was not one of Simon's partners. She was the dead bank robber's wife.

CHAPTER 43

*E*rin stared at the words, trying to figure out what that meant. Why had Juliet come to Bald Eagle Falls? What was she looking for? Juliet had asked after Adrienne, so she knew that Adrienne was Simon's partner. What did she want with her? Did she think she was owed part of the money Simon had given Adrienne from the bank heist? If so, she was out of luck because it was long gone. But Adrienne did have money of her own. Would Juliet distinguish the money she had earned herself from the bank take?

Erin tried to figure out what to do with the new information. She should let Terry know, of course. He was sleeping after a double shift and Erin wasn't going to wake him up. It wasn't actually urgent, even though it had set her heart pounding like a train engine. Erin hadn't seen Juliet since Friday when she had come to the bakery. She had probably given up and gone home. She'd realized that it was a wild goose chase and that even if she found Adrienne, she wouldn't give her any money.

Except that after she had traveled all the way from Ohio to find Simon or Adrienne, it seemed unlikely that Juliet would give up after just asking around.

Erin tried calling Adrienne on her phone, but there was no

answer. It was not surprising. When she wasn't using it, Adrienne kept it turned off for privacy and to conserve her battery and minutes. Because it was turned off, Erin wouldn't be able to text message her either. The text might go through, but it wouldn't wake the phone up. Adrienne wouldn't get the message until she turned the phone on next.

Erin tried Bella's number. It rang through to voicemail. Was Bella avoiding her because she was embarrassed about her confession? Or because she was angry with Erin for making her talk to Terry and tell him the truth? She might just be studying or doing something with friends, but Erin had never had a problem reaching her before.

She tried Cindy Prost's number. Even though she didn't get along particularly well with Cindy and avoided talking to her if she could help it. This was different. She felt increasing concern over not being able to reach anyone. What if Juliet were out there? What if she had done something terrible to Adrienne, Bella, and Cindy? And what about the children? Surely Juliet wouldn't do anything to hurt the children.

Erin tapped Bella's name again. She listened to the ringing, a knot growing in her stomach. Maybe she would have to wake Terry after all. He could judge whether it was important enough to call in the other law enforcement officers. Whether he should go to the Prost farm to see if anything had happened to them.

"Hello?"

Erin blew her breath out in relief. "Oh, Bella. Thank goodness you're there. Is everything okay?"

"Uh... yeah, everything is fine," Bella said cautiously. "Why? What's wrong?"

"I couldn't get any of you. I was worried that something might have happened to you."

"Something like what?" Bella's tone took on a tinge of fear.

"I just figured out who Juliet is."

"Juliet? Who is that?"

Bella hadn't been at the bakery when Juliet had come around

looking for Adrienne. "Juliet is—" Erin cut herself off. "Did Adrienne tell you about what Simon did?"

Bella grunted in exasperation. "What are you talking about, Erin? I know who Simon was."

"But did she tell you what she discovered about him… in Ohio?"

"Oh…" Caution entered Bella's voice. "About… that bank thing? Yeah… she said it was the only time, though, that it had never happened before. That was the only time."

And how did Adrienne know that? She couldn't know what Simon was doing when he was across the country. She hadn't known about all the other families. She certainly hadn't known what he had been up to with them.

"Maybe it was," Erin said flatly, not expressing her doubts. "But here's the thing… one of the other robbers was killed in that heist."

"I know," Bella agreed.

"Juliet was his wife. The wife of the guy who was killed!"

"Okay…?"

Erin realized that Bella was still missing a step. "Juliet is in town. Or she was a couple of days ago. She's been looking for Adrienne."

"Why would she be looking for Adrienne?" Bella sounded more alarmed, the situation starting to become more clear.

"That's exactly my concern. All I can think of is that Juliet wants the money. Just like Simon did. Just like the other guys who were looking for Simon and then Adrienne. Everyone is looking for Adrienne because they want her money."

"But it isn't the bank heist money. It's Adrienne's settlement. It doesn't have anything to do with Simon. She wasn't even going to give any of it to Simon. It's for the children. For building a house."

"I know, but no one cares about that. They think that since Adrienne has money, she should give it to those Simon owed money to."

"Why would Simon owe anything to Juliet?"

"I don't know. Maybe they didn't give Denny Martin's share to his wife. Maybe she never got anything for that heist, even though she lost her husband because of it."

"Maybe," Bella said doubtfully.

"Where is Adrienne?" Erin asked. "Is she with you? We need to let her know about this."

"No. She's not here. She was going into town."

"Here? What for?"

"I don't know. She needed to pick some things up from Scarlett."

"Why didn't she turn her phone on?"

"Adrienne never does," Bella sounded irritated. "She doesn't want anyone to be able to trace her movements, so she never has it on when she's driving. She only turns it on if she needs to make a call."

"She was going to Scarlett's? Was that the only place?"

"I guess. Everything is closed on Sunday. She knows that. She couldn't go to any of the stores."

"Did she have the kids with her? Could they be going to the park or anything?"

"She has Samuel Andrew. And the baby, of course."

So they probably weren't at the park and couldn't be at any of the stores. Scarlett's house. Maybe some other errand that didn't involve going to a store.

"I'm going to try to find her," Erin decided aloud. "I'll have my phone on. Would you please call if she gets back before I find her?"

"Yeah, sure. What are you going to tell her? I don't understand."

"I think Juliet could be dangerous."

"Why?"

Erin tried to find the words to describe the feelings she'd had from the instant she realized that Juliet was not one of Simon's past lovers, but the wife of the dead bank robber. "She doesn't exactly have any reason to feel kindly toward Simon or Adrienne. Her husband died. She might have blamed Simon for what happened. He might have bilked her out of her share of the bank take. I just... if she is going after Adrienne and I don't do anything about it, I could never forgive myself."

"I'll come into town and help."

"It will take you half an hour to get here," Erin looked at her watch. "You'd better stay there and make sure nothing happens to the kids."

"Get help from Terry. Don't go after her yourself."

Erin looked impatiently toward the bedroom where Terry was sleeping. She wanted to get out of the house, and he would make her wait while he woke up, got ready, and called the police dispatcher or Sheriff Wilmot to let them know what was going on.

"I won't," she agreed and ended the call.

CHAPTER 44

$\mathcal{E}$rin really hated to wake Terry when he had just put in a double shift. She should probably call the dispatcher or Sheriff Wilmot instead, to get someone who was fresh and could be fully alert for the job.

And what? Leave Terry there sleeping while she went off following a lead? He would want to be there. First and foremost, he would want her to be safe, and she could be by taking someone else, but he would also want to be there. He would want to be the one going in with her. He'd be really upset if he woke up to find that everything had gone down while he had been asleep and no one had bothered to wake him and at least let him make his own decision.

Erin nudged Terry's shoulder.

Terry didn't move or make a sound at first. She gave him a couple more nudges. Terry groaned in his sleep and pulled away from her.

"Terry. Wake up. You need to wake up. I need to ask you something."

"Whatever you want," he mumbled. "Jus' go ahead."

She laughed to herself. Wouldn't he be ticked if she took him at his word and went ahead based on his sleep-talking?

"Terry." She shook him harder. "Terry."

K9 had followed Erin into the room and started to whine. He didn't like this unusual behavior.

"It's okay," Erin told him. "He'll be awake in a minute. Then you can go out for a walk with us."

K9 sat back on his haunches, panting. He seemed to think this was a good idea.

"I guess I'll just call the sheriff," Erin said, looking down at Terry.

He stirred. "The sheriff? What's wrong?"

"You need to wake up. I need to talk to you."

Terry rubbed his eyes. "Erin? What's going on?"

"Are you awake?"

"Well, I guess I am now," he said grumpily.

"I'm worried about Adrienne. We need to find her and warn her."

"What?" He rubbed his eyes again and shook his head, trying to wake himself up. "You need to go out?"

"Adrienne might be in danger."

"What's going on?"

She watched his face, waiting until she knew that he was truly awake and paying attention to her. He was still tired, but he wasn't just going to drift back into sleep.

"It's Adrienne. The woman looking for her isn't one of Simon's other women. She's the wife of the dead bank robber."

Terry blinked at her, processing this slowly. "She's the..."

"The bank robber that was killed when Simon robbed the bank in Ohio."

"We don't have any proof that he was one of the men who committed that robbery."

"I know," Erin said impatiently. "But there are enough connections that he could have been. And the woman who was here trying to track down Adrienne was the wife of the man who was killed. Why would she be here if Simon *wasn't* involved in the bank robbery?"

"How do you know she was his wife?"

"I found his obituary. And she was listed as his wife. It says right there, Juliet Marsh. And that's how she introduced herself to me. Juliet. I looked for her photo online, and it matches. She is the dead bank robber's wife. It doesn't matter what else we can prove. I know she's his widow."

"It *does* matter what else we can prove. We can't just arrest the woman or ask her to come in for questioning based on the fact that she is the widow of someone who *might* have known Simon and been involved in a bank heist with him. There's absolutely no evidence of that yet."

"I don't care about arresting her right now. I just want to protect Adrienne!"

He rubbed his hand over his face. "Where is Adrienne?"

"She turns her phone off, so I can't call her. Bella said that she was coming into town. To get something from Scarlett."

"Coming into town? When?"

"She's probably here already. I want to go over there, but… certain people think I should wake you up first."

He gave a quick smile at that. "Yes, certain people would be right. Give me a minute to dress."

"Just pull on some pants. I'm worried."

He slept in his boxers and t-shirt, so it wasn't like he was indecent. He would want to pull on his full police uniform, and Erin was raring to go. It would take time to get on his full gear.

He gave her a look and climbed out of bed to get dressed.

"Running into something like this without being fully prepared can be dangerous," he warned. "Taking a few extra minutes to ensure I am properly prepared can be the difference between failure or a successful outcome."

Erin groaned.

"I'm getting ready," he pointed out. "I'll go, but not in a panic or only half ready."

She noticed that he said "I" and not "we."

"I'm coming too."

"If you think that Adrienne is in danger, then you have to acknowledge that it could also be dangerous for you. And I'm not taking you into a situation where you could be hurt."

"I'm the one who told you what was going on."

"That doesn't mean I'm going to put a civilian in harm's way."

He was quick and efficient in getting dressed and assembling his equipment. He put in a call to the police dispatcher to warn that he was going to Scarlett Simpson's house to look for Adrienne and a possibly armed suspect, Juliet Marsh.

The dispatcher promised to send one of the other LEOs over to back him up.

At least he still let Erin in the truck. She had been beginning to wonder if he would just leave her at home and expect her to wait for him to report to her when it was all over.

Adrienne's car was not in front of Scarlett's house. Terry parked his truck and called K9 out behind him. He leaned back in the window to address Erin.

"Just stay here. I'll check to see if Juliet is inside or if anyone has seen either. Don't come in, even if you think it is safe. Do you understand? Stay outside and out of the way."

Erin sighed and nodded. This was becoming an all-too-familiar situation. It was her own fault for doing what she was supposed to. She knew that Terry was absolutely right to be cautious and she *didn't* want to walk into a dangerous situation. But she did wish that she could see what was going on inside. If she could see what was happening *and* be safe from any violence…

She watched Terry and K9 walk up to Scarlett's door and knock. The door opened a few seconds later and they walked in, looking relaxed and casual. No drawn weapon, no tensing as Terry looked around and realized that his quarry was there.

One of the marked squad cars pulled up, and Stayner climbed out. He reported in on his radio, looking around for anything out of place, then returned the mic to its holder. He saw Erin sitting in the truck and nodded at her but did not come over to talk. He walked around the house and entered the backyard, out of Erin's line of view.

There were no fireworks. Within ten minutes, Terry was back at the truck. "Everything looks fine," he told Erin. "Scarlett does have some things for Adrienne, but she hasn't shown up to pick them up yet. Scarlett doesn't know Juliet, but said she'll keep an eye out and report any unusual activity. Any strangers in the area, male or female."

Erin looked around, wishing that she could spot something herself. It was a letdown. She had been expecting a lot of action and drama, and all was quiet. It was good, of course. Adrienne was safe. Scarlett was safe. Erin was safe. She blew out her breath.

All was quiet.

"What about Adrienne?" Erin asked. "You need to find her and let her know about Juliet so she isn't taken off guard."

"I don't think anyone is in any danger. I'll contact Adrienne when I can, but she isn't answering all the calls from the Bald Eagle Falls police department right now. You might have better luck reaching her."

Erin frowned. "I can at least talk to Bella. Some of the kids are at the farm right now, so Adrienne will be going back there."

Terry nodded. "Talk to Bella. That's probably the best approach right now."

He walked over to talk to Stayner at his squad car for a few minutes before going home. Erin wondered whether they would put any surveillance on Scarlett's house to see if Juliet Marsh would show up there.

Eventually, Terry returned. He opened the door for K9, who jumped up into the cab. Terry climbed into his seat and rubbed his face tiredly before starting the engine.

"I'm sorry... I shouldn't have woken you up," Erin apologized. "I really did think that they would both be here. And I don't know what Juliet wants from Adrienne or what she might do if she doesn't get it. Do you think she's the one who killed Simon?"

"Why would she kill Simon?"

"Because of the bank heist... she blamed Simon for her husband's death, or because he didn't give her Denny's share."

"Well..." He nodded. "It's as good a reason as any, I suppose. We'll investigate it further. But like I said... we don't have any evidence that Simon was part of that bank heist."

"Except that Juliet Marsh showed up asking for Adrienne. That's pretty good evidence that Simon was involved."

"A couple of leaps of logic there. We need to tie it up nice and neatly to get any warrants or to make an arrest."

They drove home in silence. Erin was sorry she had gotten Terry out of bed. Hopefully, he would be able to get back to sleep right away and would not be too wound up because of the interruption and checking out Scarlett's house.

"Sorry, I won't bother you again," she told him as he settled down to go to bed again.

Terry gave her a peck on the cheek. "You did the right thing. I'm glad you didn't just go out there yourself."

She waited until she was sure he was asleep again, listening for his heavy sleep breathing before leaving the house.

CHAPTER 45

*E*rin couldn't wait around and do nothing. She knew that Bella would call her when Adrienne returned to pick up the kids, but she couldn't sit waiting at home. She took her own car and headed out on the route she had followed several times before.

Hopefully, Bella wouldn't be doing a lot of chores. Morning was the usual time for farm chores, wasn't it? Though Erin knew Bella might have to move the goats to a different pasture or their barn for the night.

Bella should be watching TV or doing her homework. Or maybe having a late dinner. She and Erin could talk while they waited for Adrienne to get home. Perhaps Bella had been wrong and Adrienne had not been going to Scarlett's house. Or maybe she had a series of errands and was going there last. There were a lot of reasons that Adrienne might not be where she was expected to be.

And Juliet might be gone. Maybe she had already talked to Adrienne and then headed back for Ohio. Just because Adrienne hadn't chosen to talk to either Erin or Bella about it, that didn't mean she hadn't seen Juliet. She might prefer to keep that information to herself. She certainly wasn't required to tell anyone else her private business. Erin was sure Adrienne didn't want everyone to know that Simon had been involved in such nasty business. The citizens of Bald Eagle Falls already had a low enough opinion of him, with the little they knew. If they knew everything, they might shun Adrienne. The woman was already considered an outsider. She didn't need to be alienated further.

The day was cooling, the sun going down. The scenery was green and peaceful. Erin should be getting ready for bed if she were going to take the early shift at Auntie Clem's.

But she couldn't stop thinking about Juliet and what she was doing in Bald Eagle Falls. Had she killed Simon? If she had, why was she still there? Because she wanted to kill Adrienne too? Because she wanted her money from the bank heist?

Or was there something else, another piece of the puzzle that Erin hadn't yet put together?

Erin was nearing the Prost farm when she saw a vehicle pulled into the ditch on the other side of the road.

Adrienne's car.

At first, Erin was filled with relief at the sight of it. That was why Adrienne hadn't shown up at Scarlett's. She'd had car trouble and hadn't been able to get into town.

But if she'd had car trouble, why hadn't she turned on her phone and called Bella for help?

Even if her phone was out of power or out of minutes, it wasn't that far back to the Prost farm. She could have turned around and walked back in the time since she had left.

And maybe she had. She had probably left the car there, walked back to the farm, and was there now with the children. Bella hadn't called Erin back to tell her, but she didn't really have to. Maybe she had been busy and hadn't had the chance to yet. There were a lot of kids to be managed.

Erin pulled over and crossed the quiet highway to the other side to examine Adrienne's car.

The beaten-up old thing wasn't pretty, but it didn't have to be pretty to get them from one place to another. It just had to be running. Which obviously it wasn't, now. Adrienne would have another unexpected expense to deal with. But at least she had some money now. It wouldn't mean the kids wouldn't be able to eat this week.

Erin wouldn't have let them go hungry anyway. She would have made sure that they got all the baking they needed from Auntie Clem's freezer.

The driver's door hung open. Adrienne must have intended to return immediately to deal with the car. She'd had two of the kids with her, Bella had said. Sometimes, that could be two too many. It was hard to deal with whining kids and car troubles at the same time. She had probably taken the children back to the farm and then would walk back or drive one of the tractors back to take care of the car.

As Erin got closer, she heard the thin cry of a baby in the distance. Adrienne must still be close by with Sarah. Could Erin hear all the way to the farm from there? Was she on her way back, having dropped Samuel Andrew at the farm? The night was quiet. There were no traffic sounds to cover up the noise.

Erin looked up the highway but couldn't see Adrienne or anyone else walking on the shoulder. Then where was she?

Erin covered the distance to the car and looked inside. Her heart sped as she saw that Sarah was still in her baby seat in the back. Her face was red and streaked with tears.

Erin hurried around the car and opened the back door. She poked her head in.

"Hey, Sarah," she said with a big, reassuring smile. "Hi, baby! How are you? It's okay. Everything is going to be fine. Let's get you out of there."

She wasn't used to the buckles on child seats. They always seemed awkward and difficult to get the child out of without bending her arms in strange contortions. But Erin was as calm and reassuring as possible, smiling and cooing at Sarah and working the straps and buckles until she could finally pull the girl free from the car.

"There! Doesn't that feel better?" Erin asked. She cuddled and bounced Sarah, looking around and trying to figure out what had happened. Why had Adrienne left Sarah behind in the car? Where had she gone?

Sarah's wails settled down to quieter sobs. Her little baby fists grasped Erin's shirt tightly, pulling herself into Erin's body and clinging to her. Her thin face still showed her distress, and she was as light as a bird in Erin's arms. She'd been thin since she was born. Erin had often worried that she wasn't getting the nutrition she needed.

"There, there. It's okay," Erin reassured her, patting and rubbing her back.

She looked around for some sign of Adrienne. She couldn't imagine that Adrienne would have returned to the farm without her baby.

"Adrienne? Adrienne, are you here?" she called out, trying to project her voice into the trees. Maybe Adrienne had taken Samuel Andrew into the trees to relieve himself. Perhaps they had been waiting for a tow, but Samuel Andrew couldn't wait and didn't want to go right by the road. So they had left the car for two minutes to take care of business.

But it felt like Sarah had been alone for longer than that. There were a lot of tears on her face. Her diaper was heavily saturated.

But they could have been sitting there for a while, waiting for someone to rescue her. Maybe Adrienne hadn't been able to call Bella and couldn't walk that distance because of the children. It was one thing to make a hike like that by herself. Another to do it with two children, one a babe in arms. Erin got the feeling that Samuel Andrew was frailer than the other children. If he couldn't make it that distance, Adrienne couldn't very well carry him.

CHAPTER 46

*A*drienne?" Erin called again.

She strained her ears and thought she heard a faint reply. That was reassuring. Adrienne was close by. They could all pile into Erin's car and go back to the farm. Adrienne would be grateful for the rescue. And grateful to be warned about Juliet. Everything would be fine,

There was another distant cry. Erin looked toward it. Was Adrienne coming back? Did she want Erin to go to her to help her with something? Sarah was still sobbing and prevented Erin from being able to hear the call very clearly. She felt her phone in her pocket, wishing that Adrienne would turn hers on so they could talk to each other and Erin would know what to do.

She held Sarah against her to muffle her sobs for a second to try to get a fix on where Adrienne and Samuel Andrew were.

"Adrienne?"

Another distant cry. Erin started to walk toward it. Toward the farm and into the trees, if she were pinpointing the voice correctly. Erin wasn't sure what she would do when she got there. Call for help, probably. She had a working cell phone, and Adrienne apparently did not. Erin would drive everyone to the farm, and they would get Bella to tow Adrienne's car with the tractor. Adrienne would feed Sarah and Samuel Andrew and put them to bed. Then they could have the talk that Erin had come out for. To tell Adrienne about Juliet and discuss what precautions they could take to prevent her from finding Adrienne and bothering her.

Covering the rough ground while carrying a baby was more challenging than Erin had expected. She couldn't always see where she was putting her foot down and would land on a rock or thick tuft of grass that threatened to trip her. And despite how skinny and light Sarah was, she got heavier the farther Erin walked.

"We're almost there," she reassured Sarah, trying to keep herself calm at the same time. "You'll get to see your mommy again. You'll be really glad to see her, won't you?"

She could hear voices. Adrienne talking to Samuel Andrew. Maybe he was sick and couldn't go anywhere, and that was why they had failed to get back to the car. Poor guy, getting sick out in the middle of nowhere, when all he probably wanted to do was lie in his bed and sleep.

Erin could see something large in the clearing ahead. At first, she thought it was another car, though it didn't make sense for it to be back there so deep in the woods, so far away from the road. Then she realized she was looking at a tent. She laughed at herself for being so worried about everything. It was Adrienne's camp. Her tents. Erin had known that it was somewhere close to the Prost farm, but Adrienne didn't like people to know exactly where she was. They'd been harassed by those who didn't like the little family squatting, even if they had the owner's permission to be there.

And of course, Adrienne hadn't wanted Simon or anyone else who was interested in her windfall to be able to find her. He had succeeded in seeing her when she was in town, but she had been able to keep her campsite hidden from him. That was why it was so far back in the trees instead of somewhere she could pull the car up. Moving the heavy tents and tarps over that distance must have been difficult. She must have borrowed a wagon or dolly from Bella. Erin couldn't see her being able to carry all of that equipment that distance by hand.

"Adrienne?" she called out to let the woman know she was approaching the camp. It wasn't good to walk into someone's campsite unannounced. Especially if that someone might happen to have a rifle for hunting wild game and protecting them from visitors.

"Erin?" It was the first time Erin could make out what Adrienne was saying. She was relieved.

"I'm here. I've got Sarah."

"You probably shouldn't come any closer."

Erin froze.

Not come any closer?

Her mind flashed back again to the idea of Adrienne holding a hunting rifle, protecting herself from intruders.

"It's Erin," she repeated.

"Erin Price," another voice observed, "the baker who doesn't know to mind her own business."

Yes, that was probably an apt description.

Erin looked around, trying to spot the owner of the voice. She sounded like she was close by. There was a movement in the trees, and she focused on the shape of a woman.

Juliet.

Of course.

No one had believed that Juliet might be a danger to Adrienne, and now here she was at Adrienne's camp. She had figured out where it was despite everyone's attempts to keep her from finding out.

"Juliet," Erin tried to make herself sound surprised. She had a role to play. If she could keep Juliet off balance and make her think that Erin didn't know what was going on, maybe Erin or Adrienne could find a way to overcome her. "What are you doing here?"

"You people think you are all so smart," Juliet sneered. "You think that I'll just give up and go home. You don't know anything about me. I'm patient. I plan things. I think. It's the power of the brain. People like you just don't understand." She looked toward where Adrienne was standing. "People like Simon."

Erin moved closer, hoping to be able to see them more clearly and figure out what to do. Maybe there wasn't any danger at all. Juliet just needed to be heard. And when they heard her and made her understand that Adrienne's money was from a settlement and was for a house for the children, she would go home. She would leave them alone and that would be the end of it.

Adrienne wasn't standing. She was sitting on a stump. Samuel Andrew was in her lap. Juliet stood nearby, looking threatening, though Erin couldn't see if she had a weapon.

"I don't understand what you are doing here," Erin told Juliet, feigning ignorance about Juliet's connection with Simon and the robber who had been killed. How would a baker in Bald Eagle Falls know anything about that? "Do you and Adrienne know each other?"

"Oh, we know each other all right," Juliet said in a threatening tone. "We know each other all too well."

"Did you go to school together?"

Juliet looked at her, scowling. "You need to just stay out of this. I don't know what you're even doing here. I expected that cow Bella to show up, but not you."

"Bella said that Adrienne had gone into town. But when she wasn't there, I thought I would come out to the farm and talk to her when she got back."

"What about?"

About her.

But Erin didn't say that. She shrugged. "Just gossip. See how she was doing since her husband died."

"Her husband," Juliet snarled. "Simon was never much of a husband. Or he was too much of one, all over the United

States." She looked at Adrienne. "Only, he never married you, did he, dear?" she asked snidely.

Adrienne just stared at her and said nothing. Erin watched the two of them, trying to decide what was going on and if they were in any danger or if Adrienne had just been forced into an awkward conversation.

But Sarah had been left in the car. Adrienne would not have chosen to leave Sarah in the car by herself.

Adrienne held herself rigidly, not moving a muscle. Her face was pale. Erin couldn't tell whether she was holding on to Samuel Andrew to comfort him or to keep him still.

What exactly had she interrupted?

$\mathcal{E}$rin felt her phone in her pocket, trying to figure out what to do next. How to de-escalate Juliet or to get the help that they needed. It was pretty hard, coming into the situation blind, to know what would help and what would make things worse. For the moment, Juliet did not appear to be violent or threatening. But anything Erin said might change that.

She felt for the home button on the phone. She was going to have to take a chance.

"Is everything okay, Adrienne? Do you want me to... call the police?"

"No," Adrienne shook her head, her face pale and pinched. "Don't do that."

"Yes," Erin acknowledged. "I understand."

Juliet gave her a confused look, frowning. "You just stay out of this," she told Erin. "No one asked you to come here. You're not a part of this."

Erin cuddled Sarah and kissed the top of her head. "Well, when I saw Adrienne's car stopped beside the highway on the way to the Prost farm, I had to stop and help. And I couldn't leave baby Sarah in the car, could I? I'm glad that Adrienne and Samuel Andrew are okay. I'm glad you didn't hurt them, Juliet."

"Shut up," Juliet said crossly. "I don't like the sound of your voice. Adrienne and I were just having a woman-to-woman talk about her husband's responsibility in the death of my husband. She owes me. She owes me big for her part in Simon taking my Denny from me."

Erin swallowed. She had wondered whether Juliet blamed Simon for what happened to Denny. Now she had her answer.

"You mean in the bank heist?" she asked. "Adrienne didn't have anything to do with that. She was here in Bald Eagle Falls. Simon was off in Ohio."

"Is that what she told you?" Juliet demanded. "You think that this is all just on Denny? He would never have been in that bank if it wasn't for Adrienne."

Erin looked at Adrienne but just got a frozen stare from her. She didn't fill in any details to make it easier for Erin to understand.

"How is it Adrienne's fault that Denny was in the bank?"

"Because she's the one who called Simon and told him that she had to have money. That the baby was in the hospital and he was going to die if she didn't get the money for his treatment."

This squared with Adrienne's comment that Samuel Andrew had been in the hospital two years ago when Simon had brought her the money. He hadn't been a baby, but he was still a toddler or a preschooler, and Erin supposed that they probably referred to the youngest as a baby even if he wasn't an infant anymore.

"Adrienne couldn't help it if Samuel Andrew was in the hospital. And I'm sure she didn't tell Simon to go rob a bank to get the money."

"She might as well have," Juliet snapped. "Suddenly, Simon needs money and he needs it fast. Too fast to put a proper plan in place." She shook her head, jaw clenched in fury. "I've put together dozens of jobs, and nothing ever went wrong. And do you want to know why? Because I know how to plan. I know how to put together the right crew, to research and reconnoiter the target, to make a plan to get us in and out of there safely. But no, Simon has to have money right now. There isn't any time for us to set it up properly. He has no patience. Goes in there with no plan. He's participated in enough jobs to think he knows how it all works. And you know what happened?"

Erin knew what happened. They had gone in without a proper plan and there had been a firefight. Denny had died. The security guard had died. They got out with the money, so Simon had been able to get back to Tennessee and pay for Samuel Andrew's medical treatments, whatever that had involved. And Adrienne never knew the heartache she had caused by insisting she needed money from Simon right away.

"It wasn't Adrienne's fault," Erin tried to use a calm, soothing voice that would persuade Juliet of the injustice of her accusation and make her see that Adrienne hadn't really had anything to do with it. "She was just trying to take care of a sick baby."

"She shouldn't have pressured him like that. The hospital wouldn't have let the baby die just because she didn't have the money. They have to give lifesaving treatment whether the patient can pay or not. Do you think I don't know that?"

"They won't do everything," Adrienne argued. "They'll do emergency procedures, and they did, but he needed more. And you know what they did? They told me to set up a crowdfunding campaign. If I want to be able to afford the antibiotics and everything he needs, then I have to raise the money myself. And not just the medicine, but the room at the hospital. Meals. Supplies. Doctors. They charge for everything. And they just keep racking up the charges. If I could raise the money for it. If not, they would send him home. He could be treated as an outpatient at some public clinic."

Adrienne looked down at Samuel Andrew and gave him a squeeze.

"They were going to send him right back to the hole we lived in. The place that made him sick to begin with. They would call public health to report it and get it shut down. Then we'd have nowhere to live. But we could go to the clinic for the treatments," she sneered.

Adrienne shook her head emphatically.

"He would have died. He wasn't strong enough to be released from the hospital. He was still coughing. He could hardly move. And they said the danger was over. As long as he stayed on the drugs, it would eventually clear up. Do you know how long they said?"

Erin shook her head in answer. "No. How long?"

"It might take months or years. They would have to keep cycling through other antibiotics if it was resistant. We're not talking about a week of amoxicillin for strep!"

"Maybe he wasn't meant to live," Juliet said cruelly. "Maybe you should have just let him go. You had enough other kids. And Simon had loads. Why should he care so much about one little sick baby? He should have planned the job properly! He should have listened to me! Instead, he insists that we go in there blind. He says that he's scoped the place out and it is a piece of cake. Walk in and walk out."

But Denny had never walked out.

Juliet laughed, sounding a little hysterical. "A piece of cake," she laughed. "Well, I showed him. *A piece of cake!* You'll think of him the next time you're cutting up and serving a cake with one of those knives," she told Erin.

Erin swallowed, feeling sick. She forced the words out of her mouth, even though she wished she could blot out what Juliet had just said. She didn't want to remember it. She didn't want to think of Simon and his rotting remains behind the bakery whenever she cut and served a cake.

"*You* killed Simon?" she asked in a tone of disbelief. "Why?"

"I just told you why," Juliet shrieked. "I killed him because he killed my husband! He thought he could just walk away from there! He got what he wanted, and he never had to see any of the rest of us again. He could just walk away."

"Were *you* part of the heist too?" Erin had a hard time wrapping her head around this thought. She had never imagined that one of the bank robbers had been a woman. How sexist was that? She had simply assumed that all of the bank robbers were men.

Juliet hadn't just lost her husband in the bank job. She had seen him killed in front of her eyes. On a job that she knew if she had planned herself, would have gone off without a hitch. But Simon had rushed things through too quickly and had screwed everything up.

"You think I would let Denny go in there without me?" Juliet asked. "I would never send him into a job that I wasn't taking part in myself. We were partners in every sense of the word. I thought that if things went wrong, I would be able to get him out of there safely. I'd done more jobs than he had. Before we even met. I thought we'd be able to get out."

"I'm sorry," Erin told her sincerely. Her mouth was dry and she wished she had a bottle of water. A drink of anything. "But... Adrienne couldn't have known that any of that would happen. She didn't know that Simon would commit a bank robbery to get the money!"

Juliet stared at Adrienne, who remained sitting as still as a statue. "Of course she knew."

CHAPTER 48

*E*rin didn't know whether to believe it or not. Adrienne had said that she had never wanted to know what Simon was involved in. But sometimes people knew and refused to admit it, even to themselves. It was too hard, so they just curled up into themselves and, like a possum, pretended they had seen and heard nothing.

"Adrienne knew what she was asking when she called to demand money from Simon," Juliet insisted. "She knew it would be a bank. And she knew it would have to be a rush job. That it wasn't one we could spend weeks planning. She wanted that money *now*. No time to set everything up properly. Adrienne knew. And when it went bad, she knew she'd killed my husband."

Adrienne shook her head. "No. No, I never knew anything about it. Simon just brought me the money. He didn't tell me where it came from. He didn't tell me what had happened. I thought maybe..." she trailed off, trying to decide what to say.

What she had told Erin previously? That it was some scam or scheme? Gambling? Had she really known that Simon was involved in armed robbery?

"I didn't know any of this," she insisted. "I wouldn't have

asked Simon to do something like that." She hugged Samuel Andrew to her tightly, making him squirm. "I just wanted to save my baby. I needed money for the drugs to make him better. They weren't cheap, and it was months before they said it was all cleared up and he wasn't testing positive anymore."

She loosened her grip and stroked his hair back from his face.

"He's always been fragile. If anything was going around, he would be the one to get it. They were all positive, but he's the one that got sick. The nurse said that it was because of the place that we were living in. Those tiny, moldy rooms in a flophouse… I thought it was best for them to have a roof over their heads, but it turned out it wasn't. They need space and fresh air. No more confined spaces. No more disease-ridden rooms where they can't breathe."

And so Adrienne had turned to living outside in tents instead of flophouses or shelters. Trying to provide the children with the best, healthiest environment to keep them well and strong.

"You're stupid," Juliet railed. "If you can't afford kids, can't afford to raise them, then why are you having them? How many of the little rug rats do you have? Five? Six? Why did you keep having them if you couldn't afford them?"

Adrienne just looked at her, saying nothing.

Erin's anxiety was rising. She had hoped that her distress signal would bring help, but there was no sign that anyone was coming to rescue Adrienne and her children. Darkness was falling rapidly. She could hear the hoot of an owl nearby. In the dark, no one driving down the highway would notice Adrienne's abandoned vehicle. No one would know there was anything wrong and come looking for them.

Except for Bella, and would she know to look at their campsite? She had the other kids with her and thought Adrienne had gone into town. She wouldn't know where to find them. Even if they raised the alarm, the police would search for

Adrienne and the children in Bald Eagle Falls, not the wilderness.

But Erin's yellow bug was out there too, it would stand out like a beacon if they realized something was wrong and searched for them. *When* they realized something was wrong.

Sarah was fussing in Erin's arms. She could hear her mother close by and wanted to go to her. She was wet and probably hungry. The air was getting cooler, and she would need a sweater or blanket.

"Why can't you keep that one quiet?" Juliet asked irritably. "I don't know why you brought her here. I told Adrienne to leave them both in the car."

Erin looked at Adrienne holding Samuel Andrew and understood. He was big enough that he wouldn't stay in the car when she left him behind. He had followed her. Sarah, of course, was not independently mobile and could not get out of her seat.

Erin couldn't imagine Adrienne obediently leaving her children behind in the car without a physical threat. She eyed Juliet, but it was getting harder to see her in the failing light. Erin still didn't know what kind of weapon Juliet had. A gun? Another knife? If she had performed the dozens of armed robberies that she claimed, then she was used to handling a gun, and it could easily be held at her side where Erin couldn't see it. She had to assume that Adrienne knew what she was doing. If she had decided that the best thing was to sit frozen on the stump, Erin had to assume any movement on her part could draw fire.

Especially if the baby kept fussing and irritating Juliet.

"Juliet Marsh." The amplified voice made them all jump.

Juliet looked all around, her face an angry mask. She couldn't spot anyone. Erin finally saw the handgun. Juliet had been holding it at her side, but now that she was cornered, she needed to identify the soft spots in the net closing around her, and she held it in front of her as she completed a full circle.

Erin was relieved to see Juliet beginning to back toward the woods instead of threatening Adrienne. Erin didn't want a hostage situation. She couldn't stand to see the gun held to Samuel Andrew's head. After all Adrienne had done to save the boy's life when it had been threatened by disease, it would be unfair for them to lose him to this madwoman.

Juliet was heading deeper into the bush, and Erin had a sudden sinking feeling that she had been here before and she knew exactly what Juliet was about to do. Erin dashed toward Adrienne and handed her Sarah. "Quick, take her!" She fumbled the pass, but Adrienne managed to get a good grip on Sarah and avoided dropping her.

Erin raced after Juliet.

"Erin!"

She ignored the call behind her. They might not know what Juliet was doing, but Erin did. She wasn't concerned about the gun. She couldn't let Juliet get away.

Adrienne or Terry might tell her that she should just let Juliet go. At least if she were in the wind, she wouldn't bother Erin or Adrienne.

But that hadn't been true of Theresa. When Theresa had escaped, she hadn't stayed away. She had harassed all of them, causing as much pain and fear as possible. Juliet was cut from the same cloth. She hadn't stayed in Ohio where she was safe. She had chosen to come after Simon and Adrienne instead. She had demonstrated she could hold a grudge for two years, without any apparent cooling.

CHAPTER 49

*E*rin wasn't the fastest runner. But she put everything she had into it, moving as quickly as she could after Juliet without tripping over the rocks, tufts of grass, sticks, bushes, and logs. It was an obstacle course, but she gave it her all.

She was right behind Juliet when she broke into the clearing where she had parked her motorcycle. Erin had known that it would be there. Juliet was a planner. Of course she had arranged for a way to escape and wasn't just randomly running into the forest thinking she could hide behind a tree. Just like crazy Theresa, she figured she could escape through the goat trails and back roads that the police couldn't block off. It had worked for Theresa. But Juliet had to be able to get on her motorcycle to escape and Erin wasn't about to let her.

Apparently, neither was Beaver.

As Erin chased Juliet wildly through the trees, breathing raggedly, her lungs feeling like they were about to burst, Beaver leaned lazily against the bike, her strong jaw working away at the gum in her mouth.

Juliet stopped abruptly. "Who are you?" she demanded, breathing almost as heavily as Erin. She fumbled to raise her gun, which she had holstered before running. Apparently, she knew enough about firearm safety not to go belting through the woods with the gun in her hand.

But Beaver was already holding a large gun herself. She trained it on Juliet.

"I wouldn't do that if I were you."

Juliet stared at her and tried to decide what to do.

"You're under arrest, Juliet Marsh. How about you take that gun out with two fingers and drop it on the ground? Kick it away from you. Then lace your hands behind your head."

Juliet's mouth opened and shut. "You can't do that! You have no reason to arrest me. Where is your cause? This is a licensed weapon and I can carry it wherever I want to."

"Well, let's start with the murder of Simon Simpson. We can go from there. I am sure there are other charges we can lay, but I don't want to take all of the Bald Eagle Falls PD's fun away. Gotta leave them something that they can charge you with."

Juliet just stood there, thunderstruck. Beaver chewed away on her gum, waiting for Juliet to react.

"You have no proof I murdered anyone," Juliet asserted.

"I've told you you're under arrest, ma'am. I suggest you do what you're told if you don't want to end up with a hole in your belly."

Juliet's face turned red with fury as the implications of what was happening started to click into place. But she followed Beaver's instructions and dropped her gun to the ground.

"Put your hands behind your head," Beaver told her in a bored, lazy tone. Erin knew that despite Beaver's relaxed demeanor and exaggerated laziness, she was alert to every movement and fully aware of how dangerous Juliet might be. Beaver's act was just that, the act of a highly trained special agent who occasionally made Bald Eagle Falls her home.

Juliet laced her hands behind her head and, by the time any of the law enforcement officers who had arrived to rescue Adrienne and Erin made it to the clearing, Beaver had her handcuffed and was checking her pockets and person for any hidden weapons.

Stayner was the first to arrive, apparently a better runner than Terry, who was close behind him with K9 at his side. K9 could have run faster, but Terry had apparently not sent him on ahead despite the fact that his girlfriend was running pell-mell after an accused murderer with a gun.

Terry and Stayner both stopped and watched Beaver, who gave them a lazy grin. "Little late to the party, aren't you, gentlemen?"

"How did you get here?" Terry demanded.

Beaver shrugged. "Just out doing some hunting." Her smile made it clear that she was teasing him. Beaver looked at Erin and raised her brows.

"You followed me?" Erin asked.

She thought back to her drive toward the Prost farm. She couldn't remember seeing any other vehicles behind her. But apparently, Beaver had followed her at a distance. Either that, or she had some kind of tracking device on Erin's car. Or maybe her phone. It would appear that Erin had led Beaver right into the hostage scene.

"If you followed me here, why didn't you help Adrienne and me? She could have killed us!"

"You seemed like you had things under control for the time being." Beaver shrugged. "And I knew that the PD was on their way, since you managed to get a call into the Bald Eagle Falls dispatcher before I did."

Erin let out her breath. She hadn't known at the time whether it would work. She couldn't key the police dispatcher's number into the phone while it was in her pocket. Not with a touch screen rather than hard buttons. But she could hold down the home button and give voice commands. She had held it down while asking Adrienne if she wanted Erin to call the police, so that the command the phone received was "call the police." Of course the voice assistant wouldn't call the emergency number without confirmation that it had heard the command correctly, so Erin had told it "yes" despite the fact that her response hadn't exactly made sense in the conversation.

After that, she did her best to give the police dispatcher the necessary information. Where she was, having found Adrienne's car by the road on the way to the Prost farm. The presence of Adrienne and her two young children, in addition to Juliet. The fact that Juliet had not hurt them.

Juliet had also obliged by admitting that she had been involved personally in the bank heist and that she was the one who had killed Simon Simpson for his part in Denny's death.

Apparently, the dispatcher had been able to hear enough of this information through the muffling effect of Erin's clothing, and the police had quickly arrived on the scene.

Erin looked at Terry, his eyes red-rimmed with dark bags underneath. He had been awakened shortly after getting to sleep again. That was twice she had woken him up after he'd put in a double shift. He must be about ready to drop.

"I'm sorry…"

"Sorry for what? That you managed to get yourself into the middle of this? You came out here on your own without anyone to back you up? Why would you do that? You know that I went with you to check out Scarlett's house. You knew that any of the Bald Eagle Falls police department would back you up even if I was unavailable. Why would you come out here all on your own?"

"I didn't come out here looking for Juliet. I didn't think she knew where Adrienne was. I just wanted to talk to Bella and wait for Adrienne to get back so I could tell her about Juliet. So she knew to be careful of her."

Terry studied Erin closely, looking for any sign of deception. Erin didn't drop her eyes or look away. She hadn't been looking for trouble. She hadn't planned on meeting up with Juliet and ending up a hostage at gunpoint along with Adrienne and her two young children.

"But then you ran after her instead of leaving it up to the police. Why would you do that? You knew she was armed and you aren't. What were you going to do? Tackle her? You should have waited for the police department to take her down. Stayed with Adrienne where it was safe."

"I was afraid she would get away. Like Theresa."

"We would have..." Terry looked at the motorcycle, maybe reconsidering. When Theresa had gotten away, he had been disabled, knocked unconscious and tied up. He hadn't seen how quickly she had disappeared into the trees, but he knew the results. He had read all of the reports of what had happened that night. He knew that despite all of the law enforcement officers who had been dispatched to the scene, they had lost her when none of them had been able to follow the motorcycle through the trees and onto the trails and back roads that led away from her family farm.

"I didn't know that Beaver would be back here," Erin pointed out. "I was afraid Juliet would get to the motorcycle and get away."

"How did *you* get here?" Terry asked Beaver.

"Followed Erin in," Beaver advised around her wad of gum.

"What made you think she was going to lead you to Simon's killer?"

"Erin had already been targeted twice, which was a good sign that she was close to figuring out the identity of the killer."

"Twice?" Stayner repeated. "You mean the vandalism of the bakery?"

"That and the evidence left behind that linked the killing to Erin or the bakery."

"You think Juliet was the one who vandalized the bakery?" Erin repeated.

Beaver looked at Juliet. "Well, you were, weren't you?"

Juliet remained tight-lipped, exercising her right to remain silent.

"She was trying to point to me as the killer?" Erin asked.

"I think she already did that by leaving the cake knife in the body and the body behind Auntie Clem's Bakery. But I think that the vandalism of the bakery was more subtle. I think," Beaver looked at Juliet for confirmation, "She wanted people to know that *Simon* was a murderer. That he had gotten Denny Martin killed in the bank heist."

"You all act like Simon and Adrienne were innocent bystanders," Julie snapped. Her venom was aimed at Erin rather than Beaver. "It was Simon's fault that Denny was killed. And Adrienne's fault. You can hold her up as a model mother all you like, but that isn't who she is. She is culpable in the killing of my husband, just as if she had been there. She signed his death warrant herself."

"She was trying to get her son medical treatment," Erin pointed out.

"She is a cold-blooded killer. She killed him for the money. She admits it."

Erin shook her head. Adrienne had confirmed that she had been trying to save her baby. Not that she had intended anyone to die getting him medical help.

"Why did you come over here instead of rescuing Erin and Adrienne?" Terry challenged Beaver.

"She was doing a good job. When I called for backup, the dispatcher already had her on the line and patched me in so I could listen in. Things were staying calm and she had Marsh talking, so I didn't think I needed to interfere. But I didn't want her to get away."

"You knew about the motorcycle?"

"I knew they used motorcycles to escape after the heist. Motorcycles have several advantages over cars in traffic or densely wooded areas like this. Even an ATV would have a challenge getting through here. But a motorcycle will outstrip a runner even at low speeds and, with all the back roads around here... it would be very easy to slip away."

Terry looked at Erin. "Did you know that they used motorcycles to get away from the heist, or did you just guess that she might have one?"

Erin shrugged. "There wasn't a second car with Adrienne's. Juliet had to have gotten here somehow, but there was no other vehicle around. I guess she could have been dropped off by an accomplice. But I just… I remembered Theresa getting away, and I didn't want to go through that again."

CHAPTER 50

"Well, enough chatter," Beaver said. "Let's get this sweetheart booked and secured for the night." She grasped Juliet by the arm and, though Juliet attempted to pull back, she did not appear to be any match for Beaver's strength. Though Beaver's arms were currently covered by her camo jacket, Erin had previously seen how well-muscled they were. They were impressive. Beaver guided Juliet away from the motorcycle and the clearing back toward Adrienne's campsite.

Sheriff Wilmot and Tom Banks were there. All of the members of the Bald Eagle Falls police department were out in force. Adrienne was nursing Sarah, Samuel Andrew standing at her side, cuddled close to her rather than in her lap. Adrienne watched the police march Juliet past her, back toward where Adrienne's car and the police cars were now parked. Her eyes went to Erin.

"I guess I owe you one. Again."

"You don't owe me anything," Erin said. "I'm just... glad that I could help."

Adrienne stroked Sarah's head and cuddled her and Samuel Andrew close. "Thanks to you, they are both safe, and she will…" Adrienne looked in the direction Juliet had gone. "She will be put away, won't she? She'll go to prison?"

Erin nodded. "She admitted to murdering Simon and being part of the heist—and dozens of others. They got all of that on tape. And then kidnapping you and holding you at gunpoint. They'll be able to put her away for a long time."

Of course, things didn't always work out the way they were supposed to. No one could guarantee that Juliet would be put behind bars forever and that there would be no problems with convicting her on all counts. But Adrienne didn't need to hear that. She needed to hear that she and her children would be safe.

Adrienne nodded her appreciation.

More people were coming out of the woods into Adrienne's campsite and, at first, Erin thought they were professionals there to process the crime scene or offer medical care to the hostages. But as they got closer, she saw Bella and Cindy Prost. Cindy looked grim and Bella concerned, her eyes wide.

"We need to talk to Adrienne. This is my property," Cindy insisted when the sheriff attempted to keep her at a distance.

But there wasn't any evidence to be collected or any reason to keep Cindy and Bella from Adrienne. The sheriff would need to get Adrienne's statement as to what had happened, how Juliet had gotten her out of the car and held her at gunpoint, but that could wait. They already had a recording of what had happened while Erin was there and there were plenty of other charges to file against Juliet.

So Sheriff Wilmot conceded, stepping back and letting Cindy and Bella approach.

"Adrienne, are you okay?" Bella asked worriedly, leaning over her immediately to give her a hug. She reached down and tousled Samuel Andrew's hair. He made a noise of protest but didn't pull away or look frightened. He knew Bella.

"We're okay," Adrienne confirmed. She looked at Erin. "No one was hurt. Erin came and… how did you call the police? Did you call them before you showed up? When you saw the car?"

On reflection, Erin realized she probably should have. Instead she had gone waltzing into a probably dangerous situation.

"Uh, no. I called them while I was talking to you. In my pocket."

Adrienne shook her head. "I didn't even know you could do that."

"Well, you have to turn it on first," Erin said pointedly.

Adrienne looked down at Sarah as she nursed. "I have good reasons for keeping it off most of the time. Not everyone can afford big phone bills, and I need to keep it charged when I'm out here." she made a motion indicating the tents in the clearing. "I did have it on when I left the farm, but… Juliet made me turn it off."

Juliet was a good planner. It was lucky she hadn't forced Adrienne to drive the car deep into the trees where it couldn't be seen from the road. Or fortunate that the forest was too dense to drive the big car into.

Without a word, Cindy put her arms out for Samuel Andrew. He launched himself at her. Cindy picked him up and held him to her shoulder, not interrogating or babying him, just holding him close. His arms closed around her and he settled his face against her neck.

"We need to get back to the house before long," Cindy declared. "Hope is looking after the others, but it is bedtime and they won't go to bed on their own. Is everyone ready?"

Adrienne detached Sarah from one breast and turned her to nurse on the other side. "Just give me five more minutes, and then we can go."

CHAPTER 51

*E*rin didn't know whether to expect Bella to make it for her shift the next day. Bella didn't have to be there early, of course; her shift was never during the school day. But after all that had happened, Erin thought she might want to go home after school and just be with her family. The last week had been hard on everyone, but especially Bella. She had been under suspicion, worried about whether she would be found out or arrested. She also carried the burden of concern for her friend and had to face the aftermath of the break-in and vandalism at the bakery. It had been hard for Erin, but not nearly as hard as it must have been for the teenager.

But Bella was there on time after school, her smile uncertain but otherwise seeming like her usual self. She did some pre-closing tidying up in the kitchen, then took over the till from Vic for the rush of customers that always took place between school letting out and the bakery closing, as people made last-minute purchases before suppertime.

It had been a busy day. Not as busy as the day after a murder, maybe, but people were still excited to hear all of the details they could get about Juliet taking Adrienne and the children hostage and Erin rescuing them. At least, that was the way they wanted to spin it. Erin wasn't sure she had actually been a hero. She had been at the right place and managed to place a call to the police department but, other than that, she had done nothing heroic. She hadn't disarmed Juliet or put herself between Juliet and the hostages. She had never really been in danger.

Those who were regulars at Auntie Clem's knew that if they wanted to see Bella, she would be there between school and closing, so the pre-dinner rush was even busier than usual as people showed up to see her and to talk to her about what had happened. Erin had been there, but Bella was friends with Adrienne and could offer the best insight into what had happened and how she felt being held hostage.

Not that Bella had much to say about it. She was trying to protect Adrienne's privacy, just as they had all been doing both before and after Simon and Juliet had shown up in Bald Eagle Falls.

At closing time, Bella went up to the door to lock it, then let in one last customer. Cindy Prost led Adrienne's four oldest children into the bakery. They looked around with wide, interested eyes.

"They're here for their kid's club cookies," Cindy said sharply. "And... I'll have a couple of pizza shells. We'll have a treat for supper tonight."

"Yay!" the boy who was older than Samuel Andrew cheered. Erin couldn't remember his name. The children gazed into the display case with wide eyes and wanted to know which they could choose. Erin had been running the kids club for a couple of years, but Adrienne's children had never participated. Adrienne generally kept them away from the bakery and either Adele or Adrienne picked up the baking they needed from the day-old bread program. Erin understood Adrienne wanting to keep the children out of the bakery, where they would beg for all the sweets they were looking at in the display case now.

But they were well-behaved and didn't make demands for all of the different treats they saw.

"You can have one cookie each. Whichever kind you choose," Erin told them.

"Chocolate chip?" the boy demanded, pointing at them.

"Yes, chocolate chip. Is that what you would like?"

"Peanut butter?" one of the girls asked.

"Sunbutter," Erin corrected. "Yes. Whatever you would like."

The children each pondered the cookies they wanted and Erin handed them out. Bella rang up the order for the pizza shells. Erin was tempted to tell Cindy there would be no charge since they were for Adrienne, but she refrained. Cindy might be insulted at being offered "charity." She worked and owned the farm and had the money needed to buy a couple of pizza shells for dinner.

After paying, Cindy gathered the children around her like a mother hen. It always warmed Erin's heart to see Cindy interacting with the children. On her own, Cindy was blunt to the point of rudeness. She was judgmental and had targeted Erin more than once with her critical comments and Vic with religious condemnation. But in her interactions with the children, she was almost grandmotherly.

"Tell Miss Erin thank you," Cindy instructed the children.

As the children chorused their thank yous, Cindy nodded to Erin and spoke over their piping voices.

"Thank you for everything," she said, and no critical comments followed.

Did you enjoy this book? Reviews and recommendations are vital to making a book successful.

Please leave a review at your favorite book store or review site and share it with your friends.

Don't miss the following bonus material:
Sign up for mailing list to get a free ebook
Read a sneak preview chapter
Other books by P.D. Workman
Learn more about the author

PREVIEW OF MUFFIN
TO HIDE

Beaten and battered.

Erin thought she had weathered all the trouble Bald Eagle Falls could throw at her. She never would have guessed that the Auntie Clem's Bakery could be in jeopardy.

But when acclaimed food critic Gerald Montgomery is found dead in his room at the B&B with the crumbs of one of Erin's Morning Sunshine Muffins still on his lips, she worries that her bakery's fate is sealed.

But like a good bread dough, Erin is beaten down only to rise again, and she is determined to clear her name and save Auntie Clem's Bakery. With the help of her friends, she will whip this challenge once and for all.

CHAPTER 1

"$\mathcal{D}$o you really think there is a possibility that Gerald Montgomery would come all the way to Bald Eagle Falls?" Vic asked. Her tone was doubtful, but her eyes were bright. She was, Erin thought, trying to tamp down her excitement over the idea, not wanting to get her hopes up for something she considered to be unlikely.

"I didn't think it was possible," Erin admitted. She and Vic sat at the table in Erin's kitchen with their heads together, going over their plans for the next week. "It seems like a stretch that anyone would want to come way out to rural Tennessee to a little bakery like Auntie Clem's. But my sources say we are on *Montgomery's Muffin Mania* tour route." She shrugged, holding her hands palms up. "If he's going to be in the area, then he's coming to Auntie Clem's. It's the only bakery around that makes gluten-free muffins. Even in the city, only one place makes its own gluten-free cupcakes and muffins. Everyone else either orders from them or gets commercial stuff shipped from Nashville."

And that meant that they weren't fresh. Gerald Montgomery wasn't interested in something pulled from the freezer or sitting on the shelf for a couple of days. He had criticized restaurants or bakeries in the past for trying to pass something off as fresh when it was a day or two old. It wasn't worth his attention if it hadn't just come off the stove or been baked in the last few hours.

"Your sources?" Vic swept her long blond hair back, tucking it behind one ear. "How reliable are these *sources?*"

Erin Price couldn't blame her young assistant for being skeptical. Rumors that came over the grapevine in Bald Eagle Falls were plentiful but not necessarily accurate. The women of the town—and many of the men, too, Erin suspected—enjoyed gossiping about their neighbors. If there wasn't anything legitimate to discuss, they didn't seem to have any scruples against speculating or flat-out making something up. Some of the rumors that got back to Erin about herself or Vic or another friend or employee of Auntie Clem's Bakery were so far from the truth that Erin wondered whether the person who had started them was testing to see just how bizarre a rumor had to be before people would begin to question what they were hearing.

"Well, you know Cherise, the woman who runs the restaurant supply store in the city?"

Vic nodded, leaning forward with interest.

"Well, her nephew works in Gerald Montgomery's office. He saw Montgomery's travel itinerary for this tour and Bald Eagle Falls was on it. He figured she probably knew the bakery he would visit, so he called to share the news."

"And Cherise called you."

Erin nodded. "She knows I run the only bakery operating in Bald Eagle Falls and that everything here is gluten-free, so it was a no-brainer that if Montgomery is coming to Bald Eagle Falls, he is coming to Auntie Clem's Bakery."

"How did her nephew know he was coming through Bald Eagle Falls rather than just staying in the city? His itinerary is that detailed?"

"He's staying at the B&B."

"Which one? Mrs. McClung?"

Erin nodded. She had already confirmed the booking with Mrs. McClung. There wouldn't be any reason for Montgomery to stay at the B&B in Bald Eagle Falls unless he was planning to go to Auntie Clem's Bakery. If he wanted to go to the bakery in the city that made gluten-free muffins, he would have stayed in the city. The accommodations would be more convenient than staying in Bald Eagle Falls.

"Well…" Vic drew the word out long in a drawl. "Don't that beat all. He's coming to Auntie Clem's Bakery!"

"Who's coming to Auntie Clem's Bakery?" a male voice asked.

Erin didn't need to look up to know it was Officer Terry Price, her… significant other. She really hated the word boyfriend. Partner sounded too much like business. Spouse wasn't right since they were not married, much to the dismay of the church ladies who patronized Auntie Clem's Bakery.

Erin sat back in her chair and stretched her back and shoulder muscles. Terry entered the kitchen to fetch a bottle of beer to drink while he watched the game on TV. Erin wasn't sure what game he was watching or even what sport. He had told her, she was sure, but she had been too distracted by the news of Gerald Montgomery's tour to retain any details.

"Just Gerald Montgomery," Vic said, her voice high and dramatic. "Just one of the most famous food critiques in the country, coming to taste muffins at Auntie Clem's Bakery."

Terry looked at Erin. "Really? That sounds pretty prestigious."

"If he likes it, yes. If he doesn't like what he tastes… a review from a guy like Montgomery is enough to make or break a bakery. And he's very tough."

"Sounds like the plot of a Hallmark movie," Terry said. "If you can just find the right recipe to impress him, he'll give you your five gold stars and you can save the bakery from certain ruin and pay off the mortgage and fix all of the appliances in need of repair…"

"Well, there's no mortgage to pay off or appliances needing repair, but we *do* need to figure out what to serve him when he gets here. We can't just serve him an everyday rice bran or blueberry muffin and expect him to be impressed."

"Why not?" Terry challenged, "Your baking is the best. You shouldn't need to do anything special to impress him."

He removed the cap from the beer and had a swig.

"He'll be expecting something special," Erin said. "The everyday fare at Auntie Clem's is just fine—"

"Outstanding, even," Vic inserted.

"—But this guy is testing gluten-free muffins all across the country. You think he will be impressed with just any old muffin?"

"I don't think you sell 'any old muffin.'" Terry said generously. "You can't even tell them apart from a muffin made with regular wheat flour. And when you dress them all up with icing and other little bits…"

"Decorate them," Erin advised.

"When you do that, it takes them to a whole new level."

"Those prepackaged gluten-free blueberry muffins you can get at the store," Vic said slowly, "they don't even have real blueberries in them. They have *simulated blueberry nuggets…*"

Erin shuddered. "Well, anyone can make a muffin better than that. But we have to make a muffin that's better than them all."

Terry and Vic both looked at her. "That's a pretty tall order," Terry said. "You're not baking these muffins in the fires of Mount Doom."

It was Erin's turn to stare. "What?"

"Lord of the Rings," Terry advised. "The one ring to rule them all…"

"Oh." Erin gave a nod. "Yes, you're right. I won't be baking them in the fires of Mount Doom." she paused for dramatic effect, "but it *will* be the one muffin to rule them all."

CHAPTER 2

"What kind of muffin are you going to make?" Terry asked.

"I don't know, that's what we need to work out. We need to create something truly special. He'll take some of the other varieties, too; he always explores your range, but we need something that is… new, different, and special." Erin looked at Vic. "What do you think?"

Vic nodded, pursing her lips. "We should probably look over what he has liked at other restaurants and bakeries. Get a feel for what he likes or dislikes. Some people like a lot of rich sauces or rare ingredients, and some really like simplicity and making sure you have a solid grasp of the basics."

"Good," Erin nodded. "That will give us a good place to start. I've heard he also has allergies, so we'll need to get a list of what he can't eat. We want to have lots of options available to him. It wouldn't do to have a specialty bakery where he can't eat anything."

"It must be hard for him to be a food critic if he has multiple allergies. It can be really hard for some people to find anything they can safely eat."

Vic had learned all about how complicated it could be

working with Erin at Auntie Clem's Bakery. People who needed to eat a gluten-free diet due to celiac disease often had other food allergies as well, and Vic knew of a few customers who came to Auntie Clem's—some from quite a distance—because they knew that Erin would work with them to find or create something they would be able to eat.

The Fosters were one of their favorite customers in town. The oldest child had celiac disease and was very sensitive to any traces of gluten, and they were still trying to sort out all of the sensitivities of the youngest Foster child, Allan, could eat without digestive distress.

"I guess it would give him a chance to test out the service level of the restaurant, too," Erin suggested. "He can get a feeling for how they treat people with allergies or special needs, whether they have the right protocols in place to protect people who have allergies. Or else if they are sloppy and act like they don't want to deal with a customer who is particularly demanding."

Vic nodded. "I'll do some internet research and start pulling together a dossier. We'll get it all pinned down so we have plenty of safe choices for him."

Terry nodded at the two women and headed back to the living room as the commercial break ended and his game started up again.

"He *shore* likes his football," Vic drawled, drawing the word out.

"Is that what he's watching? I wasn't even paying any attention."

Vic laughed. "Growing up with so many boys, there was no escaping the almighty pigskin in the Jackson family. And I was right in there with the rest of them. My poor ma!"

Vic was transgender and had grown up as one of the brothers in the Jackson family before running away at seventeen to live as Victoria instead of James. Even knowing Vic as well as she did, Erin had a hard time remembering that the pretty young blond had once been a rough-and-tumble, shotgun-toting farm boy in the Jackson clan, one of the notorious organized crime organizations in the area. Vic had certainly transformed her life in the short time she had been living in Bald Eagle Falls.

"Did you want to go check the score?" Erin offered.

"I'm fine!" Vic assured her. "I'll watch the highlights with Willie later."

Erin nodded and glanced across the backyard toward the loft apartment over her garage, where she assumed Willie was sleeping or doing computer work. Willie still had his own house but hadn't been there much lately. Since he had started chelation protocol to reverse heavy metal poisoning, he had been in Vic's apartment most of the time, too tired and ornery to see to his own meals and other needs. Willie had always been totally independent, and none of them had expected the chelation to affect him as much as it had.

The doctors had suggested he would be dealing with "flulike symptoms." But Erin felt like it was more like going through chemotherapy. He was constantly exhausted and nauseated, along with a whole host of other symptoms, not the least of which was "irritability." Vic was a saint for putting up with his whining, demands, and moodiness.

"How is he doing?"

"Well, William Andrews ain't the best patient in the world. But he *does* try my patience."

Erin chuckled. "I'm sure he does."

Vic looked at the clock on the wall. "He should be good for a while yet. Let's spend a few more minutes on the muffins and Mr. Montgomery before he wakes up from his nap."

"Have they said how long it will be before Willie is done with the chelation and can return to normal?"

"They just say he's progressing, still clearing heavy metals from his system, and sooner or later…" Vic sighed and held her hands up in a gesture of surrender. "Sometime…"

Erin grunted. Wasn't that the way it always worked? The doctors had a prescribed protocol, but how long it would take and what the side effects would be were far less predictable than they would have liked.

"So this Montgomery," Vic insisted on turning the conversation back to the critic, "I've seen the guy on TV. He's tough. You sure you want him coming to Auntie Clem's?"

"Well, it isn't like I can tell him not to! I didn't arrange for him to come and can't exactly turn customers away. If I told him I wasn't interested in a review, he'd just give me a bad one."

"You have the right to decide who to serve."

"And he has the right to say whatever he wants to in his show."

Vic grunted and nodded. "Do we at least know when he's coming?"

"We know *Montgomery's Muffin Mania* has already started, though they're not revealing where he has been or where he is going next. I have the dates that he has reserved a room at the B&B, but I'm sure he doesn't plan to be here more than one night, so he must not be sure exactly when he will arrive."

"So we need to be prepared that whole time."

Erin nodded. "And it's not so bad. We can make a special muffin several days in a row and just not roll it out until he gets there. I want it to be a surprise, for him to be the first person to try it out. If we make a batch each day and those just go into the freezer if he doesn't show up, that's fine. Then when he comes, we roll them out and he gets to tell the world what he thinks of them."

Even though Erin said it casually, breezy, her stomach tightened at the thought of it. What if Montgomery didn't like them? What if he *really* didn't like them and gave them one of his trademark horrible reviews and everybody thought that Auntie Clem's Bakery was sub-par?

"Everybody here knows Auntie Clem's is a great bakery," Vic assured Erin, reading her expression. "They love your baking. If moody Montgomery doesn't like the baking, that won't change."

Erin knew that was true. Her customers already knew her

product. But it would cut down on the number of people out of town who made the trip to see what she had to offer. If Montgomery gave her a rave review, the traffic from the surrounding areas would increase. Maybe by quite a bit.

"We'll get a good review," Erin declared, making a positive statement like all of those build-your-success books said to. She didn't know if she believed in all of the positive-affirmations-lead-to-success stuff. But it couldn't hurt. "He'll give us a great review, and it will be great for the business."

∾

Muffin to Hide, Book #23 of the *Auntie Clem's Bakery* cozy
mystery series by P.D. Workman
can be purchased at pdworkman.com

∾

DON'T MISS A THING! GET THE LATEST NEWS AND A FREE EBOOK

Your First Taste

PDWORKMAN.COM/SIGNUP

ABOUT THE AUTHOR

P.D. Workman is a USA Today Bestselling author and multi-award winner, renowned for her prolific output of over 100 published works that span various genres. With a knack for crafting page-turners, Workman captivates readers with everything from cozy mysteries like the Auntie Clem's Bakery series to gripping young adult and suspense novels.

Her stories resonate deeply as she masterfully weaves sensitive themes—such as childhood trauma, mental illness, and addiction—into compelling narratives that evoke a powerful emotional response. Readers are drawn to her unique voice and empathetic portrayal of complex issues.

With each new release, fans eagerly anticipate another thrilling blend of thought-provoking storytelling and relatable characters that define P.D. Workman's brand as an author of unforgettable page-turners—gripping tales that leave a lasting impact long after the last page is turned.

> P. D. Workman, does not shy from probing the deep psychological scars of childhood trauma, mental illness, and addiction. Also characteristic of this author, these extremely sensitive issues are explored with extensive empathy, described with incredible clarity, and portrayed with profound insight.
>
> ——KIM, GOODREADS REVIEWER

Some of Workman's titles have been translated into Spanish, French, Portuguese, German, and Italian.

Workman began writing at an early age and is a prolific reader as well as writer. She is also passionate about teaching and learning, expresses her creativity through art and cooking, and loves exploring the Calgary parks and green spaces where the Parks Pat Mysteries are set. She was a legal assistant for many years and has done extensive charitable work.

Workman was born and raised in Alberta, Canada, and is married with one adult son.

Please visit P.D. Workman at pdworkman.com to see what else she is working on, to join her mailing list, and to link to her social networks.

If you enjoyed this book, please take the time to recommend it to other purchasers with a review or star rating and share it with your friends!

tiktok.com/@pdworkmanauthor

facebook.com/pdworkmanauthor

x.com/pdworkmanauthor

instagram.com/pdworkmanauthor

amazon.com/author/pdworkman

bookbub.com/authors/p-d-workman

goodreads.com/pdworkman

linkedin.com/in/pdworkman

pinterest.com/pdworkmanauthor

youtube.com/pdworkman

patreon.com/pdworkmanauthor

reamstories.com/pdworkmanauthor

Find P.D. Workman's books at

PDWORKMAN.COM

Scan the QR code below